"Ryan. I can walk."

"You shouldn't. Not barefoot," Ryan insisted. "Not around here." He half gestured to the field and ranch yard beyond.

"I've been barefoot for a while now." Elsie wiggled her mud-coated toes. But that only stirred those butterflies more. "And I'm fine."

"You're lucky." Ryan frowned, tightened his hold on her and headed to his truck. "You have no idea what's out here. Barbed wire. Nails. Thorns. I can keep going."

"I got it." Elsie felt him tense. And then she gave in. Wrapping her arms around his neck, she settled in closer. Just for a moment. Just to calm him. And herself. After all, she'd never been swept off her feet. Not in any sense. Right now, it was heady and thrilling. A little bit irresistible. And this seemed as close as she was ever going to get.

Best to take it all in.

Dear Reader,

I confess that I've been known to fall down more than one research rabbit hole during the course of writing a book. It has in fact happened with each book I've written, despite my best intentions and repeated warnings to myself not to get too sidelined by horse videos or the latest wedding dress styles.

In *The Rancher's Secret Crush*, reserved city girl Elsie Parks takes after my own heart with her penchant for reading and learning before she jumps into anything. When Elsie ends up on a working farm, it's not the steep learning curve that unsettles Elsie. It's professional bronc rider Ryan Sloan, with his passion for adventure and his soft spot for Elsie, who has her researching ways to guard her heart. Now if these two opposites can realize that their hearts are meant for each other, they just might discover a love they never expected.

It's springtime in Three Springs, Texas, where the bees are buzzing, the tractors are tuned up and there's always room on the porch swing. So, grab a tall glass of iced tea and come on over. We'll leave the porch lights on.

Cari Lynn

HEARTWARMING

The Rancher's Secret Crush

———

Cari Lynn Webb

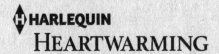

HEARTWARMING

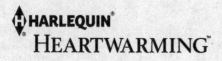

HARLEQUIN®

HEARTWARMING™

ISBN-13: 978-1-335-47572-5

The Rancher's Secret Crush

Copyright © 2024 by Cari Lynn Webb

Recycling programs
for this product may
not exist in your area.

Harlequin Enterprises ULC
22 Adelaide St. West, 41st Floor
Toronto, Ontario M5H 4E3, Canada
www.Harlequin.com

Printed in U.S.A.

Cari Lynn Webb lives in South Carolina with her husband, daughters and assorted four-legged family members. She's been blessed to see the power of true love in her grandparents' seventy-year marriage and her parents' marriage of over fifty years. She knows love isn't always sweet and perfect—it can be challenging, complicated and risky. But she believes happily-ever-afters are worth fighting for. She loves to connect with readers.

Books by Cari Lynn Webb

Harlequin Heartwarming

Three Springs, Texas

Falling for the Cowboy Doc
Her Cowboy Wedding Date
Trusting the Rancher with Christmas
The Texas SEAL's Surprise
His Christmas Cowgirl

Return of the Blackwell Brothers

The Rancher's Rescue

The Blackwell Sisters

Montana Wedding

The Blackwells of Eagle Springs

Her Favorite Wyoming Sheriff

Visit the Author Profile page
at Harlequin.com for more titles.

To the readers who believe opposites attract isn't only for science.

Special thanks to my fellow writers for their friendship and encouragement. To my husband for explaining those tractor videos to me and my daughters for offering plot solutions on demand. I'm grateful for your enthusiasm and continued support.

CHAPTER ONE

LEAVE IT INSIDE the gate.

Those had been Elsie Parks's exact but haphazard words not twenty minutes ago to Trey Ramsey of Ramsey and Sons Auto & Heavy Machinery Repair. Elsie had been moderating a dispute between her two young nieces over crayon ownership and checking the visitor policy at Belleridge Regional Hospital. That was where Elsie's brother—and her nieces' dad—was currently a patient.

Not that any of those details mattered if Elsie couldn't even get out of the driveway. She put the car in Park, told the girls to stay buckled and stepped out to confront the massive green tractor standing in their way.

The very one that Trey Ramsey had repaired. And the same one the very nice mechanic had left just inside the gate like Elsie had instructed. Completely blocking the driveway. Elsie squeezed her forehead. Behind her, car doors opened, and footsteps scrambled across the gravel drive. Soon enough, her two nieces bracketed her on either side.

Gemma smashed her polka-dot bucket hat lower on her blond head and bumped her skinny elbow into Elsie's side. "You gotta drive it, Auntie."

Elsie gaped at the giant tractor. One tire was wider than her six-year-old niece was tall.

"She can't," Autumn countered. At eight years old, Autumn was already proving to be analytical and serious-minded, same as her father had always been. Autumn pointed toward the tractor. "It's headed for the ditch. If auntie doesn't turn it just right, she'll end up in the ditch too."

The ditch was the least of Elsie's issues. The main one being Elsie had never operated a tractor, let alone sat in one. She wasn't even sure how to climb aboard to get inside the enclosed cab. Elsie turned and surveyed her surroundings.

Her nieces moved with her. Gemma rolled up onto her tiptoes and whispered loudly, "What are we looking for?"

"Another way out of here." Elsie tracked the thick three-rail wood fence that framed the acres upon acres of Doyle Farm. Her aunt and uncle had started with twenty acres and expanded during their thirty-year marriage. The property was now well over a hundred acres.

"There isn't another exit," Autumn declared, her words tinged with pride. "Dad says it's like a castle here. One way in. One way out."

"Can we have a tea party when we get home? It's what all princesses who live in castles do."

Gemma jumped and clasped her hands together. "Pretty please. We can invite Cowboy Prince since Dad can't come."

The sun beat down on Elsie's head, making her wish she'd grabbed a hat like Gemma. She could already feel her skin tightening and her face heating. Even though it was spring in the Panhandle and that Texas heat hadn't even been dialed up quite yet. Still, spring or summer, she'd never tanned gracefully. Simply turned a fascinating shade of beet red before peeling and returning to pale. *Remember to take care of your porcelain skin, Elsie. You must always protect your assets.*

Elsie touched her cheek. Sunscreen certainly wasn't going to help her now. Besides, she'd grown up and learned to rely on things like hard work, wise decisions and determination. She said, "Gemma, let's table the tea party until after we visit your dad, okay?"

Gemma opened her mouth to argue.

Autumn leaned around Elsie and added, "We have to see Dad, Gem. 'Cause he's lonely and bored in the hospital without us."

"Don't forget you promised your dad you'd bring him pictures for his wall." Elsie touched Gemma's thin shoulder and added more cheer to her words. "Maybe you could go draw another one inside the car while I move the tractor."

"Can't we watch?" Autumn yanked on the waist

of her shorts, tugging the baggy denim higher on her hips. "I could help guide you."

"I want you both to wait inside the car. Where it's safe." Elsie cringed. But it was too late to take back her words.

"You can't move the tractor, Auntie. You can't." Gemma knocked her hat off, latched her arms around Elsie's waist and clung tight. "It's not safe."

Unfortunately, two days ago, Gemma's dad had told both his daughters that it was perfectly safe for him to be up on one of the greenhouse roofs on the farm. It had been mere minutes after his bold declaration that one of the older rafters gave way and Elsie's brother fell through the roof to the cement floor below. Miraculously, Bryce had only suffered several badly bruised ribs and multiple fractures in his ankle. Now Bryce was in room 414 at Belleridge Regional Hospital, preparing for an early morning surgery on his ankle. As for Bryce's six-year-old daughter, well, Gemma now fully distrusted all claims about safety.

Elsie lifted Gemma up into her arms and hugged her. Her nieces had been through so much. First their parents' divorce that was finalized just before last Christmas. Then their sudden move at the start of the new year from the only home they'd known in the suburbs of Philadelphia to a farm in the Texas Panhandle. Now their dad's accident. More than anything the girls needed stability and reassurance. Elsie walked closer to the silent tractor. Autumn trailed beside Elsie, her shoulder brushed against Elsie's arm every other step.

"The tractor is safe." Bold statement. Up close the tractor loomed into even more intimidating. What could her brother possibly need with a tractor that massive? He'd never even owned a riding lawn mower before. What was she supposed to do with it? Elsie worked a confidence she wasn't entirely feeling into her words. "See, it's turned off right now. It can't hurt anyone."

"We should leave it off." Gemma rested her head on Elsie's shoulder.

"We could," Elsie started. "But then we wouldn't get to see your dad today."

"Then he'll be really sad." Gemma wiped her hand under her nose. Her voice descended into pitiful. "I miss my dad."

"I know you do." Elsie squeezed the little girl harder and reached for her own resolve. So what if she didn't know anything about tractors. She had to do something. She hugged Gemma once more. "I promise I'm going to get you to the hospital this afternoon so you can give your dad the biggest hug ever."

Gemma nodded and swirled Elsie's ponytail around her fingers. "The tractor won't hurt you, right?"

Elsie shook her head then lowered her niece to the gravel. "Now head on over to the car. I put your backpack of coloring supplies on the front seat."

Gemma picked up her hat and raced to the bright blue Jeep Bryce had purchased for what he'd dubbed his career pivot from financial advisor to full-time farmer.

Autumn lingered beside Elsie. Her hands on her hips, she studied the tractor then tipped her head toward Elsie. "Maybe you should call like Dad did."

"What do you mean?" Elsie studied the tractor and searched for a way inside. Her brother had hit the height gene jackpot in their family. What would've been a simple extended step up was more like a big leap for Elsie. She rolled onto the balls of her feet. The soles of her cute sandals had little flex and even less bounce. Perhaps a running start then.

"Dad made a phone call, and a cowboy came over. Then the cowboy drove the tractor for Dad." Autumn tucked her brunette chin-length hair behind her ear and nodded sagely at Elsie. "You should call a cowboy too."

Elsie rocked back and forth. *Run. Jump. Grab.* Nothing to it. Surely, she could reach the door handle on the tractor cab. It was just one jump. *Ouch.* Elsie winced and brushed away the sharp pebbles that slipped between her sandals and bare toes. "I don't know a cowboy to call."

"All the cowboys live next door," Autumn added.

"One of 'em has a beard whiter than Santa." The little girl paused and patted her stomach. "But his belly is too flat so he can't be the *real* Santa. We get to call him Cowboy Santa, even though his real name is Sam."

Sam Sloan and his family had property that bordered her aunt's farm. The two families had been neighbors for decades according to her aunt. Elsie's brother always hung out with the Sloan brothers during their summer trips to their aunt and uncle's farm. As the younger sister and only girl for miles around, Elsie had often stayed with her aunt. She'd always preferred reading on the back porch and helping her aunt in the greenhouses. Until the summer after Elsie's freshman year in high school. When she'd encountered one Sloan brother alone at the Sloan family pond.

Elsie tightened her ponytail and pushed her memories aside. "Well, we don't have Santa or Santa's helpers right now. It's just us and a tractor."

"But Auntie." Autumn tapped Elsie's arm. "What about Cowboy Prince?"

"We don't need a cowboy rescue." Especially not from some cowboy prince Elsie didn't know. All she had to do was jump. Grab the handle. Climb inside. On three. Elsie inhaled a deep breath and fixed her gaze on the tractor. Target set, she shook her arms out at her sides and crouched lower. "Watch. I'll show you. We got this."

One. Two. Three.

Elsie sprinted to the tractor and leaped. Miraculously her fingers wrapped around the door handle. She gripped tight and managed to find a place to prop her feet. Adrenaline propelled her upward. Autumn clapped and cheered her on. Swinging the door wide, Elsie climbed inside, albeit awkwardly. Scraping elbows and knees on her way in. She'd have more than one bruise from this exercise. No matter. She'd made it.

But her victory celebration was immediately cut short. The inside of the tractor looked more technologically advanced than a space shuttle cockpit. And at least as complicated. Elsie dropped onto the captain's chair. Sweat beaded along the back of her neck. The heat wasn't too stifling inside the enclosed cab. Yet the air was stale. Defeated? Not yet. All she needed was an instruction manual. Good thing she excelled at online searching.

Propping the door open with her foot, she called out, "Autumn. Look for a name on the tractor."

"But Auntie," Autumn hollered. "You can…"

Elsie's foot slipped the same time she jostled her phone from her back pocket. The door slammed shut on Autumn's words. And her cell phone landed with a *thunk* up under the console. Elsie scrambled to locate her phone. And the cab door swung open behind her.

"Well, if it isn't Elsie *won't-dance-with-me-ever* Marie Parks."

Elsie stilled. No one had called her that in forever. Not since that one particular summer. When only one person—with a very similar deep Texas drawl—had ever dared.

Slowly twisting around, she took in the full-fledged cowboy propped in the open doorway. His chestnut-colored cowboy hat rode low on his forehead, shadowing his bearded face. Dust and pollen stuck to his plaid shirt, with the sleeves rolled to his elbows, and his jeans as if he'd been walking through a dry field. Oh, but she knew him. Her heart raced. Her mouth felt as dry as the dust caked on his worn boots. "Ryan Sloan."

His grin lifted into both cheeks. His teeth flashed white. "You remember me."

Ryan was hard to forget. Even though he'd only ever been nothing more than her one-time crush. When she'd been young and foolish enough to accept his dares at his family pond one summer evening. She'd been excited and giddy and thrilled to have his undivided attention. Until his girlfriend had arrived. Then Elsie had discovered firsthand why it was called a crush. The pain had been oddly difficult to dismiss. And Elsie had decided cowboys weren't worth the trouble of a real heartache. Her voice cracked. "Ryan. What are you doing here?"

He nudged the brim of his hat higher on his forehead. Revealing a pair of all too dreamy, but deceptively shrewd, hazel eyes. "Sundancer and I were just passing by."

Elsie glanced out the window. Saw a stunning palomino grazing not far from Autumn. Not surprising. Ryan had always been a cowboy first. And his partner his trusted horse.

"I tried to tell you, Auntie." Autumn's enthusiastic shout reached Elsie clearly and concisely. "Cowboy Prince is here. Now he can rescue you." Autumn skipped over to Sundancer, tore a fistful of grass from the ground and carefully fed it to the horse.

Except Elsie rescued herself these days. No prince, cowboy or otherwise, required. Still, she couldn't quite clear the surprise from her words. "You're the cowboy prince I've been hearing about."

"One and the same." The corner of his mouth hitched into his beard. "We can talk about all that later."

Talking later. With Ryan. That sounded appealing. Or would have if Elsie's crush on Ryan hadn't expired well over a decade ago. If she had returned to Three Springs for more than her family. If she wanted to get entangled in some sort of cowboy situation. *With him.* More sweat dampened the back of her neck. Despite it not being midsummer and the temperature not even close to sweltering.

Ryan eyed her. "Well, are you going to tell me?"

"What?" *That you've strolled through my thoughts over the years. Slow and unrushed. Like the spark of a good memory. The kind worth revisiting again and again.* Elsie rolled her lips together and willed the flush she felt out of her cheeks.

"Tell me what exactly you are doing in here," Ryan said.

"In case it isn't obvious, I have a bit of a tractor situation." And definitely *not* a cowboy one. Elsie waved her hand around and tried to stir the suddenly stifling air. "Now, all I need is an instruction manual to get out of it."

"That's your plan then. Reading your way out of this." He braced his arm on the door frame and looked her over. "I see some things haven't changed much."

Elsie refused to squirm and instead returned his steady regard. Eye for eye. Beat for beat. Same as she'd met his stare years ago. *You read too much, Elsie Marie. You can't really want to be alone all the time. Come on. You might have fun.* Elsie had only ever grinned and turned the page of her book. *I'm not alone. I have my books. You should try sitting still once in a while, Ryan. You might like it.* Ryan had always laughed. *Only place a cowboy sits is in the saddle.* And then he'd hop onto his horse and leave her alone. Like she preferred. Until she hadn't.

She lifted her chin and nudged aside her memories. "Yes, that's my plan. Read the instruction manual. Drive the tractor."

"Still doing everything on your own too," he

mused, seeming intent to point out what hadn't changed about her.

While Elsie couldn't help but notice what had changed about him. Specifically, the boy she'd known had grown into a man. Where he'd once been cute and boyishly charming, he was now so very handsome, in a rugged, outdoor, hands-on kind of way. The exact kind of way Elsie had no business noticing. Elsie crossed her arms over her chest before she reached out, touched his arm. Tested her theory that beneath his sun-soaked skin was all muscle.

He rubbed his hand over his mouth. "What's your plan B then?"

"What?" Elsie met his gaze.

"Elsie Marie, I know you." He leaned farther into the cab, closing the distance between them.

And Elsie almost leaned toward him. As if she meant to meet him halfway.

Those gold flecks in his gaze sparked. His words were wry. "You always have multiple plans, Elsie. So much so, your plans *have* plans."

Only she hadn't planned on running into him so soon. So quickly. With barely enough space between them to draw a decent breath. Let alone think clearly. She swiped at her damp neck. Wanting desperately to blame the unrelenting sun for rattling her. "There's nothing wrong with being prepared."

"Let me see your phone." He extended his arm toward her. Palm up.

Now was her chance. To finally know. To take his hand in hers and know for certain if his grip was as strong and secure as she'd always imagined. To know for certain if their hands fit in that easy, perfect way that just felt right. The way she'd always wanted her hand to fit inside her ex-husband's and never quite did.

Definitely not a chance she would ever take, especially with Ryan Sloan. Who took relationships less seriously than a bear took a bee guarding its hive. *Love. Why would I want that, Elsie Marie? I have bronc riding. That's my life. All I'll ever need.* And given that Ryan was currently ranked number one in bronc riding and very single according to her brother, Ryan had certainly proven his words true.

Besides, everything Elsie needed waited in New York. The city was her calling. The country his. Their time together would only ever be temporary. As always. It was best not to hold his hand. Best not to know. After all, she never liked starting things that could not be finished.

She set her phone carefully on his palm. "If you can tell me what kind of tractor this is exactly, I can read the manual on my own."

"You don't need a manual." He tapped quickly on her phone screen, then handed her phone back.

His expression was neutral. His voice causal. "You have me."

Have him. No. He wasn't hers. She didn't want to think of him like that. That implied things like dating and relationships and those extra messy emotions. The ones she'd gotten completely wrong before. No matter. She'd filed away love in the *been there, don't need that again* folder along with her divorce papers more than a year ago.

"I added myself to your contacts. Now one of your plan B's can be calling a cowboy." A close-lipped smile worked across his face. He motioned toward her. "Scoot over."

Elsie never budged. "Why?"

"So I can give you your first tractor driving lesson." He folded his tall frame into the suddenly too-small cab.

Sweat dampened her entire back now. Yet he looked unbothered as if he was somehow immune to the heat. Elsie blurted, "We can't."

He paused and arched an eyebrow at her.

He was close enough to hug now. Without any effort. Just a small stretch. For a welcome back embrace between friends. First, she wanted to hold his hand. Now hug him. What was next? *Exit now.* She had to get out. Get herself back together. She rushed on, "I can't leave Autumn alone with your horse."

"Sundancer is gentler than a kitten and better trained than a show dog." He motioned toward the window. Outside, Autumn picked a dandelion and blew the fluff into the air all while the horse grazed calmly beside her.

"Still, I should wait here. Gemma is coloring in the car. She might need me." Elsie scooted to the edge of the chair and shifted toward the door. Only to pause when her toes touched the tips of his boots. Two problems faced her. Getting around her cowboy. And getting down.

He lifted his arm as if reaching for her.

Elsie held her breath and waited. Braced herself for the connection. She had always wanted to know...

But he simply touched his hat and adjusted it lower on his forehead. "Let me get out of your way first. Unless you need help climbing down."

Elsie exhaled and shook her head. "I can manage."

With a quick nod, Ryan backed out of the cab and was on the ground in seemingly one agile leap. Elsie on the other hand found herself indecisive about how to even climb down. Forward or backward. She finally chose backward. Only to have her sandal slip off the first step. She would've fallen unceremoniously into the dirt if Ryan hadn't reached up, caught her around the waist and set her safely on the ground.

One shift. One lean back against him. Then she would be inside his embrace completely. One more thing she didn't need to test. She took a quick breath and released it. Finally, she glanced over her shoulder and worked to keep her words light and easy. "Thanks for the assist."

His fingers flexed at her waist. His mouth opened.

But Autumn's excited words filled the silence. "Cowboy Prince, did Auntie stall the tractor like she does Dad's car?"

Elsie cringed. Then stepped away from Ryan. She set her hand on her niece's shoulder. "We only stalled twice."

"In the driveway," Autumn supplied.

Elsie glanced at Ryan. He smoothed out his grin. Elsie shoved her shoulders back. "It's been a minute since I've driven a stick shift." More like years since she'd driven her own car. Let alone one with a manual transmission. She'd lived in Seattle until last week. Walked to work. To restaurants. To everything. And if she'd wanted a ride, she opened the app on her phone and scheduled a pickup.

"I offered to give you driving lessons all those summers ago," Ryan teased. "Maybe you should've said yes."

She'd been fifteen and more worried about what Ryan thought of her outfit than perfecting her shifting skills. And he would've been a distraction she hadn't needed. Then or now. "It's coming back to me."

"I'll be happy to give you a refresher," he offered.

More time with Ryan. Not what she came for. She was there to watch her nieces. Until her Aunt Marlena and Elsie's mom returned from their extended overseas vacation. Then the two sisters would care for Bryce and look after the girls. For now, Elsie would do what she always did. Keep her senses about her. "If you could move the tractor so we can get to the hospital to see Bryce, that will be more than enough."

"Well, the offer stands," he said. His gaze gleamed. "You know how to reach me if you change your mind."

Not happening. One cowboy rescue was more than enough.

Ryan shifted his smile toward Autumn. "Want to take a ride in the tractor? Think of it like a carriage for a cowgirl princess such as yourself."

"Can I, Auntie?" Hope widened Autumn's eyes. "Please?"

Elsie looked at Ryan.

"She'll be fine," he assured her. "I know what I'm doing."

That made one of them. Elsie finally nodded.

Ryan guided Autumn up into the tractor. Elsie walked over to Sundancer on the other side of the driveway.

Within seconds, the tractor engine started. Autumn waved excitedly from her perch next to Ryan. He maneuvered expertly around the Jeep, missing the ditch entirely, and stopped beside the car. Autumn shouted out the window at her sister. Gemma cheered from the front passenger seat. The tractor rumbled up the driveway and out of sight. The large wheels kicked up a dust cloud in their wake.

Minutes later, the pair finally appeared on the crest. Ryan held Autumn's hand while she skipped beside him.

"I finished two drawings, Auntie," Gemma shouted and waved the papers at Elsie. She was out of the Jeep and racing up the drive toward Ryan and Autumn in a blink.

The girls' bright laughter floated like the plump white clouds across the spring blue sky, drawing out Elsie's own reluctant smile. It was the first time she'd heard her nieces truly laugh since she'd arrived late yesterday afternoon. It rankled slightly that it was their cowboy prince, not Elsie, who was responsible for her nieces' sudden good moods.

Watching the animated trio, Elsie's smile expanded. Before she checked herself.

Sundancer nickered and pawed the ground beside her as if wanting Ryan's attention too.

Elsie patted the horse. "Don't worry, Sundancer. He's all yours."

After all, the very last thing Elsie wanted was her own cowboy situation.

CHAPTER TWO

"COWBOY PRINCE. COWBOY PRINCE." Gemma hopped toward Ryan like a chirpy house finch flitting through his late Gran Claire's gardens. Gemma's spindly arms flapped at her sides. Her drawings snapped in the warm breeze. "Look. I put you in my pictures too, Cowboy Prince."

Cowboy Prince. Ryan still hadn't quite adjusted to his newly anointed nickname. Cowboy he was, from his old, broken-in boots to his bloodlines. But a prince? Never that. Cowboy daredevil would've been more appropriate. At least until recently. He sidestepped his current identity crisis, knelt and caught Gemma as she careened into him. Taking the crinkled paper from her, he said, "I haven't been in a drawing for a really long time."

Gemma braced her small hands on his shoulders and tipped her head to study him. "Why not?"

Ryan worked his expression into serious then shrugged. "I suppose because no one in my family draws pictures anymore."

Although with his sister-in-law Tess expecting

twins soon, he supposed that would change in the coming years. As for Ryan, coloring for fun had ended in grade school around the time he had discovered the thrill of the rodeo. And rodeo became the only thing he ever wanted to do.

Gemma's nose crinkled. "Then how do you make your walls happy if you don't have any pictures on them?"

He was happiest outside. Covered in dirt, horsehair and nature. Not a wall in sight. He glanced at the thick layer of dust stuck on his boots. Not exactly the polished look of a prince. Still, the concern in Gemma's fawn-wide brown eyes caught his attention. Unsure of the right answer to soothe the sweet little girl, he asked, "Do you think my walls are unhappy?"

She chewed on her bottom lip and nodded solemnly.

"What should I do?" he asked.

"Put pictures on them, silly." Gemma tapped her drawing and grinned. "You can have this one."

"But this is for your dad," Ryan countered.

"I'll make Dad another picture on the way to the hospital. I don't get sick reading and stuff in the car like Gem and Auntie." With that declaration, Autumn leaned against Ryan's shoulder and pointed at her younger sister's artwork. "Besides, you gotta have that one. You're in it."

"I'll put it on my wall tonight." Ryan grinned and looked at the picture. Two stick figures, one with a cowboy hat and the other with a crown on her yellow hair, stood in a field of bright sunflowers. Each flower had a smiley face drawn in the center. Even the sun in the corner beamed. It was a burst of happiness on paper. He added, "I like the crown you're wearing in this picture, Gemma. You look just like a princess."

"That's not me." Gemma giggled. "That's Auntie Elsie and you."

Ryan shifted and glanced down the drive where Elsie stood beside his horse. Elsie stroked her fingers down Sundancer's muzzle. The horse leaned into her touch as if already drawn to her. Ryan knew the feeling. He'd always been aware of Elsie. Too aware. And at all the wrong times. Like now for instance. When he was lingering for no apparent reason. When what he needed was to get back to his career. Back to the circuit. Where he belonged.

"You can look at my picture when you fall asleep. And dream about holding hands with Auntie Elsie." Gemma twirled around in several circles, wobbled to a stop and speared her arms over her head. "Then you'll wake up happy."

A belt buckle. A jackpot. A perfect eight-second ride on a bucking bronc. That had been Ryan's dream for as long as he could remember. Now certainly wasn't the time to go looking for some new dream. Or worse someone. He was good as he was—riding through life solo. On his own terms.

Besides, the truth was Elsie and Ryan only worked in a dream. Elsie was high-rises and corner offices. Sophisticated. Polished and poised. He was backroads and pastures. Straightforward. Rough and unrefined at times. Those roads weren't meant to intersect. Let alone connect. Ever. He pulled his gaze back to Gemma's picture. "So, this is me and your Aunt Elsie then."

"Holding hands." Gemma beamed then grew serious again and lowered her voice. "Auntie used to hold Uncle Andrew's hand, but no more. I think she cried a lot too. Now she won't be sad if she holds Cowboy Prince's hand."

Maybe not in a colorful picture. But Ryan was far from a prince. Never claimed to be one. He rubbed his palm on his jeans. As for Elsie, she should be holding a real prince's hand. One who would care for her heart properly. She certainly deserved that. Deserved more than a reckless cowboy like Ryan with calloused fingers and a heart too cordoned off to ever find. The last thing he ever wanted was to make Elsie sad. Nothing for it but to keep his distance.

"Well, thank you for my picture. I'm sure my wall will be very happy to have it." He folded the picture, tucked it into his shirt pocket and stood. Then walked between the girls back down the drive. "Now it's time to get you two to the hospital to see your dad."

And past time for Ryan and Sundancer to get

on their way. There was no need to stick around as if he was suddenly interested in reconnecting more with Elsie. As it was, he already knew the highlights reel of her life.

He'd kept low-key tabs on Elsie over the years. Never asking her aunt or uncle or even Bryce about her directly. Yet whenever Elsie's name came up in conversation, he always paid attention.

He knew Elsie had earned both her college degree and master's degree in hospitality and event management in an impressive five years.

Knew she worked in Seattle as an event manager for an upscale worldwide hotel chain. She'd always been driven and hardworking.

Knew also about her private wedding in Paris. Even in a simple black-and-white bridal photograph her aunt had shown him, Elsie had taken his breath away.

Lastly, he knew about her divorce.

He frowned. That was the only piece that didn't quite fit. Surely her ex-husband regretted his decision every single day. Because that was the thing about Elsie. Beyond her pretty looks and natural poise, Elsie Marie Parks was what his grandpa would call a keeper.

Which made her entirely wrong for Ryan of course.

The only thing Ryan was interested in keeping was his top ranking in bronc riding. Yet to do that, Ryan had to rediscover his edge and get back in the saddle. The one he hadn't been in for more than a month. After he'd messed up during a stunt on a Western movie set and ended up injuring Sundancer. His stomach pitched sideways. And that edge—the one that had kept him razor-focused and at the top of his bronc-riding game for so many years—remained silent and flatlined. Same as it'd been since the accident.

Gemma rushed over to Elsie and showed off her artwork.

Ryan reached for Sundancer's reins and tipped his hat at Elsie. "Looks like you're clear to get on your way." Same as him.

He needed to get on his way to finding himself again. Time was running out. He had two weeks until he had to be back in the saddle. Back in the chute. Anticipating that first jump of his horse for an eight-second ride at Belleridge Rodeo Rides for A Cause.

If only the rodeo wasn't a charity event. If only Ryan hadn't agreed to compete for Martha Claire Horse Haven. The very same horse sanctuary named after his own late Gran Claire. The one he volunteered at whenever he was home. The one that needed another new stable. Because Ryan had promised homes to five aged-out broncs from the circuit. Then perhaps he could've bowed out. Blamed an old injury. But he refused to let down his family, his hometown or those circuit horses. He had to ride. But first he had to figure out how.

"But you can't leave." Gemma turned toward him. Disappointment widened her already impossibly round eyes. "You'll miss the tea party later."

Ryan rubbed the back of his neck. "I could come back."

Gemma's eyebrows pinched together. "You said that last time and didn't come back."

Bryce had granted Ryan a tea party rain check last week. Because Ryan had told Bryce he was finally getting back in the saddle. Finally practicing for the upcoming Rodeo Rides for A Cause at the newly restored Belleridge arena. Bryce had believed him. Heck, Ryan had believed it too.

Until he'd gotten home. Saddled Mischief, his mustang. Walked to the practice arena. Started overthinking. Second-guessing. And backpedaling. Not a good look for a supposed champion bronc rider. Fortunately, he excelled at keeping things like that to himself. He tapped Gemma on the nose. "But I apologized for missing the tea party and even brought you a box of chocolate peanut butter candy. Your favorite."

Gemma's face softened.

"You could come to the hospital with us now, Cowboy Prince." Autumn snapped off a dandelion and handed it to her sister. "You and Dad can talk about the bees."

"They always talk about the bees," Gemma added. Her words rushed out in a forlorn breath that scattered the dandelion fluff into the air.

The girls weren't wrong. It was entirely intentional on Ryan's part too. If his friend was thinking about the bee business and his own life, then Bryce was less likely to go poking into Ryan's problems. Ryan switched the reins to his other hand and his gaze caught on Elsie.

She studied him closely. Suspicion crossed her face. "I should've known this was all your idea."

What? That he wasn't there by chance. That he'd purposely walked by the farm. Yesterday. And today. That he would've walked by again tomorrow. And the day after. All for a not-so-impromptu run-in with her. Ryan smoothed his expression into impassive.

"The beekeeping," Elsie clarified. "You're the one who gave Bryce the bee business idea."

No. He couldn't claim that one. But he had helped Bryce refine it. Showing her brother several other potential income streams for his bee-keeping endeavor. Ryan took in Elsie's flushed cheeks and the flash in her silver gaze like the start of a spring storm brewing. Her mind was already set. No use arguing now. He pressed his lips together and waited. He'd always been partial to a midnight storm.

"You convinced my brother to do all this. To take such a risk," Elsie charged. "You could always convince him to do anything."

But not Elsie. Never her. Despite his best efforts. Which had only intrigued him more. Yet it was for the best he hadn't succeeded. Then saying goodbye to Elsie might've actually hurt once upon a time. But Ryan had vowed long ago that goodbye would never get to him. Never hit him hard enough to ever matter.

Elsie rolled on. "Then you talked Bryce into uprooting his entire life and family to relocate here."

"You say *here* like it's a bad thing." But it was. To her. *I won't be back. There's nothing here I could ever want.* Those had been Elsie's parting words that last summer she'd spent at her aunt and uncle's farm. After Ryan had made the mistake of asking when she'd return. He tapped his hat up, met her gaze. Didn't back down. "I won't apologize if that's what you're looking for. Bryce is better off living here."

She stepped toward him. Her gaze sparked again. "That's debatable, given my brother is currently in the hospital."

"Bryce is happy here, Elsie." *You could be too.* Strike that thought. Her happiness was *so* not his concern. Still, beneath the frustration he saw the worry for her brother on her face. Heard the unease in her words. And just like that he wasn't quite ready to leave her. He said, "Since you clearly don't believe me, there's only one option. I'm going with you to the hospital. Then we can ask Bryce together about his recent life decisions."

Autumn and Gemma cheered. Then Gemma

shouted, "We'll go make room for Cowboy Prince in the car." The two girls raced toward the Jeep.

Elsie lost her bluster. Touched her forehead. Searched his face. Relief and resistance clashed in her gaze. "You can't come with us."

Try and stop me. His grin was gentle. "Sure, I can. You know I care about Bryce too." *And you if only from a distance.*

"What about your horse?" Elsie flicked her wrist toward his horse. Then rubbed the back of her neck. "You can't just leave Sundancer here."

Ryan peered at her closer. She looked flustered now. He turned and guided Sundancer up the drive. Time to get moving before she came up with more excuses to deny him. "I'll put Sundancer in the pasture. There's nothing he can get into there."

"But no one will be here with him." Elsie caught up to him and followed Ryan to the back gate of the pasture. "To look after him."

"He'll be fine." Ryan released the halter from Sundancer and checked his gait. The gelding's limp wasn't visible. It hadn't been for the past few days. Of course, Sundancer hadn't been saddle tested yet. Or ridden. Still, the horse certainly seemed to be on the mend faster than Ryan.

Elsie gripped the top post of the fence. Her attention was on Sundancer. "It doesn't feel right."

There was a distance in her tone. A tension in her fingers. Even more in her words. Nothing he would have noticed if he wasn't so aware of her.

And so very intent on not facing his own predica-
ments for a little while longer. Ryan checked the
lock on the gate and turned toward her. "What's
really going on, Elsie?"

"We aren't meant for farming, Ryan." Elsie
pushed away from the fence and rounded on him.
"We weren't farm raised. You know that better
than anyone."

"Neither was your Aunt Marlena." Ryan motioned behind him. Only the roof of the striking
stone two-story house was visible in the distance.
He knew the land and the house as well as his own.
Bryce and Ryan, along with Ryan's four brothers,
had spent as much time roaming these acres growing up as they had exploring the Sloan land. He
added, "Look at what your aunt built here."

"This was all my Uncle Robert," Elsie countered. "Aunt Marlena and Uncle Robert built all
this together. Bryce is alone now that my mom and
aunt seem to have acquired an insatiable travel
bug."

"Not really." Ryan lifted one shoulder and
stepped around her, heading back to the Jeep.
"Bryce has good neighbors and friends here. People looking out for him."

"Except no one was here when he fell through
the greenhouse roof." Frustration was thick in
her words. And in the crunch of her steps on the
gravel drive.

"You'll have to take that up with your brother,"

Ryan said. "In the meantime, give this place a chance. It might change your mind."

Elsie flipped her ponytail back over her shoulder. Certainty coated her words. "My mind is set on New York."

He shouldn't have been surprised. Her gaze had always been fixed well beyond Three Springs County lines. He tried to sound indifferent. "What's in New York?"

"My new job." She slanted her gaze toward him. "I was going there when I got the call that Bryce was in the hospital."

This was a detour. A temporary stopover on her way to where she wanted to be. This was what his Gran Claire would've called good information. *Any information is good, Ryan, even when it's not what you want to hear. Can't expect to make good decisions without knowing all the facts.* He asked, "When do you start?"

"I'll leave when Aunt Marlena and my mom get back from their vacation late next week," she explained.

She would be back on the road. Alone. But who would be watching over her? Not him. With luck, he would be on the road too. Getting back to his own life on the rodeo circuit. The only one he ever wanted.

"I want you to know." She glanced at him. "If Bryce is truly happy here, I'll do my best to support him."

Ryan nodded. Did his best to do the same for her now and pushed more positivity into his tone. "Congratulations on your new job, Elsie. I'm sure you will be very happy in the city."

"That's my plan." Her smile was small and brief. "To be happy."

Before he could press her about *not* being happy, she tossed the car keys at him then quickly added, "I think it would make everyone in the car happy if you drove us to the hospital."

Ryan caught the keys and opened the front passenger door of the Jeep for Elsie. "Your chariot awaits, my lady." That drew out her laughter. To his delight.

"Thank you, Cowboy Prince." Her gaze gleamed before she climbed into the car.

Ryan grinned, more than glad to spend a little bit longer with Elsie.

As for his own happy, he'd always found it in the saddle. And that was exactly where he would find it again. Because a horse and a rodeo were all a cowboy like him ever needed.

CHAPTER THREE

"TURN IT UP, AUNTIE," Gemma chanted from the back seat. "This is my favorite song *e-v-e-r*."

"Dad says he can't think with the radio turned up too loud," Autumn chided her sister.

Elsie was starting to think too much. And worry. About her brother. Her nieces. Herself. Four years separated Elsie and her older brother. When their parents divorced, Bryce had preferred their father's quieter house. Elsie had shuffled between houses yet never quite found her footing in either place. And the siblings grew further apart. Attending different colleges hadn't helped. Neither had job relocations that widened the distance to state lines. Now they weren't exactly tight as far as siblings went. They cared for each other. Albeit from afar. Showed their affection mostly over text and occasional phone calls on holidays and birthdays. But Bryce's accident had scared Elsie. A lot. Elsie wanted to change things between them before it was too late. She only hoped her brother did too.

That worry swirled around her racing thoughts.

Elsie reached for the volume button on the radio and slanted her gaze at Ryan. "Do you mind?"

He shook his head and grinned. "It feels like a volume up, windows down kind of day."

That sounded carefree. Worry free. She couldn't remember the last time she'd enjoyed a day like that. Certainly not with her ex-husband. They'd been too focused on their careers and work goals to ease off, even for an afternoon. She eyed Ryan. "Do this often?"

"Not as much as I should," Ryan admitted.

Surprise filtered through her. The boy she'd known had hardly ever been serious about anything, except his horses. The man now looked guarded as if he carried secrets that weren't so light and easy. But Elsie was there to mend things between her and her family, not discover more about her cowboy. She tapped her finger on the volume button and said, "Sing it if you know it."

With that, the windows rolled down. The radio went up. And the girls belted out the words to the pop song and wiggled their shoulders to the up-beat tune in the back seat. Slowly, Elsie's shoulders relaxed. By the next song, she was tapping her foot to the beat.

Two songs later, she was windblown, singing with her nieces and urging her cowboy to join the chorus. He didn't shy away and instead matched the singer's deep timbre with his own equally rich voice. All to the girls' delight and Elsie's disbelief.

Ryan Sloan could sing. And his was not a voice reserved only for showers and solo car karaoke sessions. She wanted to find another song. One of his favorites perhaps, if only she knew it. She wanted to listen to him sing more.

But he pulled into the hospital parking lot. And Elsie remembered there was nothing else she wanted when it came to her cowboy. Certainly, no further singing sessions that might make her wonder what else she didn't know about him. Oh, her curiosity was certainly caught now.

That was bad. Elsie was a learner, and the more puzzling something was, the more she wanted to understand it. But there was no manual on cowboys. Besides, her cowboy looked more like a closed book. Best all-around if she reined in her curiosity. She worried if she started learning about her cowboy, she might not want to stop.

The windows went up. And that worry stepped forward again. Searching for a distraction, Elsie unbuckled then leaned around her seat. She asked, "You need help picking up those crayons?"

The girls had spilled their crayons and markers when they'd started dancing. "No thanks. We got it." Gemma bent down, reached under her seat, and handed a green crayon to her sister.

Autumn arranged the crayon in the large box and frowned at Elsie. "Dad says if we make the mess, we gotta clean it up too."

"That's the rule." Gemma sat up, holding several more crayons. "And we gotta follow the rules or Dad gets mad."

Elsie left her nieces to their cleanup, opened her door and stepped out. Suddenly restless yet rooted in place.

Ryan rounded the front of the Jeep and approached her. "You okay?"

"Hospitals. Nerves." Elsie stuck to the obvious reasons for sudden hesitation. The ones easiest to explain. Admitting she was anxious to see her brother for the first time in person after more than three years, well that would only lead to questions. Especially from Ryan, who always put his family first. Elsie was trying to do that now. She wanted to get it right. She just wasn't certain how. She added, "Not the best combination for me."

Ryan lifted his cowboy hat and ran his fingers through his hair. "I think I should warn you."

"Hospitals make you nervous too." She winced at the hope she heard in her words. As if she wanted that to be what connected them. What made her feel not quite so alone. Not so completely out of sorts.

"They don't bother me anymore." He settled his hat back on his head.

"How did you get over it?" she asked.

"Too many injuries." He touched his thigh as if testing an old injury. "Been here more than I'd like to admit."

"Still, you keep competing." Same as she kept

proving she was alright alone. "I admire your resolve." And she liked to think she had some herself. She released the car door.

"Rodeo is what I do," he said simply. Firmly.

The edges of his mouth tightened. A brief tensing. There and gone. She would've missed it if she hadn't been watching him so closely. Locked on to him as if he was somehow her anchor inside all her sudden insecurities and uncertainty.

Ryan scratched his fingers through his beard. "But back to your brother. Bryce is pretty banged up. He's going to tell you he looks worse than he feels."

Elsie was still missing a few details about Bryce's accident. But she knew Ryan had gone to the hospital after her brother's fall. While a volunteer EMT had stayed with Autumn and Gemma at the house until Sam Sloan, Ryan's grandfather, had arrived to watch the girls. It had been Sam who'd called Elsie to tell her what had happened. It was several more hours before she'd been able to speak to Bryce. Elsie frowned. "How bad is it?"

"Lots of bruises all over. Stitches on his face. Cuts and scratches on his arms." Ryan motioned toward his boots. "And some sort of drain in his ankle that Grant can explain a lot better than me."

Grant was Ryan's younger brother and one of the best orthopedic surgeons around. Fortunately, Bryce was under Grant's care and Grant would be handling her brother's ankle surgery the following morning. Elsie's nerves stretched tight. Surely once she saw her brother, the worry would even out.

"I just wanted you and the girls to be prepared," Ryan added.

She hadn't prepared the girls. She wasn't certain they'd ever been in a hospital before. Let alone to see someone they loved. She'd been so focused on getting *to* the hospital, she hadn't given much thought to what happened *when* they arrived. "What's the process here?" Elsie drew a breath and glanced at the girls slipping on their backpacks in the back seat. "Do I go in first? Do we all go in together?"

"How about I take the girls to the gift shop," Ryan offered. "They can pick out balloons for their dad, while you go see your brother."

She was supposed to be looking after her nieces. That was why she came. But she could use the help. And a moment alone with her brother would be welcome. "I owe you."

"It's no big deal." Ryan's eyebrows lifted. "Believe it or not, the gift shop sells the best caramel almond popcorn around. Gran Claire always got us some to share when she had to bring me here as a kid."

Claire Sloan had been full of warmth and welcome. The first time Elsie had met Ryan's grandmother, she'd hugged Elsie tight. Then told her: *We only use the back door around here. The front door is for strangers. If you've come inside my home, you're no longer a stranger.* Elsie had always marveled at how instantly she'd felt at home in the Sloan farmhouse. She'd never felt that anywhere else, not even the house she'd shared with her ex-husband. Yet she searched for that feeling. Even still.

Ryan stepped around her, opened the car door for the girls then glanced at Elsie. "I think I'm going to reserve the right to call in that favor."

The smile in his words paired perfectly with his half grin. And the combination was much too appealing. Before Elsie reconsidered that expiration on her old crush, she said, "Call it in soon or I'll be gone."

Her words hovered between them. More like a warning than a casual reminder. Still, she needed to hear it out loud. She was leaving. Whatever she felt now was surely just as temporary.

Minutes later, the girls were spreading hand sanitizer all over their palms in the hospital lobby then heading to the gift shop with Ryan. While Elsie pressed a visitor's sticker onto her shirt and tapped the elevator call button. On the fourth floor, she greeted the nurse behind the desk and located her brother's room at the far end of the hall.

One deep inhale. One longer exhale. Then she stepped over her nerves and walked inside. Only to pull up short. Ryan hadn't exaggerated. If anything, Ryan hadn't been detailed enough. Her brother looked as if he'd crashed through multiple roofs headfirst.

"I look so much worse than I feel." Bryce watched her from behind two black eyes. One cheek was swollen. The other stitched from his hairline to his jaw. He started to smile, then lifted his hand toward his cheek and added, "I promise."

"That's exactly what Ryan told me you were going to say." Elsie moved to her brother's bedside and took his hand—the only part of him not bandaged—and squeezed his fingers. "The girls are in the gift store with Ryan. They'll be here soon. But seriously, are you in a lot of pain?"

"Not right now. Thanks to the pain meds." Bryce tipped his head at the IV bag hanging on the pole beside the bed and connected to the line in his arm. "And if I don't move too much. Or breathe too deeply, that helps."

Elsie winced.

"I'll be fine soon enough." Bryce tightened his grip around her hand. "I'm just glad you're here, Els. I can't thank you enough for changing your plans for us."

It was the first time Bryce had ever called Elsie and asked for her help. The first time she'd ever heard her brother say: *We need you, Els.* She couldn't have refused. Wouldn't have even considered it. Now that she was with him, she was even more certain she'd made the right decision. She was exactly where she needed to be.

"Everything okay with work and your new job?" Concern shifted through his words.

"I pushed back my start date." Elsie straightened the covers on Bryce's bed and avoided looking at the contraption holding his swollen ankle off the bed. "My new boss was very understanding."

"Well, I'm grateful to you and your new boss." Bryce dropped his head back on the pillow and tugged at his hair. "I don't have time to be down like this. There's so much to do. It's the start of the bee season."

"I'm here now," Elsie said, adding more reassurance to her words. "That should help, right? You can concentrate on getting better."

"I can't believe you're so open to helping." Bryce's gaze brightened inside his black eyes. He pressed a button and raised the head of his bed until he was sitting up. "But I really need it, so I'm taking you up on it."

Elsie fussed more with his covers and ignored the pinch of guilt in her chest. Had he needed her help before and been afraid to ask her? Afraid she would've turned him down. Or perhaps he simply hadn't wanted to bother her. It was just that Elsie and her brother always fended for themselves. They had, she supposed, ever since their parents' difficult divorce, when, in the chaos and uncertainty, it had become abundantly clear it was everyone for themselves.

Still, she was there now. This was her chance to make things right. To be there for her brother and nieces. Perhaps even make up for the years when she hadn't been.

Bryce rolled the small table closer with his good hand and tapped on his notepad. "I've got spread-sheets all prepared for you."

Detailed and task oriented were two of her mathematically-minded brother's top skills. Spread-sheets one of his superpowers. Finally, something felt familiar. Elsie grinned. "You actually created individual spreadsheets for how to care for the girls."

Bryce lifted his gaze from his notepad briefly. His thoughts preoccupied. "No, the spreadsheets are for the farm."

"The farm," Elsie repeated.

"Didn't you check your email?" Bryce asked. His fingers tapped against the computer screen again. Surprisingly quick given the rest of him was bandaged and hurt. His mind, it seemed, was still in overdrive. "I sent you an overview about an hour ago."

When she was trying to teach herself to drive a tractor. "I haven't had time to look at my email."

"Open it now." Bryce motioned toward the empty chair but kept his attention fixed on his notepad. "We can talk it through together quickly before the girls get here."

Elsie pulled her phone from her pocket and double-clicked on her email app. Sure enough Bryce's email was at the top of her unopened list. The subject: Farm to Do.

Monitors beeped in the quiet room. Elsie scanned the lengthy email. Paused and read it again. Only slower. Still, she couldn't quite wrap her mind around any of it. She looked at her brother, searched his head for a wound that the doctors might have missed. Maybe a concussion that made him forget her skillset was hospitality, not horticulture.

Only Bryce stared back at her, patient, calm and expectant. His pale blue gaze surprisingly clear and lucid, despite the pain medicine. He didn't wince from pain. Or smile and tell her he was only kidding. Her brother had never been much of a joker. And his email was no prank. She was there for more than babysitting. But she wasn't even confident she had the childcare piece in hand. Her time spent around kids was limited. Unease slipped through her.

Where to begin? Elsie glanced at her Farm to Do email and decided the only place to start was at item one. "Let me make sure I've got this straight. That I'm reading this right." Elsie searched for her most composed expression. Her most coolly collected tone. "You want me to make more space for the bees." Whatever that meant.

Her brother's eyebrows lifted. His barely-there nod encouraging.

Elsie cleared her throat and focused on item two. "Then you want me to expand the pollinator gardens." No matter she was an at-home houseplant killer. Not intentionally. She either overwatered or under watered. After her latest plant flop, she'd decided it was best for nature if she admired the flowers in the botanical gardens instead.

"It's more like a pasture than a garden," Bryce explained. "We want to add more mountain mint and white clover along with the flowers I've listed for you. The different blooming times allows extended harvesting and foraging for the honeybee colonies in the bee pasture."

"Right. Bee pasture." Elsie inhaled around the panic stirring inside her. She was there to watch her nieces. Not sow a pasture.

"The local nursery, Cider Mill Orchard, doesn't have the plants I want," Bryce continued. "I'll email you a list of other nurseries that aren't too far of a drive from the farm. We need those plants in the ground this week or we'll really be behind schedule. We can't afford that."

Elsie was already feeling behind. Far behind. She dropped her free arm to her side, forcing herself to look open and receptive. Not stubborn and resistant. She could do this. For her brother. "And item three."

"The seedlings." Bryce ran his hand through his hair and ruffled the light brown strands on the top of his head. "I updated their care spreadsheets this morning too."

"The seedlings have spreadsheets." It seemed the entire farm had its very own spreadsheet. Her brother was nothing if not thorough.

"I've got several seedling test groups in the greenhouses. Different food. Water schedule. Light." Bryce's voice got more animated. "It's all on the spreadsheet."

Color coded, she would bet. When her brother focused on something, he went all in and gave it his full attention. His clients from his financial advising days had certainly benefitted from his dedication. She asked, "What are these seedlings for exactly?"

"Bee garden starter kits," Bryce said. "We'll give out the seedling starter kits with every honey purchase. That was Ryan's idea."

Ryan. The cowboy seemed to be full of ideas.

"No, that's not entirely accurate." Bryce chuckled. "Ryan suggested harvesting the seeds and selling the kits as another way to monetize our beekeeping business."

What did a rodeo cowboy with a fondness for adventure and adrenaline rushes know about monetizing beekeeping? While Elsie felt like she suddenly knew nothing. She ran her fingers over her forehead. "You keep saying *we* and *our*. Whose business is this exactly?"

"It's mine." Bryce lifted his eyebrows up then

stiffened as if the action stretched his bruises too much. "Well, it was Aunt Marlena's, but I took it over. But you already know that. It's a family thing."

She shook her head at her brother's uncharacteristic rambling and bumped the bewilderment from her words. "Selling seeds is a profitable business then."

"You'd be surprised." Bryce tapped on his notepad again. "But we need quality seeds, which means we grow and refine our flowers and seeds to produce the best product. Then we sell those."

"Of course." Elsie studied her brother. He sounded excited about growing seedlings. Looked happy, despite his banged-up face, about it too. Ryan hadn't been wrong.

Now it was up to her to stand behind her word. She'd told Bryce she'd do anything for him when they'd talked after his accident. And she'd given Ryan her promise to support Bryce if he was happy. Time to prove she meant what she said. That her brother could count on her. Surely, he wouldn't have given her anything he didn't think she could handle.

The door to his room opened slowly. A bouquet of balloons filled the doorway before Gemma squeezed inside. Autumn close on her heels. The girls halted and slipped behind Elsie. Their eyes wide, their faces pale. Elsie wasn't quite sure what to do. Or say.

Affection spilled across Bryce's face. "Daddy doesn't look so good, does he?"

Autumn continued to study her dad and shook her head.

Gemma wrapped her arm around Elsie's waist and rested her cheek against Elsie's side. "Your face is puffy and mad, Daddy."

"Yeah. It sure is, Gem-Gem." Bryce shifted in the bed. A small smile worked across his mouth. "But those shiny balloons are making my eyes very happy."

"I picked out the balloon in the shape of the rainbow, Dad." Autumn edged closer to the bed, her hands clutched behind her back. "'Cause it has all your favorite colors in it."

"It sure does." Bryce's voice was soft, gentle.

"I picked out the sun balloon," Gemma announced and joined her sister. Then wrapped her arms around herself. "Now you'll be warm 'cause the sun is so hot in Texas."

"I'm already feeling so much better." Bryce reached his good arm out to his daughters. "And guess what?"

Autumn took her dad's hand. Gemma bounced and said, "Your face isn't mad no more."

"There's that." Bryce chuckled. "And I don't have any bandages on my right hand, which means I can still color with you."

Her brother colored. That was unexpected yet heartening. Elsie hadn't known what kind of a father Bryce would be. Their own father had been a man of few words and even less affectionate. Whereas their mother was charismatic, capricious and often unreliable. Fortunately, their father had provided a stable place growing up, even if his house felt more like a museum than a kid-friendly home.

"We got pictures, Daddy." Gemma turned and took her backpack from Ryan. Then the girls returned to Bryce's bedside to show off their artwork and debate the best wall to display the pictures on.

Elsie moved closer to Ryan and whispered, "I think I might need those tractor lessons from you after all."

Surprise crossed Ryan's face. He lowered his voice. "What did I miss?"

Before Elsie could explain, the door opened again. A nurse in light blue scrubs backed into the room with a large cart. "Okay, Bryce. I've logged into my investment website. Now, let's create my portfolio. I sure like the sound of that." The nurse turned around, touched her dark hair that was graying at the temples and blanched. "Sorry, didn't realize you've got company. Pay me no mind."

"Everyone, this is Ms. Liza. The best nurse on the floor," Bryce said. "She puts up with me."

Liza greeted the girls first, then shook her head and chuckled. "Your daddy is one of the easiest patients I've got."

"Liza and I struck a bargain," Bryce added. "Extra cookies at lunch in exchange for investment guidance. I'm getting the better end of the bargain."

"It's more like an investment tutorial." Liza laughed and punched a code into the machine on her cart. "But I can come back after lunch."

"Lunch." Gemma pressed a hand on her stomach. "Do we get lunch too? My tummy is hungry."

"Sorry, only Dad gets lunch in here." Liza leaned down between the girls and whispered, "Don't tell him, but the food is better down the street at All-Day Corner Diner. You can get fancy milkshakes there with whipped cream and double cherries."

"Dad always steals my cherry," Autumn replied. "Then pretends he didn't eat it."

"Not this time." Liza's laugh filled the room and she glanced at Elsie. "But you should hurry if you want to beat the lunch rush."

"Can we go please?" Both girls asked in unison.

Elsie glanced at her brother. He nodded then covered his yawn. "I'll check in with you guys later."

Ryan gathered the girls and steered them around the medical cart into the hallway. Elsie followed.

Bryce called out, "Els, I forgot about the wind barrier."

Elsie paused in the doorway and set her palm

flat on the door, propping it open. Then she glanced back at her brother.

"It's no big deal. I just want to ensure we've got the best wind barrier around the hive colonies," Bryce rushed on. "I'll email you the details."

Elsie swallowed her urge to holler: *No more emails*. He'd hit her email quota for the day. Then she glanced back at her brother. Watched him wince for the first time. Saw the pain he was working so hard to hide. If building spreadsheets kept his mind busy, she'd let him send another hundred. She smiled and softened her words. "That would be great. I'll email you back if I have questions."

In the meantime, Elsie needed a crash course on all things farming. Fortunately, she knew a cowboy to ask. Now all she had to do was keep her interest in check. Otherwise, she might find herself needing a crash course on how not to fall for a cowboy.

CHAPTER FOUR

RYAN WAS NO sooner in the hallway outside Bryce's hospital room when Gemma slipped her hand into his. Autumn took hold of his other hand and eased further into his side away from a complicated looking medical cart and two interns, their expressions intent and serious, standing outside another hospital room. Ryan tightened his grip as if he was a prince ready to protect his princesses from whatever scared them.

Up ahead at the nurse's station he saw a familiar figure and relaxed. He squeezed the girls' fingers lightly and said, "Want to meet the doctor who is going to fix your dad's ankle so he can go home soon?"

Both girls nodded.

Stepping up to his younger brother, Ryan cleared his throat and said very seriously, "Dr. Sloan, I've got two very important people here to see you."

Grant looked up from his paperwork on the counter, lifted his chin in acknowledgment to Ryan then turned his full attention to the girls for proper introductions. Complete with formal handshakes. Then Grant said, "Now, I believe you were just visiting my patient, Mr. Bryce Parks."

Gemma giggled, kept her hand inside Ryan's and swayed her hips side to side. "That's Daddy, Doc Grant."

"Right." Grant kept his expression neutral and ran his palm over his silk tie. "Anything you think I should know about your dad? I want to make sure our patient gets the best care ever."

Autumn lifted her hand and leaned in to whisper loudly, "He's sneaking cookies with Ms. Liza. But when we sneak extra cookies, we get scolded."

"And we gotta put the cookies back." Gemma joined in, her words solemn and grim. "Even if we accidentally took a bite of the cookie we weren't supposed to have."

Ryan rolled his lips together to squash his smile.

Grant ran his hand over his mouth. "What should I do, do you think?"

Autumn lifted her chin. Certainty filled her words. "Make Daddy give 'em back."

"But he's got to help Ms. Liza with her portfolio." Gemma stumbled slightly over the portfolio part then rushed on. "Because Ms. Liza is really nice."

"That she is. I'll see what I can do about the cookies," Grant said and shook their hands to seal the deal. "And I'll fix your dad's ankle so he can chase you two around the farm again soon."

"Dad doesn't run." Gemma giggled again, hips

swaying. "But he does play hide-and-seek if we get our chores done."

"Well, you might need to play board games until your dad is fully healed." Elsie stepped beside Ryan and smiled warmly at his younger brother. "Hello, Dr. Sloan."

"It's Grant." Ryan's brother stood and greeted Elsie with a quick hug. "We're neighbors and practically family. We used to swap science fiction books, remember?"

Elsie laughed. "Of course, I remember."

Ryan hadn't known. He started to frown then caught himself. He wasn't seriously jealous of a memory, was he? *Impossible.* Ryan had never been jealous in his life, especially not of his own brother.

"You were the only person I knew who read faster than me," Elsie added, affection in her words. "I can't tell you how many sleepless nights I had trying to keep up with you."

Grant had kept her awake. That frown worked across Ryan's face.

"I've got a well-stocked library at our new house if you need any reading material," Grant offered. "Come on over any time."

"I just might take you up on that." Elsie smiled. "I could use a good distraction."

Then why not call me? Ryan had ideas. All sorts, like a late-night stroll through Marlena's gardens. Or stargazing. Back porch swinging. He could keep going. Ryan's frown deepened. If only he'd stopped there. But his words kept falling out. "Elsie is going to be busy with the farm and the girls. Most likely won't be much time left for reading."

Elsie frowned at him.

Grant tipped his head and eyed Ryan, his gaze slightly narrowed as if Ryan was a grumpy patient withholding information.

Ryan pushed back his shoulders. *Stop talking. Don't make it worse.* "I'm just stating the obvious. There's a lot of work to be done. I saw Bryce's spreadsheets."

At the mention of Bryce, worry skimmed across Elsie's face and settled into the crease between her eyebrows. Ryan felt it like a wasp's sting—sharp and consuming. He wanted to comfort her, but his brother stepped in first.

"Bryce is going to be fine. He's going to heal and recover from this." Grant held Elsie's gaze an extra beat as if he understood she needed reassurance.

Ryan wanted to reassure Elsie too. But in a different sort of way. The way that had his arm curved around her waist. And her tucked right into his side. But not for long. She wasn't meant for a cowboy like him. And if he held her, he might not want to let go. Even when he had to. Ryan eased away from Elsie, reestablishing that distance.

Grant leaned toward the girls again. "Now, Gemma and Autumn, does your dad let you have sugar before lunch?"

"We're having milkshakes with extra cherries for lunch." Excitement widened Gemma's eyes. "My tummy can't wait."

"Then how about a lollipop you can keep for later." Grant straightened, reached behind the nurse's station and picked up a jar of colorful lollipops. He held the jar out to the girls then offered it to Elsie. Grant added, "The nurses around here try to hide these from me, but I always find them." Grant tucked one in the pocket of his white lab coat.

The brothers might not share the same clothing style, but they did share similar sweet tooths. Ryan reached for a lollipop, but his brother swung the jar out of his reach.

Grant shook his head and waggled his finger at Ryan. "None for you, big brother, until we discuss my wife."

"It's not my fault." Ryan lifted his hands. "I tried to tell Maggie and Vivian you are scared of cuckoo clocks."

Grant's face darkened.

Maggie and Grant had gotten married in a winter wedding that past February. Vivian was his youngest brother Josh's girlfriend. Ryan knew both women from the rodeo circuit and now he was grateful to have them as part of the family. Still, they were a force when they set their minds to something. And they'd set their minds to the two vintage cuckoo clocks they'd discovered in a family storage barn. Ryan added, "Maggie and Vivian wouldn't believe me. They badgered me until I got the clocks working properly."

"I should have known you turned those clocks on." Grant eyed him and wrapped his arm around the lollipop jar the same way he used to guard the cookie jar from Ryan growing up.

Ryan glanced at Elsie. "Grant here can't balance the weights precisely on the cuckoo clocks. It takes a deft hand, which is ironic given he's a renowned surgeon."

"My hands are deft enough," Grant countered. "I don't want the weights balanced. Because I do not want the clocks chirping."

"They cuckoo," Ryan corrected, more than happy to tease his brother. It was familiar and natural. Unlike his feelings toward Elsie. The ones he was putting at a safe distance.

"Call that sound those clocks make whatever you want." Grant held his hand out for the girls' candy wrappers. The girls seeming to have missed the part about lollipops later. Grant added, "There's still something creepy about those clocks."

"The clocks always scared Grant when we were kids." Ryan chuckled. The two clocks had hung in the living room of their great-grandmother's house. Their own Gran Claire had adored them. Ryan said, "Shouldn't you have gotten past this irrational fear by now?"

"I'm afraid of zombies." Autumn sucked on her

lollipop then added, "Dad says I'll outgrow it. Maybe you just need to grow more, Doc Grant."

"That is a very good thought." Grant grinned at Autumn then shot a look at Ryan. "When I grow taller than Ryan, I can hang the clocks in his house where he can't reach them. And they can cuckoo all hours of the day and night. Then we'll see who's laughing."

His own home. Ryan hadn't given that much thought over the years. But he had to now. He couldn't very well live with his older brother Carter, his wife, Tess, and their kids for the rest of his life. He just assumed when the time came, he would know exactly what he wanted to do. But now he faced decisions beyond where to live and he wanted to run in the other direction. Hardly mature, he admitted. Yet he wanted to believe entirely effective. And so, for the moment, he'd keep looking the other way.

"Maggie loves those cuckoo clocks," Ryan argued and pointed at his brother. "You love your wife. You need to learn to love the clocks too so that Maggie is happy."

"Just like that, you brought us full circle, big brother." Grant rubbed his chin then pointed back at Ryan. "Maggie isn't happy right now and it's entirely your fault."

Ryan crossed his arms over his chest.

"Maggie claims you're refusing to practice with her," Grant went on. "And she refuses to lose because you're an arrogant cowboy who thinks because he's a champion bronc rider, he can win at any rodeo event there is. Her words, not mine."

Elsie shifted and stared at him. Her surprise in her partially opened mouth. Her amusement in her arched eyebrow.

"I'm not refusing." It was more like avoiding his sister-in-law. He had agreed to partner with Maggie for the team roping event in the charity rodeo long before his movie stunt mishap and Sundancer's injury. When he'd still been in the saddle and riding without fear. He shifted and told himself not to fidget. His brother would surely notice. He said, "I've been really busy."

"I don't care. All you have to do is practice roping with Maggie for an hour. Show her you've got skills. Prove to Maggie that you guys can win at the rodeo," Grant ordered then he slowed his words as if to ensure Ryan was listening. "Just make my wife happy."

Autumn took Ryan's hand and tugged until she had his attention then she asked, "What's roping?"

"It's where two cowboys or cowgirls ride their horses and try to catch a steer with their ropes," Ryan explained. "A steer is a boy cow with horns."

"Ryan is on a roping team with my wife, Maggie," Grant added. "Maggie is a champion team roper."

"Cowboy Prince is a champion too." Gemma

grinned and turned to Elsie. "Can we watch Cowboy Prince and Ms. Maggie go roping?"

Grant's eyes widened. Oh, his younger brother hadn't missed Ryan's new nickname. And Grant wasn't about to forget it anytime soon either.

"I didn't know you roped too." Elsie searched Ryan's face. "I'd love to see that."

So would Ryan. The key to roping was riding a fast horse. But Ryan still hadn't been on a horse, fast or otherwise. But that was his secret. One he fully intended to keep to himself. "Tickets are on sale for Belleridge Rodeo Rides for A Cause. It's a charity rodeo. All the proceeds will go to the charities the competitors support."

"Who are you competing for?" Elsie asked.

"The Martha Claire Horse Haven," Ryan replied.

"It's named in honor of your grandmother." Approval was there in Elsie's sincere words.

He'd known she'd easily make the connection. Ryan nodded. "We'll compete in our best event and then there's a mixed team roping event. Only one person on the team can have competed on the professional circuit in roping before. Maggie is one of the best women ropers riding today."

"That's amazing," Elsie said. "I'd like to see Maggie compete too."

"You don't have to wait until the rodeo to see Cowboy Prince or Maggie rope," Grant offered, a little bit too gallantly. "You can come watch him and Maggie practice at our private arena on the Sloan farm."

"Can we pet the horses too?" Gemma clasped her hands together.

Grant nodded. "Maggie might even let you ride with her, if your aunt agrees."

Autumn and Gemma cheered then lifted their hope-filled gazes to Ryan. Totally not fair. How was he supposed to disappoint them? But take his first ride in over a month with an audience? Especially one that included Elsie. What would she think of him then?

"Well, Cowboy Prince, stop shirking your duties and give the people what they want." There was a challenge in Grant's growing grin. "Maggie and Vivian are painting the nursery for Tess today and then they're heading over to the arena to practice before dinner."

Vivian was a talented barrel racer. On her way to being one of the best too. Perhaps he could arrange for Elsie and the girls to watch Maggie and Vivian practice. Make it a cowgirls' day of sorts. He rubbed his chin, stalling and searching for an excuse. "Today won't work. I'm giving Elsie tractor lessons this afternoon."

"But it sounds like Maggie needs you." Elsie set her hand on Ryan's arm. "She's counting on you. You can't let her down."

He was already letting everyone down. Himself included. Ryan didn't need witnesses for his current downfall. But he hadn't hit the bottom yet. He could still turn things around. He would. On his own.

Grant handed Elsie a fistful of lollipops. "I always liked you, Elsie."

"You're alone at the farm, Elsie. You need help too," Ryan said then looked at his younger brother. "If Grandpa Sam and Uncle Roy get wind of Elsie's tractor woes, they'll want to teach her themselves."

"Good point." Grant frowned and returned the candy jar behind the nurse's station. "We definitely can't have that."

"Did something happen?" Elsie asked.

"Carter took their tractor privileges away," Ryan explained, not feeling the slightest bit guilty he'd turned the conversation away from him and roping practice. "Indefinitely."

"Because those two and tractors get into too much trouble," Grant volunteered and unwittingly helped Ryan. To Ryan's relief.

"Ryan can fill you in on the specifics of Grandpa Sam and Uncle Roy's tractor adventures." Grant tore off a piece of paper, wrote on it and handed it to Elsie. "In the meantime, that's my number and Maggie's. Call us anytime. For anything. We're happy to help too."

But Ryan wanted to be Elsie's first call. Her anytime. For anything call. Her go-to person.

"You say that now until I call you late at night after you worked all day." Elsie chuckled.

Even then, Ryan wouldn't mind. He ground his teeth together. He had bigger things to worry about than who Elsie chose to phone for assistance. He had a saddle to get into. Horses to ride. An equine sanctuary to help fund. A new stable to establish. And five horses counting on him for a home.

"I'll send Maggie if it's after hours and go back to sleep," Grant teased.

"Thanks." Elsie tucked the paper into her purse. "I really appreciate it."

"It's what we do around here," Grant said, serious and sincere. "We look out for each other." With a promise to take good care of Bryce, Grant picked up a clipboard and headed down the hallway to see his patient.

Ryan took each of the girls' hands in his and walked to the elevators.

As for looking after Elsie and the girls, he would do that through lunch. Then he'd return them to their farm, give Elsie a quick tutorial on tractor driving and finally get back to his day.

Regarding the whole keeping his distance from Elsie thing, surely, that wouldn't be hard. Nothing he couldn't manage. After all, Elsie was headed to her life in the city. Soon enough.

And for as far back as Ryan could remember, his direction had been the rodeo, not ever the city. And not even a pretty woman from the city like Elsie Parks would get him to turn around now.

CHAPTER FIVE

THE WALK TO All-Day Corner Diner was short. They placed their orders quickly after being seated at a table. And the service proved even faster. Ryan wiped a napkin across his mouth and was about to push his plate away when Autumn dropped the rest of her club sandwich on it.

"I'm full and you look hungry." Autumn grinned at him. "You gotta finish it now that it's on your plate."

"Is that a rule?" Ryan glanced at Gemma.

She nodded in solidarity with her older sister and dipped a french fry in the last of her milkshake.

Ryan picked up the sandwich. "Well, I don't want to be a rule breaker."

"Since when?" Elsie's gaze connected with his. Amusement curved around her words. "I've never known you to follow the rules."

"There's a lot you don't know about me," Ryan said. Her eyes widened. He saw the curiosity. The interest she tried to hide before she studied her phone again. Satisfied he wasn't the only one feeling something and working to hide it, he polished off the sandwich in two bites.

"Did you know the new utility tractor has a swivel captain's chair and panoramic roof? It looks like a sunroof in a car. I never used my sunroof when I had a car." Elsie swiped her finger across her phone screen. "It says the operator can view the full cycle of the loader, which has dynamic weighing technology." Her eyebrows pulled together at that last part. A cue that she was intent on learning more. Sure enough, she rapidly opened a new window on her internet app.

"It means you can get an accurate weight of whatever you've got in the bucket." Ryan set his hand over Elsie's phone screen, stopping her from reciting more tractor highlights. "What are you doing?"

"I was searching for a user's manual on the tractor dealer website." Elsie tried to peel his fingers off her phone. "But now I'm reading a utility tractor sales brochure."

"Elsie, you can't learn to drive a tractor from reading." Ryan tightened his grip. "That's not how you learned to drive a car."

"Sure, it is." She stopped trying to free her phone and sat back. "I read the driver's manual and also the car owner's manual for Dad's sedan before I ever even sat in the driver's seat of his car."

"What driver's manual?" he asked, not even bothering to mask his baffled expression.

"The *Driver's Handbook from the Department of Motor Vehicles*," she recited, her words dry and monotone. She swiped a sweet potato fry off his plate and aimed it at him. "Every state has one. If you had read it, you might not have gotten those tickets that one summer when Bryce had to drive you around."

"I got two speeding tickets that summer." Ryan held up two fingers and eyed her. "Because I was a teenager who treated the speed limit signs on the backroads as suggestions. And for the record, I don't do that anymore."

"Do what?" Elsie bit into the french fry and watched him. A faint gleam in her gaze. "Drive on the backroads or speed?"

"Speed," he replied and held her gaze. "I still like a drive on the backroads. Only slow and preferably not alone these days."

She swallowed but never looked away. "Where would you go?"

"This time of year, there's nothing like dusk at Silent Rise Canyon. A warm blanket and picnic basket is all we would need. If we're lucky, we'll catch a storm out on the plains at sunset. Incredible view," Ryan said and lifted one shoulder. "Nothing fancy, but it's a drive worth taking and definitely an evening well spent."

Elsie picked up her water, sipped then watched him over the rim of her glass. "Do you go there often?"

"Haven't been in a very long time," he admitted. And he'd always gone alone. Because he'd never been interested in sharing the moment with anyone. Until now. "What's an evening well spent look like to you?"

"My evenings are mostly spent working on the events I'm managing." She fiddled with her straw. "All work, no play tends to be true in my case, but I'm not complaining. I've always found my job really rewarding."

"While you're here, you might want to take an evening off of work just to test my theory," he suggested.

"What theory is that?" she asked.

"That slowing down can be a reward all on its own." He dropped his napkin on his plate.

"I wouldn't think a champion bronc rider has the luxury to take things slow," she countered.

"I don't." He grinned. "But like I said, the appeal is in not being alone."

Her mouth opened in the smallest O. Curiosity worked across her face. But the waitress arrived. They declined refills on their drinks and Ryan accepted the check.

"We should get to it." Ryan smiled. Elsie looked slightly distracted as if maybe she was considering the appeal of backroads and sunsets. *Wishful thinking.* And not something he gave in to. Ryan pulled out his wallet, slipped money into the billfold and pushed his chair back. Then said, "After all, the only way to learn to drive a tractor is to drive one."

Elsie blinked and picked up her purse. "You didn't need to pay for us too."

"I ate almost all the food on this table." Ryan chuckled and watched Gemma hop from her chair. "Elsie, I finished your milkshake, Autumn's club sandwich and Gemma's cheeseburger."

Gemma rushed around the table and grabbed Ryan's hand. "We were full, and you were hungry, and it was on your plate, Cowboy Prince."

Ryan squeezed Gemma's fingers. "I appreciate you looking out for me, Princess Gem."

"Well, thank you for lunch," Elsie said. "Next time is on me."

Next time. That made it sound like this was more than a one-time thing. That she wanted it to be more too. Not likely. Still, one could hope, even if it was a bad idea. And he knew it.

Ryan held the door open for the girls. When Elsie stepped through the archway, he couldn't resist. He leaned in and whispered, "I'm already looking forward to next time."

Her cheeks heated. Like she stood under a heat lamp. How he liked that. He followed Elsie, who hurried to join Autumn ahead of him. The pair led the way back to the parking lot. Elsie kept the pace brisk, and he recalculated that distance. Trying to decide just how much space he needed between him and Elsie to keep his interest in her to himself. Where it belonged.

Because following that road was only going to end in things he spent his whole life avoiding, like regret and heartache. And something about Elsie told him that she could very well be his heartbreaker. But only if he let her in. Good thing he knew better than to open that door.

Back inside the car, Ryan confirmed all seat belts were buckled then Autumn asked, "Is it still a windows down, volume up kind of day?"

Elsie shifted in her seat and considered Ryan. A challenge was there in her words. "Only if Cowboy Prince sings with us."

"Deal." He liked the surprise on her face a bit too much. If only she knew that singing would keep his interest in her tethered. Keep him from getting to know Elsie any better. He started the car and backed out of the parking space. "If we can slip in a few country songs too."

"Done." Elsie plugged her phone into the car audio system and opened her music app. "Everyone gets to pick a song they want to hear."

"Let the car karaoke begin." Ryan drove out of the parking lot and onto the main road.

Car karaoke continued all the way back to Three Springs. Ryan kept his word and sang every word in every song, even embellished several songs with a few extra lyrics to the girls' delight. They were belting out the verse of an up-beat country song about dancing in the moonlight when Ryan drove under the Doyle Farm arched wrought iron gate.

At the top of the drive, Elsie sucked in her breath. Then she simultaneously gasped and coughed. Pointed out the window then stammered, "There's a goat standing on the top of my U-Haul."

If Ryan hadn't believed Elsie earlier about New York, he had no choice now. Her U-Haul moving truck was all the proof he needed. Elsie was destined to keep on moving. Far from Three Springs. Now all Ryan had to do was be careful and avoid the kind of goodbye that could hurt.

"That's Smarty Marty," Autumn shouted. "He got out again."

Smarty Marty looked as if he'd tripped inside a white paint can. He was all black except for his tail, one back leg and his ears. And he watched them with an alertness and arrogance only a goat could perfect.

"Marty is so smart." Autumn laughed and jumped out of the Jeep. Then added, "He gets out of their pen then lets the others out to play too."

"One day, Smarty Marty walked the others all the way to Cowboy Prince's yard." Gemma's head popped between the front seats. Her gaze bright. "Cowboy Prince had to drive them all back home. Remember that, Cowboy Prince?"

Gemma was out of the car before Ryan could reply. He followed the girls into the yard.

Elsie scrambled out of the car and joined them. "How many others are there?"

"Ten. But two are lazy and don't ever leave the pen." Gemma clapped and pointed at the caramel-colored goat sitting on the front porch. "There's Butter-Belle. She's so sweet."

"We gotta gather goats, Auntie." Autumn set her hands on her hips and stared up at the top of the truck. Excitement wound around her words. "And put 'em back in their pen."

"Gather. Goats." Elsie glanced at Ryan and rubbed her throat as if that was where her words were stuck. "I've never… How exactly do we…"

"It's easy, Auntie," Gemma declared and sprinted toward the porch. "Watch me."

Except it wasn't easy. It was somewhat exasperating. Entertaining, but mostly exasperating. The girls squealed. The goats bleated. And everyone ran. It was more a game of chase than catch. And difficult to tell if the goats or the girls were having more fun. Finally, the girls wore themselves out, retreated to the porch swing and helpfully called out goat sightings.

A quick search on her phone and Elsie raided the girls' backpacks for snacks. Then she lured one goat at a time with a trail of raisins that led toward Ryan. Leaving Ryan to take care of the capturing and releasing back into the pen. After he praised each goat and treated them to bites of an apple Autumn had given him.

Finally, Elsie counted ten goats in the goat pasture and declared goat gathering concluded for the day. She walked back to the house beside Ryan and bumped her shoulder against his arm and said, "I don't know if I'm more sweaty or dirty. I need a long, hot shower. Then I'm putting my feet up and not moving for the rest of the night."

There was something appealing about the idea. Sitting with her. Their feet up. Leaning into each other. Talking the night away. They rounded the house and Ryan caught sight of her moving truck, sitting there like a giant billboard. *Right.* Best to keep on moving himself.

Elsie walked up the stairs to the porch.

Ryan stepped back. "I'm going to get Sundancer from the pasture and walk on home."

"Walk?" Elsie turned toward him. Confusion curved across her face. "Why aren't you riding?"

Loaded question that was. And not one of those truths he was about to share. He said, "Sundancer is injured. Walking is part of his rehab. As it turns out, I also aggravated an old leg injury so walking suits me too."

"But that's several miles away." Elsie set her hands on her hips and watched him.

"Sunset isn't for a while yet." Ryan continued his retreat toward the pasture. "Don't forget I know all the shortcuts between our property and yours."

"But aren't you tired?" she asked.

"Not especially." Ryan tapped the brim of his cowboy hat. "Sweet dreams, Elsie Marie."

Then he turned on his boot heels and kept walking until he reached the pasture. One loud whistle brought Sundancer to him. He picked up the halter he'd hung on the fence post earlier, adjusted it on Sundancer's head and led the horse down the drive.

And hoped he would be tired when he got home. Too tired to let his heart do any of that wishful thinking about things like backroads, slow drives and Elsie. All the things he shouldn't want.

The cowboy and the girl from the city. Impossible combination that.

Still, he patted the picture in his pocket. The one Gemma had drawn of him and Elsie. He'd hang it on his wall in his bedroom. And if he dreamed tonight of impossible things, well, what was one more secret to keep.

CHAPTER SIX

School lunches packed. *Check*.

Chickens fed. *Check*.

Goats counted and thankfully still contained. *Double checked*.

Elsie crossed off the morning task list Bryce had left her and walked back to the house. Now it was time for the school drop-off then a grocery store run. They'd decided on breakfast for dinner last night after Elsie had discovered the pantry and refrigerator were more sparse than stocked.

Only two car stall outs later—one in the school car line and the other at the only stoplight in downtown Three Springs—Elsie congratulated herself on her success and parked in front of her aunt's house. Groceries unloaded and put away, Elsie stood at the kitchen island and considered the spreadsheets spread across the granite countertop. The doorbell interrupted her, keeping her from having to decide where to get started on her brother's farm to-dos.

She opened the door to find a pair of older cowboys. Both holding their cowboy hats against their chests and wearing wide smiles.

The one with the pure-as-snow beard touched his bolo tie clasp and cleared his throat. "Elsie Marie, you most likely don't remember me."

"Sam Sloan." Elsie returned his smile. "Or should I call you Cowboy Santa?"

Sam's eyes twinkled much like she imagined Kris Kringle's would. He spread his arms wide. "It's sure nice to see you back home."

She skipped over correcting him. He'd always told Elsie that Three Springs was her home. She stepped onto the porch and into Sam's embrace. He was older, but his hug held the same warmth and kindness she remembered. "I wish it hadn't been an accident that brought me back."

"Your brother is strong. He'll recover. And you're here now. That's what matters. No use dwelling on the reasons." Sam settled his cowboy hat over his white hair and introduced her to his brother, Roy Sloan.

"Pleasure, Elsie." Roy tapped his hat against his chest then placed it on his head, covering his thick, curly, salt-and-pepper hair.

"What brings you by?" Elsie asked then frowned. Her shoulders slumped. "The goats got out, didn't they? You had to bring them back."

"Goats." Roy scratched his weathered cheek. "We don't know anything about goats."

Elsie sighed her relief.

"We're here for the tractor." Sam's eyebrows lifted.

"That one over there." Roy pointed at the green tractor Ryan had parked yesterday in front of the greenhouses. "Trey Ramsey joined us for breakfast at the Lemon Moon Diner this morning. He told us he got your tractor all fixed up and returned to you right quick."

Elsie's relief faded and a hint of unease spread across the back of her neck.

"Have you taken it for a test drive yet?" Sam asked, his words mild and pleasant.

"You need to know if it is working proper," Roy added.

"Ryan drove it yesterday," Elsie explained. "I'm sure it's fine."

"Then it's all ready to go for your lessons today." That gleam flashed in Sam's gaze again. He held his arm out as if he was asking her to take a spin across the dance floor. "Shall we?"

But Ryan was supposed to teach her to drive the tractor. Yet they'd been sidetracked goat gathering and all of a sudden Ryan had been wishing her sweet dreams and leaving. And Elsie had let her cowboy go before she'd invited Ryan to stay for dinner. To stay longer. With her. As if she wanted to spend more time with him. As for those tractor lessons, those hadn't been rescheduled.

"Ryan mentioned you needed tractor lessons." Roy hooked his thumbs around his large bronze belt buckle and lifted his chin. "So, we've come to offer our assistance."

"But I thought…" Elsie paused.

Ryan had never told her the tractor stories about the two older cowboys. No, Ryan had distracted her with talk about country backroads and sunsets yesterday at lunch. Then he'd sidetracked her with the goats. When he'd befriended each goat, he'd been so gentle and sweet. And Elsie had just stared, caught completely off guard. Her cowboy was a daredevil. A risk-taker. Not a softy.

Elsie pressed her fingers against the bridge of her nose and blocked thoughts of Ryan. His grandfather and uncle were there now. Looking so very earnest and sincere. She didn't want to hurt their feelings. She was definitely going to give Ryan a piece of her mind when she saw him again. She disliked disappointing anyone, especially these two kind cowboys. She continued, "Grant and Ryan mentioned yesterday that…"

"That we can't drive the tractor," Roy finished for her, his tone helpful, not resentful.

Elsie nodded.

"That's just a bit of a misunderstanding." Sam brushed his hand through the air as if he shooed a fly away. "We can't drive a tractor at the distillery. My grandson Carter is worried about his precious whiskey barrels."

"But out here with all this wide-open land…"

Roy spread his fingers wide and chuckled. "There's nothing to stop us out here."

"Or for us to run into," Sam added then rubbed his hands together. "How about we get those lessons started?"

"I should probably call Ryan." Elsie reached for her phone in her back pocket.

"He won't answer." Sam glanced at the watch on his wrist. "He's at the sanctuary."

"Tori, the manager at the sanctuary, picked up another rescue early this morning and the poor mare is real spooked in the trailer. Been kicking something fierce the whole ride back," Roy explained. "Ryan is there to calm her and get her settled in her new home."

"Ryan's got a touch with the wild, tricky ones. Understands them better than anyone around these parts." Pride framed Sam's words. "But it sounds like he'll have his hands full with that poor Arabian this morning."

Elsie frowned, tried to block her worry for Ryan. "Will he be safe with that horse?"

"He's got the training and the know-how," Sam said, his expression encouraging. "He just needs to keep his focus. Can't risk any distractions. That's when injuries happen."

Elsie slid her phone back into her pocket. Suddenly calling Ryan didn't seem like a good idea. "What kind of lessons are you thinking?" Something like turning the tractor on and off would be a helpful start.

"Well, what's needing to be done around here?" Sam asked and watched her, a knowing look in his gaze. "I'm certain your brother left you a list. He always was prepared and organized, even as a child. Always hoped he'd rub off on my grandsons."

Elsie pulled a folded piece of paper out of her other pocket. The one Bryce had titled Quick Reference Farm Task List.

Sam took the paper, scanned it and handed it to Roy. Then he announced cheerfully, "We can start with the bee pasture. Clearing it."

"You want to expand the bee pasture. Today." Elsie worked the alarm and surprise from her expression. "Right now."

"Just clearing it." Roy grinned. "Then we'll till it. Then we'll seed it. Can't seed with the weeds. Not a good combination."

Elsie nodded as if she completely understood.

"Gotta start someplace." Sam tucked her list in the top pocket of his chambray shirt. "Work's not gonna get done standing around reading lists."

That was true. Elsie needed to get to work. She needed to start. She'd given her word to her brother. Promised she'd do whatever it took to help him. And no one else was on her porch offering their services. How much trouble could they get into in a wide-open pasture anyway?

"We'll show you everything you need to know. There's nothing to it." Sam offered her his arm again. "We can even take pictures of the cleared field and send them to your brother. Imagine his surprise."

And then her brother could stop worrying so much. He'd already left her several voice mail reminders and sent more emails that morning when he should've been concentrating on his upcoming surgery. Now Elsie could finally prove she had things under control around the farm. That she didn't require any more cowboy rescues. That she could be counted on. Elsie curved her arm around Sam's and said, "Let's go clear a bee pasture."

"Now, that's the spirit." Roy took Elsie's other arm.

The two older cowboys hooted and escorted her to the tractor. They patiently explained the proper way to climb into the tractor. Then pointed out the different panels, switches and buttons. How to start the tractor. How to turn it off. And back on. Then it was out to those wide-open fields. Sam perched right beside her in the tractor cab.

Who got to ride with Elsie had been the only disagreement between the two older cowboys. Finally, they agreed to split up the lessons. Sam took the ride to the pasture with Elsie and Roy would take the ride back to the house. In the meantime, Roy was following behind them in her aunt's UTV.

"I'm doing it," Elsie marveled and bounced

lightly in the captain's chair. The tractor rumbled and rolled forward. "I'm actually driving a tractor."

"Nothing to it." Sam beamed beside her. "You're a natural."

"I read up on this particular model last night." Elsie peered out the window and promptly lost that thrill of achievement. She frowned. "But the manual did not go over what to do about that."

Sam leaned forward. "That's just a little mud from the storms we've been getting recently."

It was more than a little. The muddy land stretched longer than a football field, reaching the fence on one side and the wooded area on the other. And it was wider than the tractor was long. Elsie slowed to a stop. "Maybe we should go around this."

"Can't drive the tractor through the trees." Sam scratched his cheek and tipped his head toward the door. "Then there's the fence in our way over there."

"Turn around then," Elsie suggested and peeled her fingers from the steering wheel.

"Best to cut it straight down the middle," Sam said, confidence in his words. He lifted his arm and pointed out the windshield. "The pastures are just on the other side. Not too far now. All you got to do now is go full steam ahead."

Full steam ahead. Elsie had never done anything full steam ahead. She'd always stopped, assessed and reassessed. Then maybe she went ahead. *Maybe*. But never right into the mud. Into the mess. Elsie frowned and chewed on her bottom lip. "Sam, maybe you should drive for this part."

"If you're sure." Sam patted her arm.

Elsie nodded and edged toward the door. "I think I'll just wait with Roy."

"I'll meet you two on the other side." Sam slid into the chair, his words eager and excited. "You and Roy can drive through the woods and skip the mud entirely."

Elsie made her way down the side of the tractor. This time more gracefully than she had with Ryan the day before. Roy met her near the tractor. She said, "I'm letting Sam take it from here and tackle the mud."

"Might as well watch over here and make sure he gets through it." Sam motioned Elsie off to the side.

"You don't think he'll make it?" Alarmed, Elsie followed Roy. "But Sam told me it's not…"

The tractor engine rumbled, cutting off Elsie's words. And it rolled full steam ahead into the mud field. Just as Sam had predicted. Only the tractor lost steam somewhere in the middle of the muck when the tractor wheels started spinning, spraying clumps of mud in every direction. And all forward progress ceased. Worse, the rotary cutter they'd attached to the tractor hitch sank and completely disappeared beneath the thick watery muck.

Elsie slapped her hands over her mouth and caught her gasp.

Roy yanked his cowboy hat off his head, stomped toward the UTV and tossed his hat on the driver's seat. "Looks like I gotta get into the driver's seat now and fix things, as usual."

Alarmed at the barely concealed delight in Roy's words, Elsie rushed after the older cowboy. "Are you sure that's a good idea?" How in the world was he going to get to the tractor? It wasn't a swimming pool. It was a mud pit. He couldn't possibly be happy about this.

"Someone's got to get in there or we'll be out here all day. No one wants that." Roy went to the edge of the mud pit. Elsie trailed after him. Roy added, "And it's just a little mud."

Why did they keep saying that? Elsie had a little mud on her jeans. But there was nothing little about the muck facing her.

Roy waved his arms over his head until he captured Sam's attention. Then he yelled, "Come on out, so I can get in there and drive it right."

"Think you can do better." Sam climbed out onto the tractor steps. "I'd like to see you try." With that Sam jumped down into the mud. And then sank. First his boots disappeared. Then his knees. Finally, the mud stopped rising just below his waist.

Panic squeezed around Elsie. She flailed her

arms in front of her as if she intended to grab Sam's hand. But she was much too far away.

"Now look what you did," Roy grumbled.

"Don't just stand there," Sam shouted back. "Get me a rope and pull me out. I'm getting mud in places I don't want."

Roy turned and stomped back to the UTV. Elsie hot on his heels. Roy opened the toolbox in the UTV bed. "Who stocked this? There's nothing useful in here."

Elsie stepped around to the other side of the small bed and pulled a frayed rope from under the toolbox. "What about this?"

"That'll have to do." Roy managed to get back to the edge of the mud. He swirled the rope over his head as if he was catching a steer then released it. Sam lifted his arm. But the end of the rope landed several feet short of its mark.

Elsie cringed.

"You have to get closer," Sam called out. "I can't move, let alone hardly bend."

"Gimme a minute." Roy tapped the toe of his boot into the mud in front of him as if testing the temperature of bath water.

Elsie stood close enough to Roy to easily grab him around the waist. Ready to pull the older cowboy back if he waded in too far.

"Hurry up, will you," Sam said, his words surly. "It's not deep over there. I drove right through it."

"Fine." Roy tromped farther into the mud.

Elsie reached for him, but her fingers caught a fistful of air. "Roy. Stop."

But the older cowboy had already stepped in too far. And he too sank. All the way past his knees and almost to his waist. Just like that. The rope dangled from the hand Roy lifted over his head. From Elsie's angle, Roy looked to be even deeper in the muck than his brother. Elsie paled.

Sam's eyebrows bunched together. "Didn't see that coming."

Roy twisted to look at her. "Best step back, Elsie. We don't need you sinking too."

Too late. Elsie glanced down at her feet. Her running shoes were no longer visible. The muck was up around her ankles. And her shoes were practically rooted in thick sludge and sinking more. Elsie shoved her hand under the surface, loosened the laces on both shoes and worked one foot free. Then she stepped back and added an awkward, desperate lunge toward solid ground. Her other foot slipped free of her stuck shoe, and she landed with a decided thud on her backside.

"Nice dismount," Sam offered. "You okay, dear?"

Elsie nodded and stopped short of rubbing her sore backside. She'd lost both shoes and a sock, but at least she was on solid ground. Wiping her filthy hands on her jeans, she asked, "What should we do now?"

"Don't suppose there's another rope in there?" Sam said, his words hopeful.

Elsie shook her head and used the back of her hand to push her hair out of her face.

"It's probably a good time to mention that the key to the UTV is in my back pocket," Roy added. "Given how the rope toss turned out, it's probably best if I don't go throwing the key around too."

"Never thought I'd see myself stuck this far in a mud puddle," Sam said and started to laugh.

"Me either." Roy's laughter streamed out.

And Elsie shook her head. How could they laugh at a moment like this? Still, she felt her own laughter swirling inside her. But her amusement quickly soured, and her stomach turned. She had to call Ryan. Get help. And confess what she had done. How could she tell Ryan what had happened with his grandfather and uncle? How could she not? She needed another cowboy rescue, even if she didn't want to admit it.

"No one is staying stuck for long." Elsie tugged her phone from her pocket and worked to sound confident. "Not on my watch."

"Who you callin'?" Sam shouted, a hint of panic in his words.

"Ryan." Elsie wiped more mud from her fingers and tried to keep the phone screen clean.

"Not that one," Sam countered. "Call my other grandson Grant. He's always been the calm, more reasonable one."

"Grant is in surgery," Elsie said. Or would be soon. He'd texted Elsie when she'd been at the grocery store to let her know that Bryce's surgery was moved to the afternoon.

Still, Elsie had known she should've gone to the hospital for Bryce's surgery. But her brother had told her it was a waste of her time to sit in the waiting area. Even though Elsie could've been reading up on tractor ownership, best beekeeping practices and how to train goats. But Bryce had insisted between the girls and the farm there was too much for her to do in Three Springs. And Grant had promised to personally call Elsie when her brother was out of recovery and back in his room.

"Well, that won't do. Can't bother Grant when he's in the OR," Roy mused. "What about Caleb?"

Caleb was one of the youngest Sloan brothers. One of the identical twins. Caleb had always been funny and laid-back growing up. Perhaps he could break the news to Ryan instead of Elsie. *Coward. Absolutely.* She asked, "Do you know Caleb's phone number?"

Sam frowned and shook his head. "Why do I need a phone number when I can just holler for my grandson in the house?"

"Don't look at me." Roy speared his fingers into his hair and fluffed the curls higher. "My mind is good, but not my memory these days."

"Looks like it's Ryan." Sam sounded irritated. "Got no choice now."

"What happens when Ryan gets mad?" Elsie asked, wanting to be prepared.

"Ryan gets real quiet. Same as his Gran Claire used to," Sam offered. "I prefer the shouting. The heavy silence makes a person twitch something fierce." Sam watched her. "And that's when the guilt sets in something bad."

Elsie pressed her hand to her stomach then hit Ryan's number on her contact list.

Sam lifted his chin. "But we ain't done anything wrong. Just got a little stuck is all."

"Nothing to feel the least bit guilty about either," Roy charged on. "You tell him that too, Elsie. That it's not our fault."

But it was her fault. She should've stopped this. Never accepted their offer to teach her to drive a tractor. *I'm sorry. I'm sorry. I'm sorry.*

The line clicked on. Ryan's voice filled the speaker. "Elsie. Is that you? You okay?"

Elsie lost her apologetic chant and stammered, "Ryan. Hey." Elsie looked at Sam. He nodded at her, his gaze encouraging. Elsie spoke around her sudden unease. *Tell him.* "Ryan, I'm hoping you can meet me out at the farm. There's a bit of a situation here."

A scratch came across the line. "What kind of situation exactly?"

One you are definitely not going to like. Elsie started to sweat.

"Tell Ryan to bring an extra-long, heavy rope."

Sam shouted into the sudden silence. "Two ropes. Three if he's got 'em."

"Elsie." Ryan's voice rushed over the speaker. "Elsie. Is that my grandfather?"

"Yeah." Elsie pressed her lips together, swallowed. Worked her words from her tight throat. "I'm with Roy and Sam."

That silence descended across the phone line. And Elsie started to fret and fidget. Just like Sam warned.

Sam shouted again, "Tell him not to bring Carter."

Another beat of silence and Ryan asked, "Did he just say he doesn't want Carter?"

Ryan's words sounded careful and tight as if he spoke through clenched teeth. Elsie nodded and cringed, even though Ryan couldn't see her.

"Anyone but Carter," Roy hollered.

Elsie lifted her hand and made the universal shush sign, trying to quiet the duo. That silence stretched again. But Elsie was fully in it now. "Ryan," she started.

"Do I want to know what's going on?" Ryan finally asked. His words were even softer and even more contained.

Elsie hedged, "Not really."

"Is everyone okay?" The concern in Ryan's words calmed her.

"We're good," Elsie said, glad she could offer that much, then she added, "Just stuck at the moment."

Another scratch came over the line as if Ryan was on the move. Walking most likely. He asked, "Where are you exactly?"

"Hold on," Elsie said and covered the speaker with her palm. She looked at Sam. "Where are we exactly?"

"Tell Ryan to head to the north pasture and cut across toward the old wheelhouse," Sam called out. "He can't miss us."

"Got it," Ryan said, an urgency to his words. "I'm on the way."

The call disconnected before Elsie could thank him. She worked a small grin across her dry mouth. "Help is on the way."

"Now, don't look so worried, Elsie." Sam swirled his hand over the sludge-covered surface. "This is nothing but a mud puddle."

"That's right." Roy nodded. His words were confident and amused. "Sam and I got stuck in a real mudhole once before. Now, that was a real problem. Remember that, Sam?"

The two brothers laughed at the memory. Yet looking at the pair of older cowboys and the immovable tractor all Elsie could see were problems. And the biggest problem hadn't even arrived yet.

CHAPTER SEVEN

IT WASN'T LONG before the deep hum of a truck filled the air. Elsie stood and turned. Make that two trucks. Heavy duty and powerful and carrying three Sloan brothers.

Ryan emerged from a silver truck and set his hands on his hips. Elsie shifted her attention to the steel blue truck. The driver climbed out, his face set in a hard mask beneath his cowboy hat. Elsie recognized Carter Sloan, the oldest Sloan brother, from his dark hair touching his shirt collar and his commanding presence.

The passenger door of Carter's truck opened, and Caleb hopped out. His handsome face broke into an inviting grin before he released a wallop of deep laughter. No sooner did Caleb pull out his cell phone and move carefully to the edge of the muck. His brothers followed behind him.

"Caleb, what are you doing?" Sam asked, exasperation thick in his words and expression.

"First I'm taking pictures." Caleb's words were gleeful. "Then I'm going to video this. For Grant and Josh because they aren't here to witness this fiasco in real time."

"Stop messing around, Caleb," Sam ordered. "We need to get out of here."

"Should've thought of that before you climbed in." Carter's words were gruff, his exasperation an equal match for his grandfather's. And his stance was unyielding.

Carter Sloan had always been intimidating growing up. Always focused and always looking out for his brothers. Then Elsie had gotten to know Carter better and decided the oldest Sloan was mostly bluster. At least she'd thought so. Except she wasn't so certain right now.

Sam pointed at Ryan. "We told you not to bring Carter."

"Should've known Ryan wouldn't listen," Roy grumbled. "He never listens to us."

Ryan lifted his arms. "Was I supposed to bring Tess?"

"Tess is pregnant with twins, she needs her rest." Sam matched his grandson's frown.

Wrong thing to say.

Carter's face darkened more. His voice lifted. "Tess can't rest now. She's at home worried about you two."

That silenced the older cowboys. But there was no reprieve. Carter swung around and narrowed his gaze on Elsie. "Why did you let them drive a tractor? What were you thinking?"

"Don't raise your voice to Elsie." Ryan stepped to her side and faced off with his older brother. "You know how persuasive those two can be." Ryan glanced at her. His voice gentle. "It's not your fault, Elsie."

And just like that, something inside Elsie burst. Maybe it was the stress. The panic. Whatever it was, she gave into it completely and wholeheartedly. Her voice raised, matching Carter's. "Of course, it's not my fault." She advanced on her cowboy. "Because it's entirely your fault, Ryan Sloan. Yes, it is. This is all on you."

That brought Ryan around to face her fully. And caught the immediate interest of both his brothers who never hesitated to step to either side of Ryan as if to defend him. Ryan stared at Elsie. His voice lowered. "Mine? How can this be my fault?"

"You distracted me," she accused. With talk about back country roads and slow, long drives to the sunset. With him. Then he'd befriended each goat. So sweetly and tenderly. And she'd wanted to impress him. Show her cowboy that she was more than capable. More than worth his notice too. Nope, not going there either. She squeezed her forehead and searched for something not too revealing. "At lunch. You interfered with my tractor research."

A slow smile worked across his face before he smoothed it out and set his expression back to impassive.

"We can assign blame later," Sam interrupted. "Like after lunch."

"I am getting rather hungry," Roy mumbled.

"You two are lucky we're not leaving you right where you are," Carter quipped. "To think about what you've done."

"I'm really sorry about all this. I should've stopped them." Elsie reached out and touched Carter's arm. "How can I make it up to you? I can make dinner for everyone tonight."

Carter tipped his head and eyed her. His voice softened. "My wife's stomach is sensitive these days. It's the twins she's carrying. She's only been eating chicken."

Elsie nodded and grinned. "My Aunt Marlena says I make her chicken and dumplings better than she does."

Carter smiled, genuinely and openly. "What time should we be here?"

Dinner was no sooner set than the Sloan brothers focused their attention on the trio of trouble in the mud field. How best to pull out Roy and Sam, then work the tractor free. Ryan pointed out that the tractor was stuck on some sort of mound in the middle of the field, which had led to the tires losing traction. And the sunken rotary cutter was contributing to the tractor's awkward angle.

Caleb handed his phone to Elsie and instructed her not to miss a single second. Then grinned and lifted his eyebrows up and down. "Record everything, Elsie. I'm counting on you. This is bargaining power later. We'll want this."

In the end it was Ryan who came up with the plan. And then the brothers got to work, using their trucks, tow hitches and communication that told Elsie the brothers always worked as a team. Not that they didn't stop and debate several times. And laugh. That was a surprise to Elsie. They joked and laughed the entire time. As if once they knew their grandfather and uncle were not in serious danger, they relaxed and found the humor in the situation.

Roy and Sam were pulled free and waited with Elsie. Then the brothers concentrated on extracting and unhitching the rotary cutter before working on the tractor. And that laughter continued through it all. No matter how much mud covered them or how many tries failed to budge the tractor. But finally, even the tractor found purchase and rolled free of the sludge. Fishing for Roy's favorite boots brought about the most laughter and arguments on how best to retrieve them. Elsie even offered a few suggestions, happy to join in.

It was decided Roy and Sam would ride in Carter's truck bed back to the Sloan farmhouse where the two cowboys could then be hosed off out in the driveway. Caleb jumped into the UTV after Roy used his muddy hand to fish the key out of his pocket to drive it back.

The only awkward moment came when Ryan

noted Elsie's bare feet and swept her easily up into his arms. And her laughter got swept away by those butterflies flapping in her stomach. "Ryan. I can walk."

"Not barefooted," Ryan insisted. "Not around here."

"I've been barefoot for a while now." Elsie wiggled her mud-coated toes. But that only stirred those butterflies more. "And I'm fine."

"You're lucky." Ryan frowned, tightened his hold on her and headed to his truck. "You have no idea what's out here. Barbed wire. Nails. Thorns. I can keep going."

"I got it." Elsie felt him tense. And then she gave in. Wrapped her arms around his neck and settled in. Just for a moment. Just to calm him. And herself. After all, she'd never been swept off her feet. Not in any sense. Right now, it was heady and thrilling. A little bit irresistible. And this seemed as close as she was ever going to get. Best to take it in.

Ryan deposited her in the passenger seat and buckled her seat belt for her as if he wanted to keep her where he put her. Before she could protest, he brushed his thumb across her cheek, stalling her words. Then her forehead, the caress just as gentle and light, making her breath catch. And he kept right on fussing over her. Tucking her hair behind her ears. Sliding a towel under her bare feet.

Elsie willed her heart to stop racing. She always did the fussing. Prided herself on not needing to be looked after. She should put a stop to things right now. But her cowboy made her *feel*.

Feel cared for. Feel important. Feel worth the inconvenience.

Finally, his gaze tracked over Elsie from her head to her toes, slow and steady, as if assuring himself she really was fine. Then he stepped back, shut her door and came around the hood of the truck to the driver's side.

But feelings were inconvenient. And uncalled for. Ryan was a friend who'd come to her rescue again. Nothing there to let her heart get confused over. *Follow your heart, Elsie, but don't leave your brain behind.* Her mother always followed that advice up with a reminder: *If I'd stopped to think straight, I would've seen clearly that your father and I were too opposite, and that spark between us was just too weak. It blew out easier than a tea light.*

She'd listened to her mother and believed she'd been wise about her first husband. Yet she'd ended up divorced and discovered her heart and her mind were not in sync when it came to relationships and love. And could not be trusted.

Ryan climbed inside and started the truck. "Caleb and I will come back out here and get the tractor."

Elsie nodded and forced herself to think straight.

To get back to her task list. Back to the things that mattered. "I need to pick up the girls from school and head to the hospital to see Bryce. Then we'll go to the store and get started on dinner for tonight."

"Can I bring anything?" He slipped on a pair of sunglasses.

"No thanks." Elsie rubbed the dirt on her jeans. "I've got everything handled."

Or she would have everything handled. That included her growing feelings for a certain cowboy. Because falling for her cowboy would be more than unwise.

And she'd vowed not to let love outsmart her ever again.

CHAPTER EIGHT

RYAN PARKED HIS TRUCK, carried Elsie to the front porch despite her protests and because he wanted to. Because he wanted her arms around him again. Because he wanted to hold her close and tell himself one more time that she was fine. Unharmed. Safe. As if she was his to be concerned about.

When she was inside the house, he jumped into the UTV with Caleb and headed back out to the north farm fields. Caleb's fast driving and the wind blowing in his face made any conversation less than ideal. For that he was thankful.

He needed a minute to collect himself. It'd been an emotional storm from the time he'd seen Elsie's number flash on his phone screen earlier to pulling his truck in at the mud pit. He'd gone from delighted to hear her voice to concerned to bone-deep worried to riled to relieved. When he considered all the things that could've happened to Elsie and his family, that anger threatened to creep back in. He reminded himself again that everyone was good. Dirty, but good.

The mud field came into view. Ryan lightly punched his brother's shoulder. "Drop me here."

Caleb pulled to a stop and frowned at him. "The tractor is on the other side."

"I want to look for Elsie's shoes." Ryan jumped out and headed for the spot where Elsie had been sitting. He knew it'd been too much to expect his brother would leave him alone and head back to their family's farmhouse.

Caleb was quickly at his side and jabbing his elbow into Ryan's ribs. Speculation in his words. "So, you and Elsie."

There was no Elsie and him. Ryan shoved at his brother. "Just look for Elsie's running shoes so we can get the tractor, hightail it out of here and shower."

"You may not know this, but I'm an excellent multitasker," Caleb boasted, his words teasing. "For instance, I can look for shoes and talk about things like you and Elsie."

"We are not discussing that." Ryan followed several small tracks deeper into the mud. "We are just retrieving her missing shoes for her."

"Why? They're most likely ruined," Caleb said.

They wouldn't have been if Elsie hadn't been out there in the first place. She didn't belong in tractors and mud fields. She belonged in his arms. *No.* She didn't belong there either. She wasn't meant to be traipsing barefoot through the sludge. She was meant for formal affairs where she could shine, showing off her style and her elegance. Even if she'd looked happy and content with mud streaked across her face and her arms wrapped around his neck. Time to stop. Reset. Focus. She was headed back to the city soon. Ryan back to the circuit. And all this would simply become a moment. A memory. Nothing more. Ryan grumbled. "Just keep looking."

His little brother searched the muddy water and kept right on talking too. "Still, I'd like to mention that you carried Elsie twice. I really think that's something to discuss."

"That was the polite thing to do." Ryan sighed. "She was barefoot." And Ryan had seen an opportunity and he'd taken it. Selfish, sure. He'd do it again too. Without hesitation. And now he was getting in deeper and deeper. Not good. Yet he wasn't sure how to stop himself. There'd always been something about Elsie.

"You never even gave Carter or me a chance to do the polite thing," Caleb chided.

Wasn't that a fact. If anyone was carrying Elsie, it would be him. Now he sounded possessive, not polite. Ryan ground his teeth together. How could one woman turn him inside out in no time at all? "Leave it alone, Caleb." And he would leave Elsie alone too. Surely, he could manage that much.

"Fine," Caleb agreed too easily. Then grinned at Ryan. "I've other things to discuss with you anyway. Like how worried you were when Elsie called."

"We were all worried," Ryan reminded him.

"True." Caleb nodded and stuck his hand into the sludge. "But you were riled, big brother. You never get riled up about women. Horses yes. Women never. There isn't one I can recall."

"Think harder." Ryan tossed a rock across the mucky water and tried not to get irked by his brother's refusal to let things go.

"I got nothing." Caleb pulled his arm from the mud and revealed his empty hand. "Nor can I think of anyone who you've been worked up about ever."

"What about Mom?" Ryan offered.

"Mom doesn't count." Caleb chuckled. "Mom is the reason you don't get riled up about women in the first place."

Ryan didn't deny his brother's claim. Their mother, Lilian Sloan, had left her five young sons with her parents one summer and never returned. She'd gotten divorced from their father, lost focus of her family and concentrated on her medical career instead. Ryan had lost count of the nights that he'd had to soothe his upset little brothers, Caleb being one of them, when they'd cried for their mom. All while tucking away his own emotions to keep his brothers from feeling worse. That kind of thing tended to leave a mark, he supposed. Still, their grandparents had stepped in to raise Ryan and his brothers. What Ryan felt for his late Gran Claire and Grandpa Sam was more than he could ever put into words.

"It's only Elsie. She is the only woman I've seen you actually riled up about." Caleb paused, wiped the back of his hand across his forehead then added, "But then Elsie was sure riled up with you too earlier."

Elsie had been riled. Sparking like one of those midnight thunderstorms he liked so much. And she hadn't backed down. Came right at him. Right into his space. Ryan couldn't remember ever wanting to kiss a woman more. It'd taken all he had not to haul her into his arms and do just that. But he had more restraint than that. And a certain degree of self-preservation. Kissing Elsie would no doubt sink him.

Right now, he could only imagine what he couldn't have with Elsie. If they kissed, then he would know. And some things just weren't good to know. No matter what his Gran Claire had claimed. That was information he did not need.

"Hard not to like Elsie even more after she faced off with you, big brother," Caleb added, all too cheerfully. "Definitely admire her spirit."

So did Ryan. And that was a bit of a problem. There was too much he already admired about Elsie. Too much he still wanted to learn about her. His hand collided with something familiar. "Got it." He pulled one of her shoes from the mud, tossed it to Caleb, then eagerly reached for the other. "Take these back for Elsie. I'll get the tractor." And finally end their conversation.

"Don't take too long clearing that bee pasture for Elsie," Caleb ordered and turned to walk backward in the direction of the UTV. His words wry. "After all, you wouldn't want to be late for dinner. Nothing at all polite about that."

"I'm not…" Ryan stopped talking and let Caleb's laughter roll around him. Because he was. He was absolutely going to clear the field for Elsie.

MORE THAN AN hour later, Ryan parked the tractor outside Marlena's greenhouses and forced himself to look right at Elsie's packed U-Haul as he walked by it to get into his truck.

Forced himself to remember that Elsie was moving on. Very soon. And that he wanted nothing more than an uncomplicated goodbye. That meant no more carrying Elsie around. No more getting to know her. No more complicating things between them. Time to treat her like nothing more than a neighbor—friendly but respectful of each other's personal space.

Back on Sloan land, Ryan checked on his horses in the stables then headed to the farmhouse to shower and change.

Carter sat on the porch, his hair damp and mud-free. His ankles were stacked on the outdoor coffee table. His laptop was propped on his lap. And an open chip bag and bowl of salsa were within easy reach. At Ryan's approach, he glanced up and said, "Hey, little brother, it's your turn."

His turn. Ryan paused on the other side of the table and eyed the chip bag. But his hands were still filthy. He studied his brother. "Is this about Mom and her house-hunt-help text from earlier?"

As yet there'd been silence in response from all Ryan's brothers and himself. They weren't convinced their mother truly intended to move from New York City back to the Texas Panhandle. The very place she'd turned her back on decades ago.

And Ryan wasn't exactly certain he wanted to encourage his mother. He'd stopped hoping years and years ago that his mother would change. He hardly wanted to start hoping again. Although now, with Tess expecting twins soon, their mother would become a grandmother. And he couldn't stop wishing that Lilian Sloan would prove to be a better grandparent than mom. His future nieces and nephews deserved that much.

"Not what I was talking about." Carter closed his laptop and slid the computer onto the table. "But now that we're on the subject of Mom…"

"I can meet with Mom's real estate agent for her." Ryan wiped his hands on his jeans, but the dirt remained stuck to his palms.

"Why would you do that?" Carter asked, his surprise obvious.

And not all that unexpected. Ryan hadn't gone

out of his way for Lilian Sloan since she'd suddenly decided to come back into her sons' lives over a year ago. He was still adjusting to her presence. Still undecided on exactly how he felt about her return. He shrugged and decided on honesty. "Maybe if our mother sees there's nothing here for her, then she'll give up on the idea of moving back permanently."

Carter scratched his cheek. "Or you might find Mom her dream home and give her a reason to stay."

Ryan grabbed Carter's iced tea glass instead of the chips and took a long drink. "You don't actually believe that, do you?"

"I've recently decided that when it comes to our mother, anything is possible." Carter lifted one shoulder. "But if you're set on taking the lead on the house hunt thing, I won't stop you. And I doubt the others will either."

He wasn't exactly set. But Lilian Sloan provided a ready excuse to avoid roping practice and things he wasn't ready to face yet. Still, he knew the clock was ticking. Time was running out. And ready or not, he was going to have to figure out if the bucking-bronc-riding cowboy who attempted daredevil stunts was who he used to be. And the answer terrified him. Because if he wasn't *that* cowboy, who was he? And would he be enough?

Yeah, he was going to have to face his fears. Real soon. Ryan tapped a piece of ice into his mouth and crunched down hard. Just not tonight. "If you weren't referring to Mom just now, what else is going on?"

"It's your turn to watch Grandpa and Uncle." Carter dropped his feet onto the porch, pulled a chip from the bag and considered Ryan. "They're up to something."

"And you want me to find out what," Ryan guessed.

"I want you to keep an eye on them," Carter said. "Make sure they don't get into any more situations like today."

"Fine." Ryan readily accepted again. For too many reasons beyond ensuring his family's safety. Reasons like needing just one more excuse not to get in the saddle. Reasons like needing distance from a certain neighbor.

Carter chewed on his chip and studied Ryan. His gaze narrowed. "Why aren't you protesting? Telling me to ask Caleb instead?"

Ryan finished the rest of Carter's iced tea and wished for indifference to tinge his words. "Maybe I'm curious to see what Grandpa and Uncle Roy got planned now."

Carter sat back and drummed his fingers on the chair rest. "You could ask them what they are up to now."

"Like they'd tell me outright," Ryan countered. "And we both know they won't tell you."

"I already tried asking them. They told me they

were only being good neighbors and I could learn a thing or two from them." Carter shook his head and rubbed his chin. "But you're making this too easy, little brother. First Mom. Now this. You're avoiding something."

If you only knew how many things. Ryan crossed his arms over his chest, met his older brother's stare and kept his expression neutral.

"Or someone." Carter grinned and lifted his eyebrows. "Interesting."

"There's nothing interesting about anything," Ryan said. "You've got the distillery and you need to be available for Tess. The twins are due within the month. Caleb has been working at the fire station a lot. Josh and Vivian left for Arizona. Grant is busy in the operating room. That leaves me."

"Makes sense. You're right." Carter shrugged then stood and clapped his hand on Ryan's shoulder. "Still, I find I'm really looking forward to dinner tonight with Elsie. It'll be fun to catch up with an old friend, don't you think?"

There would be no more catching up. It was simply dinner with the neighbor. "I'm sure it'll be fine." Or it would be if Ryan could remember those neighborly boundaries. Besides, a cowboy with an identity crisis was hardly the kind of partner someone as successful and put together as Elsie would ever want.

"We're going to head out early," Carter said. "Tess and Maggie want to pick up a few things for Elsie. Hostess gifts they told me. Need us to get you something too?"

Ryan shook his head. "Already got one on my way home."

"Now, that is very interesting." Carter wrapped his arm around Ryan's shoulders. "Care to share what you bought for an old friend you aren't interested in catching up with?"

"Nope." Ryan shoved his brother away and walked into the house. His muddy boots dropped in the mudroom, he headed upstairs to his room.

He shouldn't be looking forward to dinner with Elsie. Not even a little bit. But he was.

And that was what his Gran Claire would've called trouble brewing. *That there is nothing but trouble brewing, Ryan. Best not go stirring it up either. Otherwise, it'll boil over and then you've got yourself nothing other than a mess. And you've never been good at cleaning up a mess like that.*

CHAPTER NINE

HER COWBOY WAS LATE.

No apology. No excuse.

He simply slipped inside the house as if he always came and went on his own terms. Even in her house. Then he slid easily into the empty chair at the head of the table on the far end. Shared a fist bump with Autumn. Then Gemma. Accepted the salad bowl from Carter and what Elsie hoped was a lecture on punctuality.

Elsie would've liked to lecture him herself. It would be long and lengthy. And detailed about how he must stop making her feel. Nervous. Excited. Irritated. Frustrated. Relieved when he finally arrived. Disappointed he wasn't closer. Exasperated by her own roller coaster of completely uncalled for emotions.

If they weren't each seated at the head of the table, but on opposite ends. If his entire family wasn't there as witnesses. If she had him alone.

Alone. With her cowboy. That she intended to avoid. Otherwise, she might forget everything she meant to tell him and do something foolish. Like run her hand through his wavy deep brown hair, tangling her fingers in the thick strands that touched the collar of his striped navy button-down shirt. A color he should definitely consider wearing more often. *Enough*. Her cowboy had gotten to her plenty for one evening. Time to put a stop to that. Elsie concentrated on her bowl of savory chicken soup and scooped a plump dumpling onto her spoon.

Sam dipped a butter knife in the whipped butter Elsie had made for the homemade biscuits and slanted his gaze along the length of the table. Then he looked at Elsie. His voice lowered conspiratorially. "Roy and I hooked up the tiller after we arrived this evening, in case you're of a mind to drive that tractor again tomorrow."

"Have to get back in the saddle, or rather the seat," Roy said, his voice just above murmur level. He lifted his eyebrows at her. "That's the way of things. Today was nothing but a little setback. We'd never get anywhere if we let those thwart us."

"But we never cleared the field." Elsie set her spoon down and kept her voice tuned to quiet. "You told me that's the first step."

Sam grinned wide. His eyes brightened. "Ryan took care of that earlier today."

"Why would Ryan do that?" Elsie whispered and worked to keep her focus on the older cowboy, not the one who already stole too much of her attention.

Sam reached over and patted Elsie's arm. "That's what a cowboy does for his cowgirl."

"I'm not his…" He certainly wasn't hers either. Elsie shook her head. Still, her gaze landed on Ryan at the end of the table and stuck.

Gemma had shifted her chair closer to Ryan. The pair was busy coloring, their heads pressed together, their focus on the paper in front of them. Gemma traded Ryan's yellow crayon for a green one. Her cowboy never missed a beat, simply kept drawing and listening to Gemma chatter away. As if he always colored with six-year-olds at dinner gatherings. And those feelings stirred again. Elsie reached for her wine glass and barely swallowed her sigh inside the chilled white wine.

"You and Ryan will have to sort out your relationship particulars." Roy squeezed her arm and drew her attention to him. "But if you'd like our assistance, we're available."

"We're quite familiar with the nuts and bolts required for a solid, strong relationship," Sam added quickly, as if not wanting to be left out. "And we know more than a thing or two about the finer points of love."

Elsie shifted her gaze from one to the other, took in their sincere expressions and wisdom-tinted gazes. Then realized they were more than serious. The pair was ready and willing to offer love advice. To Elsie. About Ryan. She sipped her wine again. A deeper, longer drink. And considered how not to disappoint the two well-meaning cowboys she really liked.

But relationship advice wasn't necessary. Elsie was putting all her stock in her career these days. Her mother had given up everything for love, including her theater career, only to have Elsie's father give her up. Fortunately, Elsie had her event manager job at the hotel when her ex-husband walked away from their marriage. A career could be counted on. Elsie couldn't claim the same about love. She said, "You'll be my first call if I ever require relationship advice."

"Just keep in mind, if you're calling about Ryan, then we might need more than one call," Roy offered and scraped his spoon across the bottom of his bowl.

"Roy isn't wrong. My grandson is like a wild mustang." Sam nodded, his expression and words resigned. "He just needs the right cowgirl with enough patience and time to understand him."

Time was not what Elsie had. As for patience, that was not always her best trait. And cowgirl she was not. She was batting zero on the list of things Ryan's cowgirl should be, according to his grandfather. The man who most likely knew Ryan best. She wasn't who Ryan needed. She knew it. Understood it. Yet her gaze drifted back to him.

Fortunately, Gemma and he seemed intent on creating their personal collection of artwork.

"Now we can help with your relationship business, but I'm afraid we can't continue with the tractor lessons." Sam rattled the ice in his bourbon glass. His words disgruntled. "Even though we'd sure like to."

"But if you have a mind for improving what we already taught you on the tractor," Roy started then paused. His bushy eyebrows lifted, widening his eyes. "There's another bit of land that sure could use your attention."

Elsie finished her wine and worked to keep her curiosity in check. "Where would that be?"

"Not two turns to the west of your bee pasture." Roy waggled his eyebrows. "Close and easy to find."

"Where exactly is that?" Elsie asked. Unsure how she was going to get the tractor out of the driveway, let alone drive it to another field. Still, she'd driven today. And Roy hadn't been wrong when he told her that she had to get back in the tractor seat. There was work she'd promised to complete.

"You head to the north end of your bee pasture and keep straight for another hundred or so yards." Sam drew an imaginary line on the tabletop then picked up the crystal saltshaker and set it down in his finger's path. "At the copse of trees, which you cannot miss, head west."

"That's left," Roy chimed in.

Elsie nodded. Sam grinned and continued, "Then follow those trees until you see the old wheelhouse near the stream. Can't miss the field."

Elsie pushed her bowl away and took in the two older cowboys. Before she could ask more about the land, Carter interrupted.

"This is the best chicken and dumplings I've had, Elsie." Carter dragged a piece of a home-made biscuit through his empty bowl. There were murmurs of approval and praise around the table.

"When did you become such an accomplished cook?" Grant helped himself to a second serving of chicken and dumplings.

"Aunt Marlena taught me to cook when I came here for the summers." Elsie wiped a napkin on her mouth. Then after her parents divorced, she always cooked at home. For herself and her mom. But not for fun, rather for necessity. Otherwise, every meal would've been breakfast cereal—her theatrical mother's preferred go-to fast food. Still, Elsie had always found a certain comfort and sat-isfaction in the preparation and sharing of a good meal with friends and family.

"Wait." Carter picked up the rest of his biscuit and eyed her. "You were making these biscuits back then and never thought to share with me. Not once. Even though I taught you to drive."

Elsie chuckled and sat back. "Would those bis-cuits have made you a nicer driving instructor?"

"I was plenty nice." Carter popped the biscuit into his mouth and grinned around the bite.

"Why do I not believe that, husband?" Tess shoved playfully against Carter's shoulder.

"It wasn't my fault." Carter rested his arm on the back of Tess's chair and picked up his bourbon glass. "If Elsie hadn't been on a mission to strip the gears in my truck with every shift she made, I wouldn't have yelled so much."

"That was not her fault," Maggie said, coming to Elsie's defense. "She was just learning. You should've been more patient with her, Carter."

Tess nodded her agreement and frowned at her husband. Elsie had only just met Tess and Maggie, yet she couldn't deny she'd felt an instant connection with the two women. They'd brought her a brand-new pair of proper work boots for the farm to replace her ruined running shoes. And white chocolate truffles handmade by Tess that, according to Maggie, solved any problem. Even more, they treated Elsie like she was already family, offering to help, take her to lunch, listen. Whatever she needed, she was not to hesitate and simply let them know.

"It wasn't all bad." Carter tipped his glass in a toast to Elsie. Laughter swirled in his gaze. "Tell them what you did, Elsie."

"I might have threatened him." Elsie felt her cheeks warm. Carter had always treated her like his little sister. In return, she thought of him as another big brother and often talked to him like she would her own brother. Elsie lifted her chin. "I told Carter that if he didn't stop barking at me, I was going to drive straight to Claire and cry all over his grandma's shoulder. Then I was going to tell Claire that her grandson was nothing but a big meanie."

Laughter spilled around the dining room.

"I'm sure that threat got him to act right." Sam tapped his glass against Elsie's.

"Gran Claire taught us all to mind our manners and be kind." Grant took Maggie's hand in his. His words wistful and affectionate. "Gran Claire definitely wouldn't have tolerated her grandson being a big meanie. I wish Elsie had told her. I would've loved to have been there for that lecture."

"You got enough Gran Claire lectures all on your own, Grant," Carter said, his words dry. "Besides, I was perfectly polite after Elsie threatened me."

"Instead of snapping, he groaned every time I stalled," Elsie added. "Which was a lot."

"But you learned to drive a manual transmission that summer." Carter pressed his hand to his chest and toasted himself. "So it seems I wasn't all bad."

"A skill that is coming in rather handy right now." Elsie lifted her wine glass toward Carter. "If I didn't thank you before, I am now."

"Wait." That one drawn-out word rolled across the table like the thud of a wild mustang galloping across a field.

Everyone shifted to look at Ryan. Gemma had moved back to her original spot and continued to color. Ryan leaned back in his chair, his arms folded across his chest. His fingers stroked through his beard. He looked casual, almost disinterested. All except for the glint in his gaze. The one fixed fully on Elsie.

You've certainly got his attention now. And those feelings—the ones Elsie refused to acknowledge—swirled faster. Those butterflies fluttered.

His fingers stilled inside his beard. His gaze narrowed ever so slightly. His words sounded careful. "You let Carter teach you to drive. But when I offered, you flat-out refused me."

Elsie swallowed and tried not to fidget under the weight of Ryan's stare. Of course, she had refused him. She always thought of Carter like a big brother. As for Ryan, she always thought *about* him. Too much. And her teenage heart was too tender back then. Elsie opened her mouth to explain.

But Caleb saved her. "Did Elsie refuse to dance with you too, Ryan?" His words were casual and almost too cheerful. "Because I taught her how to dance. Same as Carter taught her to drive." Caleb turned an all-too-innocent look at Elsie. "Remember when we danced together, Els?"

Elsie nodded. Her gaze collided with Ryan's and stuck. She felt her cheeks warming all over again and said, "Your Gran Claire taught us to dance, Caleb."

"Still, you were my partner, Elsie, for every dance lesson we shared," Caleb continued, seemingly content to keep on elaborating.

The heat in Elsie's cheeks spread to her chest. And Elsie second-guessed the sleeveless, V-neck wrap dress she'd chosen to wear for dinner.

"You must remember that." Caleb's words were persistent and ongoing. "Gran Claire always complimented me on my proper hold when we practiced together."

The extra emphasis Caleb put on together was hardly necessary. Elsie would've frowned at the youngest Sloan brother, but she couldn't quite pull her focus away from her cowboy.

Ryan's eyes widened. The briefest flare before his expression shifted into impassive once more.

She might have believed her cowboy didn't much like what he was hearing. Might have not minded his misplaced jealousy if she considered him more than a friend. If she wanted to feel something more for him. And if she wanted to know her cowboy felt something for her in return.

Instead, Elsie decided to put an end to things and said gently, "Caleb, I think my toes are still bruised from when we danced together back in high school."

There. The smallest of grins on her cowboy's face. The tiniest of twitches across his mouth that faded before it caught fully. Elsie had no time to celebrate her small success.

"I've come a very long way since high school, Els." Caleb pushed his chair back, stood and thrust his arm out toward Elsie. Then grinned and said, "Dance with me and I'll prove it to you."

"We can't dance here," Elsie protested.

"Why not?" Sam asked, his words mild. "Seems as good a place as any."

"Used to dance with my sweet Millie in our kitchen. Bumped against a cabinet or two, but we always just kept dancing." Roy smiled into his bourbon glass as if watching the replay of an old memory.

"But…" *I want to dance with…* Her gaze found Ryan again.

His arms were still crossed loosely over his chest. He looked distant and disengaged. Much like he'd been since he'd arrived. All except for his intense gaze. The one that captured hers and refused to let go.

"Don't you remember how to dance, Elsie?" Caleb asked, his words taunting and teasing. "Or are you afraid you'll step on my toes?"

Elsie held Ryan's stare. His eyebrow arched as if challenging her hesitation. As if daring her. Elsie pushed her shoulders back. She would dance with Caleb and anyone else who asked her. She would dance all night if she must. If only to prove she didn't want Ryan to be her first or last dance.

"I didn't step on your toes back then, Caleb. Nor will I now." Elsie rose and moved around the large table into the open space between the family room and dining area. "Autumn, play a country song. A fast one." Autumn ran over to the smart speaker on the bookshelves, Gemma on her heels. Then Elsie stepped into Caleb's hold and smiled. "Try to keep up, Caleb."

And he did. Led her in a two-step and country swing blend perfectly. No bruised toes. Only laughter and twirling and cheering from their audience. Caleb finished the dance with a brilliantly executed dip. She was out of breath when Caleb righted her. And told herself she was relieved when she saw Ryan had cleared part of the dining table and was already disappearing into the kitchen.

Not my concern. Still, she gathered more dishes and stalked right after her cowboy. She dropped her stack of plates in the kitchen sink and cornered Ryan between the island and the refrigerator. "What is your problem tonight?"

"I don't have one." He braced his hands on the granite countertop behind him and leaned back. "Do you?"

Oh, she had a problem. A cowboy-sized one. For certain. But that was for her to sort out herself. Later. When she was alone and not so intent on reading between the lines. Surely, she hadn't truly felt butterflies because of him earlier. Now only frustration flickered through her. "No. I'm having a delightful evening."

"That's good." His words sounded bored. He tipped his head toward the dining room. "Sounds like they are playing another song. I'm sure Caleb would dance with you again. You should head back out there. Enjoy the rest of your evening."

"What about you?" *Would you dance with me? Just once. So, then I would know...* Elsie cut off that thought. She had to stop feeling so much around him. Stop imagining what wasn't there. And start thinking straight.

"I see Marty is out of the goat pen again." His focus shifted to the wide window over the kitchen sink. "I think I'll go and gather the goats."

"Right now?" She worked to hide her exasperation.

He nodded.

"Is that really what you want?" *What if I wanted it to be me?* She searched his face.

His chin dipped, quick and certain. Then he released the counter and eased around her without making the slightest contact.

She could've reached for him. Stopped him. To what end? To ask him to dance with her only to realize she wanted another and another. But she had her own life—and career—to build in New York.

The one she'd diligently researched and mapped

out. The one that would prove she could live outside the pages of her books. Outside her comfort zone. *You're too content watching life being lived around you, Elsie. But I'm ready to go live it.* Without her, it turned out. Her ex-husband had never asked Elsie to join him. Never asked what she'd been ready for.

But Elsie was ready now. To create her own success in a big city where she could thrive. Yet a cowboy like Ryan wasn't meant for city life. He was meant for everything she couldn't offer. Like open country roads, long sunrise horseback rides and her trust.

Her trust that what she felt between them was something more than a flicker. Something worth risking her heart for. Because she was done handing over her heart only to have it returned broken. Something about her cowboy warned her that he could steal her heart and break it before she even knew it.

Elsie kept her arms at her sides. Then twisted and watched him leave. Best get used to it. After all, she would do her own leaving one day soon enough.

At the back door, he turned around and watched her for a beat. Then one more. Finally, he said, "What I really want is to kiss you, Elsie Marie. But sometimes we just don't get what we want."

CHAPTER TEN

THE NEXT MORNING, Ryan walked Sundancer up the Doyles' driveway and veered straight for the tractor. Elsie sat in the captain's chair, the cab door propped open courtesy of her new work boots from Maggie and Tess. She wore a blue plaid flannel shirt, the sleeves rolled to her elbows, and a faded burgundy baseball cap, her ponytail pulled through the back. Casual suited her. Same as the emerald green silky dress she'd worn last night had suited her. She was pretty. He supposed she would always be that to him. He'd come close enough. He stopped yards from the tractor.

"Elsie." Ryan set his hands on his hips and stared up at the tractor cab. "What are you doing?"

"Working up my nerve to drive this thing." Elsie's hands fluttered in the air then settled on her jean-covered legs. She tipped her head and considered him. "What about you?"

The same. Working up my nerve to apologize. But I meant every single word last night. Not the apology he should give her. He went with the first thing that came to mind, stalling until he found the right words for that apology he owed her. He said, "I'm worried about a mare at the sanctuary. Midnight Rose is not settling in well with the other horses. Even the stables stress her out." Details were vague on the mare up until her arrival at Martha Claire Horse Haven, but Ryan didn't need specifics to know the mare's life had been far from ideal. "I'm trying to figure out how best to help her."

Elsie adjusted the brim of her baseball cap. "Get her a goat."

Ryan gave up. Gave in. And climbed up into the tractor cab. To be closer to Elsie. Like he wanted. He asked, "Did you say goat?"

"Yes." Elsie shifted in the chair and picked up her cell phone from the cup holder. "Goats make excellent companions for horses. I was reading all about goats last night."

About last night. Up close, he noticed how ridiculously big her plaid shirt was. She'd clearly borrowed it from Bryce's closet. It was knotted at the waist and unbuttoned to her stomach, revealing a pale pink tank top underneath. The ill-fitted shirt, designer jeans and scuff-free boots reminded him she'd stepped into this life temporarily. And soon she'd be leaving Three Springs and him behind.

Yet when he looked at her, he still wanted to kiss her. Same as he had last night. That hardly meant it was the right thing to do. For either of them. Still, that apology drifted away on the crisp morning breeze.

"Listen to this." Elsie crossed her legs. The toe of her boot tapped the air in time to the tap of her finger on her phone screen. "I found this blog last night. The top five reasons to get your horse a goat as a companion."

Ryan had a top five list too. Five reasons Elsie and he wouldn't work. Five reasons he should walk away and keep his distance from her. One reason was parked in the driveway with a goat standing on it. Yet despite the logic and his common sense, Ryan stayed. If he lingered longer, then maybe he would find that one reason they were meant for more than a goodbye.

Elsie paused and glanced at him. Her gaze expectant. "What do you think?"

I think that I still want to kiss you. Very much. Would you mind so much? He leaned against the door frame and said, "The rescue doesn't have goats."

"I do." Elsie pointed out the windshield toward the U-Haul truck where Smarty Marty was currently standing as if playing king of the mountain. Elsie added, "We have an empty stable and a pasture that's suitable. Sundancer seemed to enjoy it."

"I can't bring her here." He rubbed his fingers across his bearded cheek. *I shouldn't be here.*

"Why not? There are no other horses to scare her. And she'll have goats for company." Elsie tapped on her phone screen again. "Sometimes a change of scenery is all that's needed."

Perhaps that was what Ryan needed. A change of scenery. Or perhaps it wasn't a change. It was just getting back to the circuit and back to what he did best. Back to the place where he never questioned whether he belonged or not. Where he knew the rules and the expectations. Where it wasn't about his heart, but rather his dedication. His perseverance. Being fearless. For eight seconds, not a lifetime. Because love couldn't guarantee his heart would ever be enough for someone else. After all, he'd loved his mother and that hadn't been enough for her. He sidestepped his thoughts and concentrated on Elsie. "But a horse means more work for you."

Her eyebrows lowered beneath the brim of her baseball cap. She frowned at him. "You already did my work. So, it seems I need something else to do."

There was too much irritation around her words not to be genuine. Ryan stared at her. "You can't be angry with me for clearing the bee pasture. I was helping you. You should be thanking me."

"I didn't want you to do it for me." Her frown deepened. "And I'm certainly not thanking you."

"I can see that." Amusement softened his words, but his own exasperation quickly followed and took hold. "You can't actually want to drive a tractor. Plow fields. Farm. You admitted you were not born into this life." One more reason they wouldn't work. This was never the kind of life she wanted. And it was the only life he knew.

"Of course, I don't," she charged then brushed her hand over her face and seemed to lose a bit of her steam. "But it's not about that."

"This conversation isn't making any sense." Nor was he. They made no sense together. And yet when he looked at her…

"How about this then?" She stiffened in the chair and eyed him. "It's about proving that I can do something more than read a how-to book. That I can be counted on too. That I can handle things on my own and be trusted to get it right." She paused, tightened her ponytail and adjusted her hat as if putting herself back to rights then added, "Surely that makes sense. Or maybe it does not. Because you always get things right, especially out here. Where you belong."

He'd gotten a lot wrong lately. Ryan held her stare for an extra minute then said, "Don't move." He was out of the cab and on the ground before she could respond. Within minutes, Sundancer was secured in the same pasture as days earlier, and he was back inside the tractor cab with a silent Elsie. He propped himself next to the captain's chair, motioned to the control panel then said, "Well, turn it on."

She slanted her gaze toward him. Her voice breathless and low. "What?"

"The bee pasture has only been started," he explained then added a small smile. "Now you're going to finish it."

"Right now?" Excitement and reluctance wobbled through her expression and words.

"Can't think of a better time, can you?" He sounded concise and challenging. Then he crossed his arms over his chest as if intent on waiting her out. "Time to prove yourself to yourself, Elsie Marie."

Elsie stuck her phone into the holder and scooted back in the chair. "What are you going to do?"

"Consider me your onboard help desk. Here for advice." Nothing more than a good neighbor being helpful. Ryan pushed his hat lower on his forehead and stared out the windshield, rather than at the stray piece of Elsie's hair that touched her cheek. "But you are in the driver's seat. What happens next is entirely up to you."

And that's where Ryan was going to leave things. With Elsie. Entirely. Because Elsie had always been the one to do the right thing. To follow the rules. To be sensible. And Ryan had always been the risk-taker. The jump-and-consider-the-consequences-later one.

But the consequences of jumping with Elsie, well, those were ones even he might not recover from. Good thing he knew Elsie was smart. She would know someone like him was all wrong for her. He should be more relieved. He shouldn't want to prove that he could be who she needed. Because that would be all kinds of wrong. For both of them. And that meant Ryan would do what he did best in relationships—keep things between them light, easy and casual.

Several hours later and the bee pasture prep completed, Ryan lifted his hat off his head and brushed his hand through his hair. Beside him, Elsie concentrated on driving the tractor with the same intensity she had since they'd started. She was completely by the book. Although, she'd stopped reciting proper tractor operating tips she'd collected from the owner's manual. When he'd run out of farm facts to fill the silence, he'd turned on music inside the cab. Still, her shoulders were too tight and her grip tense as if she feared relaxing.

Ryan paused the music on the console and asked, "So are you going to tell me why we are now working on Sloan land? Or do you want me to guess?"

"How do you know this is Sloan land?" Elsie kept her attention trained on what was ahead and steered in a perfectly straight line that would have impressed the most seasoned farmhand.

"Bryce and I used to have epic battles on the property line out here." Ryan chuckled. Their battles had lasted hours in the summers and often stretched over days. Truces were called for afternoon cannonballs in the Sloan family pond, lunch, or worse, chores. But the friends had always stepped in to help each other finish their chores in order to get back to the fun faster. Ryan grinned at the memory. "True turf wars were waged in these parts on more than one occasion."

"Who won?" A smile played across Elsie's face.

He liked that. Making her smile. Would've wanted to do that more if he wasn't determined to be more detached neighbor than interested friend. He said, "I won, of course."

"Of course." She chuckled, the sound natural and relaxed.

He liked that too. His own smile came easily.

"And if I asked my brother?" There was a tease in her words.

"Bryce will lie and claim a false victory," Ryan said, dryly and decidedly.

Her full laughter spilled free, falling around him like an unexpected spring shower. That sound he really liked. Far too much. And he was drawn in again, despite his determination to remain detached.

She slanted her gaze at him, her amusement faded. "Sam and Roy told me I could practice my tractor skills out here. I never got a chance last night to ask them more about this land."

Ryan ran his palms over his jeans and considered the property. Not far ahead, nestled among the treetops, the pitched roof of an old, all-too-familiar barn came into view. Ryan pointed out the windshield. "Head that way."

"Is that a barn?" Elsie leaned forward in her chair as if wanting a better view. "Why would someone put a barn all the way out here? All by itself. That's odd."

"I don't know." Ryan smiled and shrugged. "But growing up we never cared about the reasons the barn was built, only that it was here."

Elsie frowned at him.

"I'll have you know that barn served several important purposes over the years for Bryce and me," Ryan stated, unable to keep the humor from his words. "Among other things, that old barn was our hideout, neutral ground during those epic turf battles, and a dungeon when we were rogue pirates."

"There was certainly a lot going on out here." Elsie shook her head. Her grin stretched wider. "Clearly, I had no idea."

"Hey, I tried to invite you to come along." Ryan lifted one shoulder, nudging aside his old disappointment at her refusals then added, "But you were always more interested in your books than joining our adventures."

"Well, you never mentioned anything about rogue pirates." Elsie slowed the tractor to a stop.

"Well, I can't promise we'll find any pirates, but it's worth exploring." Ryan reached for the door rather than hold his hand out to her. "You can wait here or join me. Your choice."

"Lead the way." Elsie motioned to the door. "But if I find pirate treasure in there, I'm not sharing."

"Fine." Ryan leaped to the ground. He was glad to share this moment alone with her. And wasn't that far from the neutral neighbor he intended to be. Still, he waited within easy reach of Elsie and watched her climb down.

Her boots barely touched the grass when Ryan turned, heading toward the old barn. A path had been cleared toward the side door of the stone and slate rectangle building. The glass in the windows had been gone long before Ryan and Bryce had claimed the space as their own fortress. The second-story loft only covered half the space and few floorboards had remained when they'd been kids. But the waterwheel on the other side of the barn had transformed the barn into something more. And ignited their imaginations same as the water from the stream had turned the wheel in a slow, constant roll.

"That's a waterwheel." Wonder splashed through Elsie's words and expression. "You never told me about that."

There was a lot he hadn't told her. Even more he couldn't tell her. Still, he grinned. "Would that have enticed you to come out here with me?"

She ducked her head and hurried over to the waterwheel, but not before he caught the blush tinting her cheeks pink. And didn't that jump-start his own foolish thoughts. Still, he followed Elsie over to the stream's edge. The wooden wheel creaked. The water spilled gently from the wheel slates. The stream gurgled. It was peaceful and calming. And very inviting.

The perfect place to gather your thoughts as his Gran Claire would've told him. *Always good to sit for a spell, Ryan. Every now and then. Make sure your heart and your mind are in tune.*

Before he invited Elsie to sit beside him for a spell to see if they were in tune, Ryan turned and pointed at the warped wooden door. "Want to hunt for that treasure now?"

Elsie laughed and motioned in front of her. "After you."

"I haven't been inside here in years." Ryan nudged the door open then peered inside to check for fallen beams or other potential mishaps. The space was surprisingly debris-free.

"Is it the same as you remember?" Elsie joined him. Her face lifted to the pitched roof and thick rafters still bisecting the ceiling.

Ryan turned a slow circle then brushed his fingers across the stone wall. "Feels smaller than it did when we were kids."

"You've grown a bit taller since then." Elsie chuckled and moved farther into the rectangle barn.

"I suppose that's true." Ryan wandered over to the ladder still leaning against the stone wall. The one they used to scale to reach the rickety loft. Looking up at it now, he was amazed they hadn't collapsed through the worn floorboards to the cement floor below. The entire space seemed to be one safety violation after another. When had he started seeking those out first? "And it doesn't help that I seem to have lost my imagination."

She paused and considered him. Her face shadowed by her baseball cap and the dimly lit interior. "You sound disappointed."

"More nostalgic…" He looked up at a cobweb in the window. Water droplets glistened on the intricate webbing. "For those times when you believed you could be anyone or anything. All you had to do was imagine it. There was nothing to stop you."

"What's stopping you now?" Her voice was all too perceptive.

"Nothing." He shrugged one shoulder, nudging against his uncertainty. Then added more conviction to his words. "I am who I always wanted to be."

"Then there's nothing left to imagine," she said quietly.

Except when he looked at her. Then he imagined. Things like a life partner. A real commitment. His own family. All the things he never really considered. All the things he always avoided. After all, the only commitment he'd ever been able to keep was to his rodeo career. Same as his mother had only ever stayed true to her medical career. His apple hadn't fallen far from that tree. And the thought of failing Elsie left him cold. Nothing to do but tuck his foolish imaginings away. Concentrate on what he did best: rodeo.

Elsie stood in front of a wooden worktable that spanned the length of one wall. Amusement and confusion blended in her expression. "I'm trying to imagine what Sam and Roy plan to do out here. This is where they told me to bring the tractor the other night at dinner."

Ryan walked over to the table. He picked up a handful of tiny yellow flower petals from the wooden work top and scattered them across his palm. Thanks to Elsie, he now had a fairly good idea what his grandpa and uncle were up to. "My guess. They want to make dandelion wine."

"Seriously?" Elsie peered at the flower petals he held.

"They found an old family recipe a few years back." Ryan picked up an intact dandelion flower from the work top and held it out to her. "They've been wanting to brew something, but Carter hasn't let them use the distillery or its equipment."

"So, they found a workaround," Elsie said, approval in her words. She touched her fingertip to the dandelion blossom. "They certainly are enterprising."

"Among other things." Ryan brushed the petals off his hand and wiped his palms together. No use lingering and encouraging his own wayward wishes or those of his grandfather and uncle. "We should get going. I need to head over to the sanctuary this afternoon."

He had a meeting with the contractor about the new stable barn build. The one the sanctuary could afford if Ryan took home the grand prize at the rodeo in two weeks. And the same one that would house the five aged-out broncs Ryan had committed to giving a new home to. All part of his family's legacy. But it only happened if Ryan located his nerve and got in the saddle again.

Elsie walked over to him, pulled his attention back to her. She said, "We can't just leave this unfinished for Roy and Sam."

"Why not?" Ryan asked. "We can't encourage them. This barn wasn't safe when we were kids. It's undoubtedly gotten worse over the years."

"But you can make sure it is safe," Elsie countered. "Make sure they are safe out here."

For now. But who would watch his grandpa and uncle when he was on the road? Back on the circuit full-time where he needed to be. He knew how to be successful there. But Elsie tempted him to think beyond the arena. Beyond that eight-second ride. He stopped himself. He always faltered in relationships. And letting down Elsie wasn't something he ever wanted to do. Promises were something he couldn't give her.

He nudged the toe of his boot into a pile of dirt. "I don't know, Elsie. This place needs more than a deep clean."

"Come on, Ryan," Elsie urged. "You know how happy it would make them."

And her too. He could see it all over her face. Hear it in her voice. But her happiness wasn't his to ensure. He crossed his arms over his chest. "I'll talk to Josh and see what I can do." When her smile spread wide and her mouth opened, he held out his hand, palm up. "But I'm not making any promises. If it is not safe out here, then there will be no dandelion wine making happening."

"I believe in you," Elsie said, quickly and decidedly as if doubting him was an impossibility. Then she pulled out her cell phone and tapped on the screen.

But all Ryan seemed to have were doubts. Especially where Elsie was concerned. Looking at her now, he doubted they were so very different after all. Simply two people content to make others happy until they discovered a bit of their own. *I could be happy with you.* He shut down that thought and ordered his heart to get back in line. Then he cleared his throat. "What are you doing?"

"Researching dandelion seeds." Elsie swiped her finger across her phone screen. Her eyebrows knitted together. "We will want a high-quality seed for the wine."

"It's a weed," Ryan said, his voice dust coated like the stone walls surrounding him and his heart.

"It's a weed that turns into something delicious." Elsie followed him outside.

"Have you ever tried dandelion wine?" Ryan asked.

"No, but it sounds good." Elsie grinned at him over her phone. "Listen to this."

Ryan paused and considered her. He was beginning to like those three words—*listen to this*—more than he should. Every time she repeated that phrase her gaze lit up and her voice sparked. And she captured his full attention. Completely and undeniably.

"'Dandelion wine is a citrusy, floral spring tonic. Not too sweet. Its golden color is both warm and rich,'" Elsie read from her phone. "Doesn't that sound delightful."

He was beginning to think she was delightful. And wasn't that just about as unacceptable as weeds in his Gran Claire's gardens? He turned and headed for the tractor. "It's still a weed."

"It's a weed with a worthy second act." Elsie bumped her shoulder into his arm. "We should all appreciate that."

And before he got to appreciating her enthusiasm for dandelion wine and how much he liked being with her, he said, "You do realize that your family can shut down the whole operation if they choose to, don't you?"

"How is that?" Elsie tucked her phone back in her pocket.

"Water rights." Ryan hitched his thumb toward the waterwheel. "The stream is on Doyle land.

And I imagine there were disputes centuries ago right here in this very spot over the land and the water."

"Or maybe the previous owners worked together," Elsie mused.

"That sounds very optimistic and idealistic." And she looked very adorable and all too approachable. Ryan retreated.

"Perhaps I should advise my brother and aunt to demand a percentage of the profits from the sale of the dandelion wine." Elsie climbed up into the tractor cab.

"You should probably demand a bottle of dandelion wine first," he suggested. "You might not even like it."

He definitely couldn't say the same about Elsie. He liked her. Too much already.

And now he'd gone and complicated that goodbye. Only one thing to do. Demand his heart stand down.

Otherwise, he just might find himself in trouble—the heartbreaking kind of trouble.

CHAPTER ELEVEN

RYAN HAD NEVER been one to second-guess his decisions. Until recently. And the frequency seemed to be multiplying by the day. Take right now, for instance. Ryan glanced at the time on his watch. His frown deepened.

He certainly had not planned on touring houses for sale all morning with his mother's real estate agent, Fletcher Belfer. As for his mother, she was back in New York overseeing her medical practice.

Now it was well past the lunch hour and he was still looking at houses. Worse, he and his mother were also currently live on video chat. Ryan already had to postpone his visit to the sanctuary to check on Midnight Rose. And had to ask Maggie to meet Paige Bishop, the local veterinarian, at the Sloan stables for Sundancer's weekly checkup.

Adjusting his grip on his phone, Ryan moved from the office and continued to film his walk-through of the first floor of the renovated townhouse in downtown Belleridge. As for Fletcher, he'd stepped outside to take an important phone call. *Lucky him.*

"Ryan." His mother's crisp voice streamed across the speaker. "Step back and pan across the entire kitchen again. Only slower this time."

Ryan did as his mother requested. He moved farther back into the living room and lifted his phone to capture the kitchen. And kept silent.

He had not planned on this. He'd counted on his meticulous mother instantly disliking every single place. Instantly discounting each one as unsuitable for her. And that in turn would have immediately proven Ryan correct. That his mother really had no intention of *actually* relocating to the Texas Panhandle to be closer to her family.

But his mother was acting interested. And very involved. Now Ryan was second-guessing his decision to take the lead on this particular task. And seriously reconsidering calling Caleb for backup. Especially now that Fletcher appeared not to be returning anytime soon from his urgent phone call, leaving Ryan to deal with his mother alone.

"How many people can fit around that island, Ryan?" His mother's voice disrupted the silence. She added, "I can't tell from this view."

"I'm not sure. Maybe six could stand around the island." Ryan tipped his head and studied the granite-topped island.

There was room enough for two stools. Three would definitely be a crowd. But he could see the appeal. It would be an ideal spot for a relaxed evening. With room enough for a couple to cook comfortably together. Then enjoy a good bottle of wine and good food together. It would be quiet. Intimate. Romantic. With the right person. Someone like Elsie, he supposed, if he wanted a night like that. In a place like this.

Ryan shook his head. He had all the room he could want in his trailer on the circuit. "Is it really important how many people fit in the kitchen?"

"Well, I'd certainly like to know what size dinner party I can host in the space," Lilian countered, her words mystified as if she couldn't understand his question.

Or perhaps it was that they didn't understand each other. That wasn't much of a surprise. They were no more than strangers who happened to share a bloodline. He was at home in an arena on horseback. She thrived in an operating room in the city. If he hadn't been desperate for one more reason not to get back in the saddle, he wouldn't have agreed to this. But now, he was in over his head and sinking fast.

"Mother, this townhouse has the essentials," Ryan said then recited the same things he'd told her earlier. "A completely upgraded kitchen. Full-sized bathrooms and a two-car garage." *Can we please stop pretending now? Stop pretending you intend to move here.*

"What about the outdoor living space?" his mother asked, as if she was genuinely engaged and considering this property as her potential new home. "Does it flow from the living area outdoors? Or is it disrupted? It looks to be disconnected."

Ryan squeezed his forehead with his free hand, twisted to film the family room and strove to be patient. "There are sliding glass doors leading right out to the screened-in patio."

"But would there be ease of movement for my guests with furniture in place?" his mother asked, seeming far too intent on continuing to discuss the property. She added, "I need to know about the flow in the main rooms. The energy. The feel of the house."

Ryan flipped the phone around and looked directly into the camera. "It is an end unit and a solidly built townhouse." That should end the conversation. Stop the farce.

"That sounds just adequate." His mother's lips pulled together, and she shook her head. "That won't do. We'll need to keep on looking."

Why wasn't she giving in already? Ryan decided on a gentle nudge and suggested, "Or we could put this whole house hunt thing on hold."

His mother's shoulders stiffened. Then she peered closer into the screen as if he'd suggested she add ice cubes to her champagne. Her words were measured. "Why would I do that?"

Because you have no intention of following through. Of committing to mending the family fences, as it were. Those words stuck to the back of his dry throat. As if that little kid he used to be still held a shred of hope that Lilian Sloan could change. That Lilian Sloan meant to keep her word this time.

Some of his family members were more optimistic about Lilian's intentions, Ryan however was not one of them. "I just think it might be better if you were here to look at the homes personally."

"I plan to do that." Lilian's smile returned then she straightened away from the camera. She lifted her arm and flicked her ring-free hand toward the screen. "I've several things to do on my end over here. I want to ensure a smooth transition with my practice. I'll still be consulting and advising of course, but there are details I must oversee to ensure my patients are getting the best possible care when I'm not here. And I really need you to help me narrow down the search to our top five."

Five. She wanted a top five list. Ryan wasn't certain he had time to find one, let alone five possible homes for his mother. He studied her, took in her composed expression and steady stare. Surprise filtered through him. "You're serious about this."

"Quite serious," Lilian said firmly and without hesitation. "Now, call me tomorrow after you've walked through the next group of listings. We can decide if there are any places I need to see on video chat afterward."

And so it seemed the house hunt would go on

with Ryan leading the charge. He nodded. Because she seemed to be expecting his acknowledgment. And he wasn't about to back out and hand the task over to one of his brothers. If she reconsidered—which Ryan believed was still very much a possibility—his brothers would only end up disappointed in her again. And his brothers being hurt was—as it always had been—unacceptable.

"Also, you might consider bringing someone along with you to walk the properties," Lilian suggested, her thin eyebrows lifted. "Vivian or Maggie perhaps."

Both Vivian and Maggie liked Lilian Sloan. However, when it came to taking sides, Vivian and Maggie often agreed with and protected Ryan and his brothers. And in turn, Ryan looked out for the two women whom he thought of as his sisters. "Vivian and Josh are in Arizona with Vivian's family. They won't be back until late next week for the rodeo. And Maggie has been busy helping to organize the rodeo and practice."

"We don't want to take Maggie away from that." Lilian smiled fondly. "She's so very dedicated to her roping career and now rodeo management it seems." Lilian paused then tilted her head. "Surely you know someone who can join you and provide answers to my questions."

"I'll see if I can find someone," Ryan said then added a warning. "But you might just have me. And that might have to be enough." *For once.*

"Well, I'm sure you and I can learn to speak each other's house language," Lilian said, her words encouraging and pleasant. "Even if it takes dozens more house showings, I'm certain we will find a rhythm. Until tomorrow then." With that his mother wished him a good afternoon and disconnected.

Ryan would have better luck finding a rhythm on a wild mustang than with his mother. But there was nothing for it now. He had to see this through. Wait his mother out. Wait for her to change her mind and back out. Then he'd deliver the bad news to his family somehow. Because family first wasn't just something he said, it was something he lived. Just as his grandparents had taught him.

Outside, Ryan replaced the key in the lockbox on the front door then waved to his mother's real estate agent still sitting in his sedan. Arrangements made to talk about the next listings in the morning, Ryan climbed into his truck and checked his messages. And his heart sank. Midnight Rose hadn't eaten her evening feed or her morning feed. It wasn't a trend that could continue.

He opened a new text message and typed: Taking you up on your offer to use your stables. Will be by this afternoon. Then he pressed Send and told himself he was acting only on the mare's behalf. It was in the mare's best interest to be moved to Elsie's quiet, empty stables.

It certainly wasn't good for him.

To be around Elsie and pretend that he wanted nothing more than to keep his distance. That he thought of her as only his best friend's little sister. Nothing more. Still, he would do just that because it was what was in the best interest for them both. Their roads were crossing now, but not for the long haul.

Back on Sloan property, Ryan parked outside the stables. His door was only barely open when Maggie left the stable and let out an excited whoop. Ryan climbed out of his truck and greeted his sister-in-law.

"Sundancer has been cleared completely," Maggie announced. Then she raised her arms over her head, shimmied in circles and added, "Dr. Paige declared him in full health not an hour ago." Another circle shimmy then Maggie stopped and pointed at Ryan. "Now you can saddle up too. You haven't limped since you brought Sundancer home."

Ryan stilled. That was excellent news about Sundancer. Everything he'd been waiting and wanting to hear about the intelligent and hard-working gelding. Yet it was nothing he'd been prepared to hear. Because he wasn't quite ready himself.

He yanked his hat off and ran his hand through his hair then did what he was becoming rather skilled at recently. He stalled. "I can't saddle up. Not today anyway."

"But you said you would ride when Sundancer could ride." Maggie's head tilted to the side. Her lips pursed as if she was trying out her next statement. "Those were your exact words. That day is here."

The day for second-guessing was certainly here. Once more Ryan was questioning why he'd asked Maggie to meet with Dr. Paige Bishop instead of rescheduling for the afternoon. And why he ever thought it would be a good idea to tell Maggie he'd ride when Sundancer could. "Can't ride today."

Maggie narrowed her gaze. Her words sounded careful and reserved. "Why not?"

"I want Elsie to ride Sundancer first," Ryan said and quickly warmed to his off-the-cuff explanation. "Elsie is lighter, and I can check Sundancer while she's in the saddle. I don't want to push him too hard too fast." As for himself, well, he'd always been driven to push himself harder and faster than everyone else. Once he located that overdrive button, he'd press it again. And all would be as it should.

"When have you ever done that to a horse?" Maggie crossed her arms over her chest. Her brow furrowed. "You put your horse's comfort and health before your own. Always."

Except when he'd been careless and too full of himself. When he'd pushed too hard and believed he was too good for anything to go wrong. Then Sundancer had gotten hurt. And it was Ryan's fault. That guilt surfaced again. He knew the risks to himself and accepted those willingly. But injuring a horse was hard to accept. He glanced at Maggie. "Then you know it makes sense to put Elsie on Sundancer first."

"What else is going on?" Maggie asked, her words soft. Her gaze piercing and all too perceptive.

Maggie and Ryan had been friends for years on the circuit. They'd seen each other at their best and their worst and everything in between. And understood each other. Yet, Ryan hadn't told Maggie the truth about Sundancer's injury. Nor had he confessed his role in the accident. That was one burden he had to bear on his own. Ryan held her stare and tried to deflect. "Why does there have to be something else going on?"

"You're not acting like yourself." Maggie walked closer to him, her focus steady. "And I'm not the only one noticing and commenting."

"Look, I've had a frustrating day already, walking through houses and condominiums for my mom." Ryan shut his truck door, but nothing blocked the discontent he'd felt since the accident. "Can we not do this right now, Mags? Please."

"Sorry." Maggie winced. "Why did you agree to take that on for your mother anyway?"

"The truth?" Ryan said grimly.

Maggie nodded.

"I didn't think she was serious." Ryan shook

his head. Disbelief growing. "And now I'm not so sure." Despite all the reasons not to believe in his mother, there was that worrisome pinch of hope. One he couldn't quite seem to toss aside and ignore.

Maggie opened and closed her mouth. "What now?"

"We have lunch. I'll make the sandwiches." *And prove I'm not rushing off to see Elsie. That I can in fact ignore my feelings for my city girl.* He turned toward the farmhouse and said, "Then you help me load Sundancer in the trailer on your truck and come to the sanctuary with me."

Maggie took the conversation detour in stride. "What's happening at the sanctuary?"

"Midnight Rose is worse." Ryan frowned. He'd brought the mare to the sanctuary after another rescue had requested help with the overly nervous, easily spooked mare. He'd been certain she would settle right in. No problems. No more stress. It hadn't gone as planned. Something of a theme of his lately. "She isn't eating. And she's more anxious than when we picked her up. We're out of options on-site, but we need to do something for her. And Elsie offered her stables."

"So, you're bringing Sundancer along in the hopes that he'll help calm Midnight Rose," Maggie said, her words pensive.

Ryan nodded. And he was bringing Maggie along as a buffer between him and Elsie. As a reminder to him not to sweep Elsie up into his arms for a been-thinking-about-you embrace. Or worse, a been-dreaming-about-this kiss. Ryan lengthened his strides. "It's probably a long shot."

"I think it's a good idea." Maggie matched Ryan's quick pace easily and effortlessly. "Perhaps Sundancer here will be all Midnight Rose needs."

"I doubt it will be that simple." Ryan frowned then searched for more confidence. He was responsible for the mare. Surely, he could help her. Surely, his gut instinct for horses hadn't disappeared too. "If she tolerates Sundancer being in the stall beside hers then that will be a promising start."

"Sometimes the ones you think would never go together get along the best." Maggie hurried ahead of him and reached the back door first. "And seemingly mismatched pairings not only have things in common, they also find the perfect fit together." With her hand on the door handle, Maggie kept the door closed and met Ryan's gaze. "I'm not just talking about horses either, Ryan."

"If you're trying to be subtle, Mags, it's totally not working." Ryan chuckled and crossed his arms over his chest. He was more than willing to let his stomach growl if only to set his misguided, happy-to-be-in-love sister-in-law straight. He said, "Just to be sure we are clear, I will tell you this. Elsie and I aren't a pairing—mismatched or otherwise. And we definitely are not together."

"But you could be." Maggie widened her stance in front of the door as if more than ready to press her own point upon him. "You could be together. With Elsie."

"No. We can't be," Ryan stressed, pushing more conviction into his words. "What we can be—what Elsie and I are—is friends. We are two friends helping each other out. Nothing more."

Maggie considered him. Her mouth pulled in as if she was working through possible arguments.

"There's nothing more to talk about, Mags," Ryan said. "Elsie is just a friend." The same as any other.

As for wanting to kiss his friend, well, that was only a temporary hiccup. When he got back to the circuit and what he'd always done, then he'd remember where he belonged. And what he always wanted. The rush of one more ride. The thrill of one more win. A rodeo lifestyle all his own. And no regrets.

Maggie studied him then finally shrugged one shoulder and opened the back door. "If you say so."

He certainly did say so.

Not that his heart seemed to be paying him any mind. Still, there was no thrill in risking his heart.

As for those regrets, well, that was simple. He wouldn't allow there to be any.

CHAPTER TWELVE

ELSIE STEPPED OUT of the stairwell at Belleridge Regional Hospital and exhaled long and deep. Then told herself she was winded from climbing four flights of stairs, not from Ryan's text. And her heart was beating faster thanks to those same stairs, not from the thought of seeing her cowboy again. If ever there was a sign she needed to get back on a consistent exercise program, she had one now.

Elsie made her way down the hall and greeted the nurses behind the desk. Her phone she kept in her purse. Not for safety reasons, but to keep herself from texting Ryan back with something foolish like *Looking forward to seeing you*. Or *Can't wait to see you*. Or worse, *You're welcome to stay for dinner. Then we can talk about that kiss*.

Nope. That conversation wasn't happening. Elsie moved out of the path of an empty gurney and turned down the hall toward her brother's room.

For a cowboy who'd claimed he'd wanted to kiss her, Ryan had acted completely disinterested afterward. Sure, he'd been patient and attentive in the tractor the other morning. Yet despite the closed-in cab, there had been no contact, accidental or otherwise. No leaning into each other's space. No closing the distance. He'd been polite and informative. Reciting tractor statistics and farming essentials as if he understood that information grounded Elsie. That the more she knew, the less uncertain she felt.

Only her cowboy left her uncertain. And too aware that when it came to matters of the heart, Elsie often read things all wrong. For now, she'd stick to the facts. Ryan had taught her to drive a tractor then he'd left. And they hadn't spoken for several days since. Except for his recent text about bringing Midnight Rose to stay at her family's stables that afternoon. There was nothing that suggested he even still thought about wanting to kiss her. Therefore, she would stop thinking about him doing just that.

Mind made up, Elsie knocked on her brother's door then walked inside his hospital room. The laughter and animated voices caught her off guard immediately. Yet the two familiar, lively women, each one propped in a chair on either side of Bryce's bed, were immediately recognizable. The Baker sisters were long-time friends of her Aunt Marlena's and two of Elsie's favorite Three Springs residents. Elsie's smile stretched wide. "Breezy. Gayle. I didn't know you would be here today."

"We just got back from our great-niece's wedding in Austin." Breezy adjusted the fire-engine red framed glasses propped in her short, spiky white hair and laughed. "We told our niece to get married in Marlena's greenhouses. The gala Vivian staged in those greenhouses was quite stunning."

Elsie had seen the photographs from the holiday event in her aunt's greenhouses that past Christmas. It'd been quite the transformation and nothing short of inspiring for Elsie.

"Instead, our niece staged quite a spectacle, taking over every public space at the hotel." Gayle's lips pursed and she tapped her finger, the nail painted a bold purple color, against the edge of her moon-round eyeglasses. "Could've used your eye for editing, Elsie. You always know how to finesse things into just the right blend of lovely and refined."

There was nothing garish or pretentious about the Baker sisters. They claimed to be as home-grown as Texas tumbleweed and iced tea. Always looked after everyone as if they were their own. And Elsie adored them.

"But never mind all that." Breezy edged around the bed and squeezed Elsie tight. "It's been too long of a spell since we've seen you, dear. Much too long."

"But she's lovelier than ever, don't you think, Breezy?" Gayle elbowed her sister aside and hugged Elsie with a strength that belied her petite frame. Then she reached up and patted Elsie's cheek. Her gaze tender. "It's good to have you home again, dear."

"I'm glad to be here," Elsie said, surprised by how much she meant it. She greeted her brother then said, "It sounded like I interrupted quite the lively conversation. Anything I should know?"

Breezy shooed Elsie into her chair then joined her sister. The pair each perched on a side of the chair and appeared completely comfortable. Breezy said, "We have a nephew that spends his pennies before he's earned them. He could surely stand a sit-down with Bryce for a bit of financial advising."

"Don't let them fool you, Els." Bryce lifted his eyebrows slightly. The swelling around his eyes had gone down yet the bruising was an assortment of blue and purple shades. "Breezy and Gayle were taking copious notes and I have no doubt they'll do quite well with the financial advising all on their own."

Gayle preened and chuckled. "Even so, Bryce has kindly agreed to be on speakerphone during our sit-down with our nephew."

"We find it wise to always have backup. Some-times our nudges aren't enough to set 'em straight." Breezy laughed, the sound unrestrained, and waved her hand as if orchestrating the melody. "But now that you're here, dear, we can discuss the booth."

"Booth," Elsie repeated and looked at her brother. Bryce shrugged at her and didn't bother to hide his confusion. Instead, he fluffed the pillow behind his head and leaned back as if settling in for an entertaining afternoon.

"The booth at It's Blooming Spring Garden and Food Festival that's happening this coming weekend." Gayle smiled and traced her finger around the embroidered cherry blossom on the bib of her white denim overalls. "I found these at the cowgirl boutique booth last year. Then Maggie's older sister Kelsey upscaled them for me with her fancy hand stitching. You won't find a more skilled embroiderer than our Kelsey."

Elsie couldn't disagree. The overalls looked like something sold in a chic boutique in the city. She nodded and held her silence, familiar with the two sisters' meandering style of conversation. Talking to the lively duo was always a bit of an adventure, filled with detours and alternate routes that eventually circled back around to where the conversation started. All Elsie had to do was sit back and enjoy the ride.

"It's Blooming Spring is the largest spring festival in the surrounding counties." Breezy spread her fingers wide. "It draws thousands and thousands of visitors every year. There's even a live concert Saturday night. And this year is their twenty-fifth anniversary."

"Always puts me in the mood for spring," Gayle mused and tapped the toe of her slip-on foam clog as if already listening to that live band. "I look forward to this weekend every year. And there's even more to look forward to now." Gayle's foot paused. Her pencil-thin eyebrows lifted, and her voice dipped into a confidential whisper. "What with Bryce's honey being a finalist in the competition and all."

The retiree's toe went back to tapping. And Elsie hit that first speed bump. She glanced at her brother. "You entered a competition?"

Bryce shook his head and tugged on his hair, messing up the strands even more. "When would I have done that? I've been in here for days."

"He didn't enter his honey," Breezy announced then wrapped her frail arm around her sister's thin shoulders and beamed. "We did."

"And now you need a booth at It's Blooming Spring for the whole weekend of the festival and samples," Gayle added. Excitement pushed her words into each other. "Lots and lots of honey samples will be needed for the attendees."

A booth. Honey samples. The whole weekend. *Bump. Bump. Bump.* The conversation was suddenly full of speed bumps and potholes. Elsie rolled her lips together, but that unease zigzagged through her.

"You will also need product to sell." Breezy tipped her chin down and eyed Elsie. "No good giving out honey samples if no one can take any honey home, right?"

At Elsie's small nod, Breezy's grin burst free. Approval worked across her papery face.

"Monty Westwood did that one year." Gayle blinked behind her round lenses and shook her head. When she spoke she sounded woeful and aghast. "Monty refused to hand out samples. Claimed the attendees could buy his barbeque sauce if they wanted to taste it. Well, you can imagine, he wasn't invited back to the festival after that."

Elsie wasn't sure what to imagine. She rubbed her forehead and tried to extinguish her dismay. "Can we start with the competition? Maybe you can share how that all came about." Elsie slanted her gaze at her brother. He looked as mystified as Elsie, yet slightly less dismayed, and slightly more than a little amused. She continued, "I'm sure Bryce is as curious as I am."

"Oh, that. The contest is for the best new local specialty food product in the surrounding three counties." Breezy touched the rings on her fingers and lifted one shoulder. "Gayle and some of the others in town were convinced the contest was fixed."

"On account of no Three Springs businesses ever finaling in the competition for more years than we could remember," Gayle added, displeasure framing her frown.

"It certainly was quite the dry spell for our town and county included." Breezy shook her head then grinned. "Until Tess Sloan entered her divine chocolate truffles last year and finally managed to break into the finals."

"She should've won too," Gayle harrumphed.

"Verna Sanford stole first place, with her lavender rhubarb tea. But then Verna is from the same county that hosts the festival. As you can imagine, those rumors about the contest being fixed started up again."

Elsie was starting to imagine more potholes in her path.

"So, we decided we should try again," Breezy explained. "For the sake of proving our theory. And we entered Bryce's honey into the contest this year."

"Now you've finaled, Bryce." Gayle clapped then pressed her clasped hands against her chest. "And this certainly feels like it's Three Springs's year to win at long last."

"Thank you for believing in my product enough to enter it." Bryce smiled then gingerly touched the stitches on his cheek. "I'm honored to make it this far in the competition."

"You'll feel more honored when you win." Breezy leaned forward and patted his arm. "The winner receives a cash prize and a feature in *Lasso Your Lifestyle* magazine. That's good exposure for your business."

"As is the festival booth," Gayle chimed in. "Can't forget about that. I'm sure Elsie can design something for you."

"Me?" Elsie stammered.

"Who else, dear?" Gayle blinked at Elsie calmly. "Your brother certainly isn't up for the task. Besides, it needs to have flair and pizzazz. You must entice people to walk up to the booth. It must truly stand out. That's more your expertise."

Elsie coordinated conferences, corporate retreats, galas and weddings. Festival booths were nowhere on her résumé.

"And you'll need a partner," Breezy declared. "But not a silent one like your brother has."

Her brother had a business partner. Why hadn't he told her?

Bryce shifted in the bed, suddenly looking slightly uncomfortable.

"Breezy is right. You need a partner to help you work the booth," Gayle continued, drawing Elsie's attention back to her. Her grin expanded into mischievous. "Nothing for it now, dear. You need to call your cowboy."

Her cowboy. Elsie felt as if she'd tripped face-first into another pothole.

Before she could respond, Breezy jumped in. "The workload is always better when shared. And when you do it with a handsome cowboy at your side, it's always more fun."

"No need to get tongue-tied, dear," Gayle said in an understanding tone. "If it was Bryce running the booth, we'd tell him to go get himself a cowgirl to share the work with."

Bryce cleared his throat. "I've got two little cowgirls at home already. That's more than enough for me."

"You've got two sweet daughters, Bryce. There's

no denying that." Breezy chuckled and patted her palm over her chest. "But there's room in your heart for that someone special. You just haven't met her yet. But when you do, I promise you'll make room."

Bryce's gaze widened on Elsie as if seeking a silent rescue from the pair's matchmaking endeavors. But Elsie feared turning the sisters' romantically-inclined attention back on her. Elsie ran her palms over her jeans. "Anything else I should know about the festival?"

"We've already forwarded the email from the festival coordinator to Ryan." Breezy smiled.

"Already?" Elsie asked. What about calling her cowboy?

Gayle nodded. "We figured Bryce's partner would want to know too, even if he's a silent one."

"Ryan is your silent partner." Elsie stared at her brother. Waited for his nod.

Bryce looked guilty as charged. "Ryan is an investment partner."

Elsie welcomed the news. Or told herself she did. After all, she'd been right not to read between the lines where her cowboy was concerned. He'd helped her only to watch out for his business investment. He really hadn't been there *for* her. She swatted away that dash of disappointment. "Well, then I guess I'll talk to Ryan about the particulars for the booth."

And completely disregard those particulars about kissing her cowboy.

CHAPTER THIRTEEN

CALL A COWBOY. It'll be fun. That was what the Baker sisters claimed. Yet Elsie wanted to call *out* a cowboy. That, she thought, might be satisfying.

Elsie pulled into the circular driveway in front of her aunt's house. A silver truck and long horse trailer were already backed in beside the stable barn. Looked like Maggie and Ryan had arrived while Elsie had been in the elementary school car pick-up line, waiting for her nieces. And if she was of a mind to call out her cowboy, now was her chance.

"Cowboy Prince is here already!" Gemma exclaimed from the back seat, her excitement obvious. "With the horses too."

"I can't wait to meet Midnight Rose." Autumn's delight infused her words.

Seat belts unclipped and suddenly there was an unmistakable scrambling sound in the back seat.

"Everybody pause," Elsie ordered. The engine cut, she twisted around in her seat and pointed at the boots she'd tossed into the car earlier. "First things first. Take your sandals off and put your boots on. No bare toes in the barn."

The girls made quick work of swapping their shoes. Elsie nodded and used her most serious tone to keep her nieces pinned in place. "Remember what we talked about. Midnight Rose frightens easily. You need to keep your voices down and listen to everything Cowboy Prince tells you." Elsie looked from Autumn to Gemma. "Understood?"

"We won't do anything unless Cowboy Prince tells us it's okay," Autumn promised.

Gemma nodded and reached for the door handle. "He's coming this way, Auntie. I'm just gonna say hi."

"Me too." Autumn pushed open her car door.

The pair was out of the car, hollering their hellos and racing toward Ryan before Elsie could stop them. Elsie sighed into the empty car. "So much for using their indoor voices." She climbed out and closed the car doors her nieces had left open. Then paused, her gaze fixed on the trio.

Ryan swept both little girls into his arms for a group hug, drawing out their collective delight and laughter. Gemma's boots barely touched the ground when she tugged Ryan's arm, pulling him down so she could climb onto his back for a piggyback ride. He only laughed and obliged, securing Gemma on his back before standing up. Autumn latched on to his hand with both of hers. Her feet swirled in some sort of quick step in the dirt while she chatted away to her rapt audience of one.

And suddenly Elsie wanted to join her cowboy for an embrace of her own. So much for calling out her cowboy. Elsie shook her head and stayed where she was.

A familiar blonde walked out of the stable and waved to Elsie.

Elsie hurried over to greet Maggie and put even more distance between herself and her cowboy.

Maggie adjusted her cowboy hat and grinned. "You better be careful, Elsie, or you're going to have a houseful here soon."

A houseful. There was something pleasant about the idea. But nothing Elsie could afford to linger on very long. This wasn't her place to fill with all those things that would make it a home. Like family and friends. Pets and companions. Laughter and love. Her gaze skipped over to her cowboy and held. "Ryan told me the horses won't be here permanently." Neither would Elsie.

"Well, don't be surprised if you get used to having horses around," Maggie said. "And want to keep them."

She was already getting used to having her cowboy around. But there would be no keeping him. Or this life. It wasn't what she wanted, was it? "I'm worried the girls might have that problem." *Not me.* She paused, stretched the wobble from her smile then continued, "Bryce may need to give in and get them a pair of barn cats or puppies sooner than he planned."

"It would be hard to refuse those two adorable kids much." Maggie chuckled then glanced at Elsie. "Grant tells me that Bryce has been a model patient."

"Because Grant has given my brother full access to his computer," Elsie said. "Now he can build his spreadsheets, run honey sales models and forecast future earnings."

"Bryce is very talented at that. He already built a budget for Grant and me, as well as designed our investment portfolio." Maggie laughed and touched her cheek. Her wedding ring sparkled in the sunlight. "Never thought I'd have that. I feel very grown up and very prepared for those next stages in married life thanks to your brother's guidance."

"Bryce has always been good at helping people plan wisely for their futures." Elsie had planned wisely too for her own future. And her plans hadn't included a cowboy or an extended stay in Texas. She would be wise to remember that.

Maggie's eyebrows lifted above her sunglass frames, and she tipped her head toward Ryan. "Speaking of being good at things, that cowboy over there has always been good with horses and kids."

"What's he not good with?" The words slipped out before Elsie could stop them.

Maggie slid her sunglasses lower on her nose and eyed Elsie over the tinted lenses. Her words sincere. "A cowgirl's heart."

Good thing Elsie wasn't a cowgirl. Nothing for her to fear. She offered Maggie a small smile. "Well, that was honest." But hardly unexpected.

"I really like you, Elsie." Maggie nudged her sunglasses back into place. "While I think you and that charming, but extremely guarded, cowboy over there could be really good for each other, I also believe it's good to be prepared. To know exactly what you are getting into."

Ryan strolled closer and lowered Gemma to the ground. His gaze shifted from Elsie to Maggie and back to her. "What are we getting into now?"

They definitely were *not* getting into matters of the heart. Especially not ones involving a cowboy complication. And there would be complications with her cowboy. The kind caused by difficult goodbyes and inevitable heartbreaks. Best not to go there. Not now. Not ever. Elsie said, "We were about to get into proper horse care."

"And on that note, I'll take these two lovely ladies to visit Sundancer." Maggie grabbed Autumn's hand then Gemma's and added, "We're going to talk about what Sundancer can eat. What he can't eat. What his favorite snacks are. Then I'll show you how he likes to be groomed."

"What about Midnight Rose?" Autumn frowned. "Doesn't she get favorite treats too?"

"We'll let Ryan handle Midnight Rose for now," Maggie said.

"Because Midnight Rose likes Cowboy Prince the best. Do you know why?" Gemma lifted her arm, raising Maggie's arm too. She spun in a quick circle beneath their joined hands then answered her own question. "It's because Cowboy Prince makes her feel safe."

He certainly had a knack for that. Elsie tethered her thoughts before they spiraled away from her. Still, her gaze was hooked on Ryan. He was strong. Yet it was his confidence and certainty in how he carried himself that drew her to him. He knew who he was. Where he belonged. She envied that. But she was determined she would have it for herself too. In New York.

Her gaze connected with his. That awareness spiked. And that was bad. She looked away before she got tangled up in that cowboy complication after all.

Maggie spun Gemma one last time then wrapped her arm around the little girl's waist. "Once Midnight Rose gets used to you and your sister and your goats, she's going to like you best too."

That brought out Gemma's ear-to-ear grin.

Autumn scratched her nose. "Which goat do you think she'll like the best?"

"Smarty Marty will greet her first," Gemma decided. "But Auntie calls him a rascal and she uses her mad voice when she says it too. Then she says he's lucky he's so cute."

"I'll leave you two to it then." Maggie waggled her eyebrows at Elsie and laughed. Then the trio walked toward the pasture, debating who was the friendliest goat in the flock. And who would make the *best* best friend for Midnight Rose.

"Have something against rascals?" Ryan tapped the rim of his hat higher and studied her.

"Yes, especially the cute ones that make me chase them around the backyard all night," Elsie said.

"You could just let him roam around," Ryan suggested. "Save yourself the frustration."

"I tried that." Elsie wiped her hand over her mouth, but her smile still broke free. "And found him standing beside my bed the next morning, chewing on my favorite pair of leggings."

Ryan's shoulders shook. Then his laughter spilled free.

"It's not funny." Elsie failed to sound admonishing. "I liked those leggings, but now there's a hole in the backside. I'm still mad at him too."

"I'm sure he feels bad." Ryan on the other hand hardly looked contrite.

Elsie rolled her eyes. "I know he doesn't. I caught him two days later trying to eat my scrunchie."

"Could be he just wants your attention." His eyebrows twitched. His gaze warmed.

Elsie's cheeks heated. "Well, that's not the way to go about it."

"Care to tell me what is?" His words came out in a slow drawl.

This. Right here. Treating me as if I'm the only one who matters. Elsie blinked, batted away those butterflies and fluttery feelings tangling inside her. She fumbled for her phone rather than reach for his hand to anchor her. "Right. We should get to Midnight Rose." She swiped across her phone screen, but her knees still felt slightly wobbly. "I was researching anxious horses in the car line earlier. Listen to this."

Silence swirled between them.

Her breath caught. His smile was tender. Affectionate. Unguarded. And aimed directly at her. Her voice was no stronger than a puff. "What?"

The corners of his mouth curved into his beard as if he had more than one really good secret and no intention of sharing. Then one of his eyebrows arched. "You were going to tell me something you read."

Elsie blinked.

"During your horse care research," he added.

Horse care. Right. Elsie came to her senses. What could she possibly tell him about horses that he didn't already know? Silly Elsie. He wasn't the one complicating things. She was. Turning this into something it wasn't. Time to stop. "Never mind. It's nothing."

"But you thought it was important." He crossed his arms over his chest and widened his stance as if preparing to wait her out. "So, I'd like to hear it."

He didn't mean that. Couldn't mean that. She waved her hand. "I'm sure you've already covered it on your spreadsheet."

"Spreadsheet," he repeated, not bothering to mask his confusion.

"You must have made a spreadsheet for the horses and their care for me," Elsie explained, letting her own frustration roll through her words. "As my brother's business partner, you would know he puts everything on spreadsheets, especially for me."

"I'm only supposed to be a silent partner." He scratched his cheek and frowned. "But there doesn't seem to be anything silent about it."

"Why didn't you tell me?" she asked, finally calling him out. Just as she should have earlier. Then she wouldn't have gotten lost in his warm gaze. Or his charming ways. Or let herself get carried away.

He shrugged. "I didn't think it was important."

Or rather he didn't think she was important. At least not enough to be let in on the secret. One more reason not to read between those lines. It was past time to get back to matters other than her heart. There was a festival booth to build. Honey to sell. A competition to win. And an anxious horse that she felt compelled to help. "I already turned music on in the stables for Midnight Rose. It's supposed to help soothe horses. But I should warn you. The stables aren't as nice as the ones your family has."

"The stalls here open to individual paddocks," Ryan said, his words reassuring. "That will allow Midnight Rose to come and go for her food and water when she wants. On her own terms. I'm hoping she won't feel so trapped."

"That's good." Elsie started walking toward the stables. "It's important to know where you stand, isn't it? Even for a horse."

"Elsie." Ryan touched her arm and stopped her. "You're upset I didn't tell you about the partnership with your brother."

I'm upset I thought, even for a second, I could matter to you. Elsie shook her head. "It's fine." *I'm fine too.*

After all, sharing things wasn't what they did. And nothing she wanted to do. Not with him. That implied things like a relationship. That she was part of a *we*. But she was comfortable on her own. Preferred it like that, in fact. "Let's get Midnight Rose settled in. I'm sure you have more important things to be doing."

He opened his mouth then closed it. His gaze searched hers, sharp and alert, then finally he said, "I'm right where I want to be."

And for a second time those lines blurred. Until

Elsie checked herself. Tethered herself back to the facts. He was there because he'd delivered Sundancer and Midnight Rose. Reminded herself his priority was the horses. As it should be. As was hers too. The horses and the bee farm linked them. Nothing else. She said, "I'm going to have her eyes checked. I was reading about equine eye issues causing some horses to spook."

"You don't have to do that," Ryan said. "I can handle her care."

"She's living on my family's property," Elsie argued. "I will look after her." *You too if you let me.*

"Why would you do that?" Ryan asked. He set his hands on his hips. "You have more than enough going on already."

Because she was inexplicably drawn to the mare. The same as she was to him. She nudged that realization aside. "It's important to know you are wanted, Ryan. Everyone, including horses, needs to feel that."

"I agree," he said softly.

Maybe it was the sincerity in his expression or that tenderness in his eyes, but Elsie let her words slip free. "I want Midnight Rose to know that she can belong here if she chooses." She inhaled, tried not to fidget under his unrelenting stare then exhaled, revealing another truth. "If I can help Midnight Rose find her place, then maybe I can find…"

"Your place," he finished for her.

He understood her.

She nodded. "I know what it's like for her. It's unsettling and scary shuffling from one home to another. Not knowing where you fit. Then realizing you don't and probably never will."

"Was that what it was like after your parents' divorce?" he asked, his voice gentle.

"My dad didn't know what to do with me. Dresses, braids and tears mystified him," Elsie admitted. "He was brilliant at solving a math equation. But faltered when it came to soothing a scared little girl."

His only daughter who'd only ever really wanted a warm hug from her father. To have someone hold her and tell her it would be alright. Even if it'd been a lie. That was all Elsie had ever wanted growing up. Instead, her father kept her at an arm's length, providing the material things she needed growing up but without the affection.

Ryan stepped closer to her, but he didn't reach for her. "What about your mom?"

"Mom let me go to the theater with her as long as I stayed quiet backstage." Elsie lifted her shoulder as if her past wasn't of any real consequence. Yet still she shared it with him. "So, I stayed out of her way too. I would read in the prop room until the final curtain dropped." And lose herself in the pages of her books. Chapter after chapter. Book after book.

"Did you ever feel like you belonged someplace?" he asked.

"Here." Elsie lifted her arm and motioned around her. "With my aunt and uncle during our summer visits. They made me feel like I belonged." *Like I was truly wanted.* She'd forgotten just how much her time spent on the farm had meant. Until now.

His smile was soft and sincere. Surprise skimmed over his words. "There's something about this place, isn't there?"

"You feel it too?" Elsie closed the distance.

"Always." He lifted his hand.

Elsie held her breath.

"Auntie. Cowboy Prince." That shout came from Gemma.

Followed by Autumn's excited command, "Hurry up. You gotta see this."

Ryan's hand landed on his hat, smashing it lower on his forehead.

Elsie jumped away, spun around and hurried toward the pasture. Ryan kept pace beside her. Autumn hopped up and down and waved them on.

Gemma decided they weren't moving fast enough and sprinted toward them. She grabbed Elsie's hand then Ryan's and tugged them both forward. "Butter-Belle and Midnight Rose are friends now. You gotta see." Gemma steered them toward the pasture gate and pointed through the fence posts. "See."

Sure enough, Midnight Rose stood at the far

end of her paddock. Her graceful black head stretched over the fence posts, grazing on grass. Butter-Belle grazed not inches from her.

Ryan set his arms on the top rung of the fence and leaned toward Elsie. "And look who's not all that far away either."

Sundancer was grazing in the main pasture. Only ten feet from the gate that opened from Midnight Rose's paddock into the pasture. Elsie smiled at Ryan. "This just might work."

"Yeah." His warm gaze skimmed over her like a caress. "It just might."

CHAPTER FOURTEEN

EVEN THE DEVIL knows when to walk away, Ryan.

And that was the problem with Ryan, according to his Gran Claire. Despite knowing he should walk away, he never did.

Like right now.

"I'm going to head out and get in some practice before dinner." Maggie pushed away from the pasture fence and pulled her keys from her pocket. "Ryan, are you joining me for some roping practice?"

Here was when he walked away. He shook his head. "Can't. I need to build a festival booth with Elsie."

Elsie aimed a surprised look his way. "How did you hear about that?"

"I got a text message from Bryce earlier to check my email." He tugged his phone from his pocket and waved it at her. "Then Breezy and Gayle called to give me a direct order. I was told to help Elsie with whatever she needs for as long as it takes."

Elsie pressed her lips together as if fighting back her smile.

"I'm definitely not messing with an order from the Baker sisters." Maggie chuckled and lifted both her hands, palms out. "We can practice tomorrow. Should I tell Tess to expect you for dinner this evening?"

Ryan watched Elsie and waited. Here was her out. Her chance to decline his help. And send him on his way. That would've been the sensible thing.

Elsie chewed on her bottom lip, looking indecisive and adorable.

"I'm really doing you a favor and saving you a call." Ryan leaned toward Elsie and kept his voice low. Only for her. At her raised eyebrows, he added, "Now you won't need to call a cowboy like the Baker sisters instructed you to do."

Her smile finally broke free. Followed by her soft laugh as if the joke was theirs to share alone. And that indecision disappeared. He really should leave now. Before he decided he wanted to share even more with Elsie.

"Unfortunately, I don't think we will be done before dinner, Maggie." Elsie counted off the list of items on her fingers. "We still have to go through the feeding schedule for the horses. There's the seedlings to water. The goats to gather. The honey inventory to locate. Homework to complete. And that festival booth to design."

"Sounds like a busy evening for you two," Maggie mused then jingled her keys. "Don't forget to stop and eat at some point. If the Baker sisters find out that tonight was all work and no play, they just might send you two on a real date."

Elsie blushed and knocked the brim of her baseball cap lower on her forehead.

Maggie didn't bother to hide her amusement. She hugged the girls, wished everyone a good night and strolled away. Her laughter trailing behind her all the way to her truck.

Autumn tucked her hair behind her ear and studied Ryan then Elsie. Finally, she asked, "Auntie Elsie, are you and Cowboy Prince dating?"

"No. We're working together." Elsie looked everywhere but at Ryan. "And we're going to need your help and your sister's tonight."

"But, Auntie, don't you want to date Cowboy Prince?" Gemma's nose scrunched up. Confusion coated her words. "Everybody wants to date a prince."

Ryan stilled. Held his breath. And waited on Elsie.

Elsie fidgeted. Tightened her ponytail. Touched her cheek. Then finally caught herself and jammed her hands into the back pockets of her jeans.

But the girls had already moved on. To Ryan.

Autumn tipped her head and assessed him as if she was a matchmaking understudy of the Baker sisters. Her words clear and clever. "Cowboy Prince, do *you* like Auntie Elsie?"

"I do." Very much. And much more than was wise.

"Then you and Auntie should go on a date," Autumn announced. Pleasure brightened her expression.

"Autumn, thanks for finding me a date." Elsie's hand landed on Autumn's shoulder. A hint of alarm leaked into her words. "But now isn't really the time for this."

Ryan couldn't think of a better time for this. And judging from the resolve on Autumn's face, the little girl was just as undeterred. He kept his focus on Autumn. "I can take your aunt on a date, in fact." At Autumn's cheerful double fist pump, he asked, "When do you think we should go on this date?"

"Tonight," Gemma declared and sashayed between Autumn and him.

"It's a school night, Gem." Autumn frowned at her sister.

"We never get to have fun on school nights." Gemma's shoulders deflated. She nudged the toe of her boot into the dirt.

"Speaking of which, we have that work we should really be getting too." Elsie motioned toward the main house as if urging them away from a hazard zone.

"But you could go on Saturday night," Autumn offered and held her ground. Gemma clapped and jumped back into dizzying twirls. Autumn added, "That's when dates happen on TV. But then Dad always changes the channel, so we don't know what happens."

Elsie's chin dipped toward her chest. She reached up and pressed her fingers against her forehead as if she wasn't sure what was happening. And she required a moment to reset her thoughts. Or perhaps her plans.

But Ryan had plans of his own. He stifled his amusement and said, "Saturday it is."

Elsie gaped at him, then her eyes narrowed as if to warn him the conversation wasn't over.

He grinned at her and said, "Now that date night is settled, we should get on with our evening. We have lots of work to do after all."

Elsie shook her head. Her exasperation more than obvious. She spun on her boot heels and headed toward the main house.

"What about dinner?" Gemma poked her finger into her stomach. "My tummy gets hungry when we gotta do lots of work."

"We will definitely have dinner." Ryan bent down and let Gemma climb onto his back. He stood and caught up to Elsie and added, "Work makes me hungry too."

"But we can't eat and work at the same time." Autumn skipped between Ryan and Elsie. "That is Dad's rule."

"'Cause dinner is for sharing, not working," Gemma chimed in. Her words loud in Ryan's ear. Then she shifted to look at Elsie. "Right, Auntie?"

"That's the rule," Elsie said, still seemingly exasperated and slightly distracted. Perhaps by the idea of Saturday date night.

But did she want to go on a date with Ryan or get out of it? He wasn't sure he wanted the answer. Still, he wanted a date with Elsie. Knew it was selfish. Though he couldn't deny he wanted more time with her. That goodbye was looming, but it wasn't there yet. He asked, "Are we sharing our food?"

"No." Gemma giggled, and her arms tightened around his shoulders. "We're sharing stories about our day."

"Or our dreams," Autumn said then pointed at him. "But only the good ones. Not the scary ones. Nobody likes those."

"We talk basically," Elsie explained. "That's the rule at the dinner table."

He was already looking forward to the experience.

Hours later, that dinner with Elsie and the girls was looking less and less like a sit down affair and more like quick takeout.

The afternoon had slowly started to slip sideways not long after Autumn and Gemma went inside to change out of their school clothes. It began when Gemma couldn't find her favorite pair of overalls she always wore to work on the farm. That launched a full house search, only for Gem to discover them in the hall closet where she'd hastily stashed them with the bath towels.

Crisis averted and their work clothes on, the group ventured to the attic for supplies to use for the festival booth. Autumn opened a box marked Craft Supplies and discovered a large spider nestled among the colorful furry balls and tissue paper. Consequently, the girls had refused to go back into the attic. And demanded a rehoming of the spider outdoors and far enough from the house that he wouldn't be enticed to return anytime soon.

Finally, Elsie set the girls up on the lawn with the paints to fill in the festival sign she'd already traced out in pencil. That left Elsie and Ryan to locate the honey inventory. They'd found the cases neatly stacked in the storage shed near the honey house. They were each carrying the last of the cases from the UTV to the main house when the first clap of thunder cracked across the sky.

The storm rolled in quickly and chased the girls inside. That left Elsie to rescue the festival sign and Ryan to herd a screeching Smarty Marty and his escapee pals, who for reasons unknown feared even the tiniest of raindrops, back into their shelter. Then he coaxed Midnight Rose into her stall next to Sundancer's, closed the stable doors and turned up the volume on Elsie's classical station.

By the time he walked out of the stable, the rain had picked up. His shirt was damp halfway to the main house when he spotted Elsie in one of the greenhouses. Just as he crossed the threshold, the greenhouse door snapped closed behind him. A bolt of lightning streaked through the darkness. Thunder boomed. And the lights overhead flickered and cut off.

"Was that the…" Elsie glanced up, but her words were drowned out by sound of the sudden downpour of water. Inside the greenhouse. Soaking them and everything else.

Ryan tipped his head down and watched the water stream off the brim of his cowboy hat. He felt his laughter swell deep inside him. He'd always enjoyed spring thunderstorms.

Elsie sputtered and wiped the water off her face. "What is going on?"

"Sprinkler system." Ryan pointed at the intricate polished piping crisscrossing the glass ceiling.

"Why is it on now?" Elsie frowned and brushed her wet ponytail over her shoulder.

"Probably an electrical short and wiring mixup." Ryan set his hands on his hips and shook more water from the brim of his hat. "I told Bryce to have Josh check his work after he installed the new sprinkler system himself."

"Looks like we don't need to water." Elsie pulled her damp shirt away from her stomach. "What now?"

"You head on in to check on the girls. The generator should've kicked on at the main house when the power went out." Ryan held the door open for her. "I'll find the water shutoff out here and meet you back at the house."

It wasn't long before Ryan stepped under the covered porch, even his socks inside his boots were soaked. But there wasn't time to dwell on that. The thunder boomed. The lightning lit the sky. And the rain kept falling in heavy sheets.

Elsie swung the back door open. Autumn and Gemma clung to either side of her, their eyes peeled wide. Elsie held up her cell phone with the flashlight on. From the darkness behind them, Ryan already guessed what she was going to tell him.

"We don't have power." Elsie's fingers tightened around her phone. Yet her words were calm and mild as if she wasn't the least bit concerned. "The generator isn't on. The fuel level is on empty."

One more item most likely on Bryce's to-get-to-later spreadsheet. But now there would be no getting around it. Power outages weren't uncommon where they lived. Surely Bryce hadn't forgotten that.

Ryan swiped his hat off his head, shook off the water and set it on the hook inside the door. Then slipped out of his boots, peeled off his socks and walked barefoot into the house. "Then we'll just have to find as many candles as we can." Ryan tugged his cell phone out, turned on the flashlight and handed it to Gemma. "Let's team up and see who finds the most candles. Winners get double dessert."

That distracted the girls as intended. It wasn't long before they had piled quite a candle collection on the dining room table. Then declared it Princess Pizza Night thanks to Elsie having all the ingredients on hand and her brother having bought a propane pizza oven over Christmas. That announcement set the evening back on track. As did the dry clothes Ryan borrowed from Bryce's closet.

Ryan secured the last blanket over the princess fort he'd constructed in the center of the family room and let it drop over the opening. The blanket muffled the girls whispering inside. He joined Elsie on the oversize L-shaped couch.

An open case of honey sat on the coffee table. It was one of over a dozen cases she'd opened. She stared at the glass honey jar in her hand and shook her head. "I cannot believe my brother didn't notice that the labels were printed wrong."

Ryan dropped onto the sofa and picked up a honey jar. "It's hard to miss. Sweet House of Bees Pure Honey, Prefect Treat for all Ages."

"Children under one year old can't have honey." Elsie peeled the label off the jar and then scraped at the last stuck bit. "Surely he meant to put that warning on the jar."

"It's required." Ryan worked the label off the glass.

"I suppose we can have a labeling party when the new, correct labels arrive." Elsie picked up her wine glass and settled back into the sofa. "Thanks for everything today."

"Glad I was here." He wiped a rag over the jar and dropped it into a box. Then glanced over at Elsie.

Her head was resting against the cushion. Her long wheat-colored hair fell in waves around her shoulders. A soft smile teased the corners of her mouth. She'd changed into a pair of lilac-colored wide-leg pants, a cream-colored cropped tank top and a lilac cropped sweater. Comfy-chic she'd called it. Now she looked relaxed. Content. He drank his wine. "You look happy."

"I am." She leaned in toward him. "I feel like we accomplished a lot this afternoon. It's satisfying."

Ryan nodded. "Is your job in the city satisfying?"

"It's different." She sipped her wine then touched the corner of her lip. "It feels good when one of my events happens without any issues. And it's rewarding knowing that I put together something that mattered to other people. That gave them a moment to remember."

"But," he said.

She swirled the wine in her glass and stared into it as if gathering her thoughts. "But I don't get to experience those events. I don't get to take part. Those events happen at the luxury hotel I work for, but they aren't for me. Today I was part of things that mattered *to me.*" Her glass stilled and she shrugged. "Probably doesn't make sense."

"No, it does." He leaned over and tapped his glass lightly against hers. "Here's to doing more things that matter."

"With the people who matter," she added then sipped her wine and watched him over the rim. "Can I ask you something?"

Yes, you matter to me too. He straightened away from her and nodded.

"Why the rodeo?" she asked. "Why bucking broncs?"

"I'm too tall for the bulls."

She arched an eyebrow at him. "That's not what I'm asking."

They'd reached the sharing part of the evening it seemed, after all. And perhaps it was the candlelight. Or the rain pattering against the windows. Or the remarkable woman beside him. But for the first time in longer than he could remember, Ryan shared parts he rarely revealed to anyone. "I was hooked from my first ride on a pony that bucked harder than some grown bulls I've ridden. I was five. It was the summer before we moved here permanently. We were only visiting our grandparents for two weeks. I begged Grandpa Sam to let me ride every single day until we left."

And then he'd begged his parents to let him stay longer. Then back in the suburbs of upstate New York, he'd wished every night to go back to his grandparents to ride horses and bulls forever. He hadn't known then that his wish was about to come true faster than he'd ever imagined. And just what he would lose when his wish for forever was actually granted.

He sipped more wine and continued, "When we came back the following summer, Grandpa Sam had a pair of ponies waiting for me in the stables. I was good in the saddle." And in those few seconds, he was free from the hurt—his and his brothers'—that came from his parents' divorce. Their father had walked away without a backward glance. Same it seemed did their mother. But in the arena, he wasn't missing his mom or his old life. It was just him and his horse. He added, "Over the years, I realized I could be better if I worked harder. Trained more. Dedicated myself. So that's what I did. And I got better." And that hurt faded. "So, I kept pushing."

"Now you're at the top. You made it." She studied him. "What's next? Do you keep pushing?"

"You want to know if I'll ever be satisfied." He rested his elbows on his knees and cradled the wine glass between his palms.

"Will you?" Her voice was faint like the smoke from the candles.

"I don't know," he admitted. "I always had that fire in me for as long as I can remember."

"Had." She shifted on the couch to face him and

tucked her bare feet up under her. "That sounds like it's gone."

He scrubbed a palm over his cheek and beard. Finished off his wine. But apparently, he wasn't finished sharing. He said, "I never thought I'd see this day."

"What happened?" She set her arm on the back of the couch. Her fingers sank into the plush blanket draped there.

It would be a simple thing to slide his hand into hers. Even easier to tug—just barely, just enough—to pull her toward him. Into his arms. So, he could hold her and hold back those fears. But he'd always faced things head-on and alone. Until recently. And that had to stop. He might not be in the saddle, but he had to get to who he was.

He leaned back into the cushions behind him, putting her farther out of reach. "Would you believe me if I said I woke up one day and it was just gone?"

Her fingers stilled in the blanket. A shadow of disappointment curved over her face. "If that's the story you want to tell."

He let her down. That was why he was better on his own. Only himself to disappoint. "It's just that I haven't told anyone the truth."

"What truth is that?" She tucked her hair behind her ears as if she wanted to see him better. "That you're not really injured."

He lifted his eyebrows, opened his mouth.

She cut him off and said, "I haven't seen you limp once. Or even wince as if in pain. Not when you climbed into the tractor or jumped the fence or gathered the goats."

"I pulled my hamstring badly several seasons ago. It took me off the circuit for a few weeks while I rehabbed it." He rubbed his hand across his left leg. "Barely bothers me these days."

Her eyebrows pulled together. "Then why tell everyone you reaggravated your injury and couldn't ride?"

"Because I couldn't tell them I hurt Sundancer." Ryan stood, stretched his legs as if he could run from that truth. The flames of the candles swayed from his hasty movements around the coffee table.

"What do you mean?" Elsie's gaze tracked him as he paced.

"Sundancer's injury was my fault." Ryan swung around and faced her. He'd come this far. Might as well give it all up. She couldn't fix it. Or him. "I was on set for a Western action movie. For their horse stunts. It was the last day of filming. And the director decided to reshoot the pinnacle stagecoach chase scene at sunset. It was nothing I haven't done dozens of times before." Ryan stretched his arms over his head then ran his hands through his hair. "But I miscalculated. My boot hooked in the stirrup on my jump from Sundancer to the stagecoach. Not long, but enough to tip Sundancer off-balance. He stumbled and fell while I clung uninjured to the stagecoach and finished the scene."

Elsie unfolded her legs, set her feet on the floor and clasped her hands in her lap.

"The director got the shot he wanted. The filming wrapped. I brought Sundancer home to recover," he explained. "And I haven't been able to get in the saddle since."

"But it was an accident and Sundancer has healed. Maggie told me he was cleared," Elsie argued. "You've been injured in the arena too and still gotten back in the saddle. Still competed."

"This is different," he countered. "It's the first time I hurt a horse."

"Not intentionally," she said gently.

"Does it matter?" he asked then shook his head. "I told myself I was talented and fearless when I was really arrogant and reckless."

"So, you walk away from the life you love as a sort of punishment and penance." She stood up and walked over to him. "What does that prove?"

He didn't know. Knew only he wasn't sure where he belonged anymore. "I should probably go."

"You can't walk home in this weather." She closed the distance between them and held his stare. Her words direct and firm. "And I'm not driving you home in this weather either."

"Elsie." *I'm lost. And when I look at you...*

"Just don't move." She held up her hand, stopping his retreat, then came closer. "When I was a little girl, do you know what I wanted more than anything from my dad?"

Ryan was sinking. In the compassion swirling in her silver-gray eyes. His voice was rough in his own ears. "What was that?"

"This." She wrapped her arms around him. Tightened her hold when his shoulders stiffened. With her cheek pressed against his chest, she explained, "I just wanted someone to hold me and tell me it was going to be okay. That I was going to be okay."

Ryan dropped his chin on her head. Squeezed his eyes closed. Still, he was fighting.

She whispered, "You are going to be okay, my cowboy prince."

And finally, he gave in. Curved his arms around her and drew her as close as he possibly could. Then he held on. Because right there. With her. He started to believe again.

CHAPTER FIFTEEN

"Elsie." Ryan's arms anchored her against him.

Her reply was part sigh, part hum. Just enough to let him know she'd heard him. Her cheek was pressed to his chest. Right over his heart. The beat matched her own. Steady. Strong. And Elsie held on. To him. To the moment.

His embrace tightened. A gentle squeeze. She felt his exhale. Felt him settle around her. Then he said, "Thanks."

"Anytime." If only that were true. They only had this time. Elsie tipped her head up and met his gaze. She could lose herself in the warmth there. In him. If she wasn't careful. "That's what friends are for, right?" Just like that, as intended, the moment collapsed around her. With one simple word: *friends.*

Ryan released her and stepped back as if retreating behind those invisible friendship barriers.

She wanted to reach out. Capture his hand. Pull him back to her. Cross those boundaries. But that would be reckless. Careless. A risk she couldn't let her heart take. She was only passing through.

A visitor like she'd always been. Meant to leave like always. This wasn't her place, even if being in his arms felt so very right. This was for the best. Friends was all they could ever be.

She stuffed her hands into her pockets. "We should probably get to work on those mislabeled honey jars. We've got hundreds of labels to remove."

"We could do that." He rubbed his fingers across his bottom lip and watched her.

"Or there's the new labels to create and order." Elsie hurried into the kitchen where she'd left her laptop on the table. "We also need a new sign for the booth. And the booth layout. We should probably design a flier or brochure. Postcards. Something to give out at the festival that tells people where to find us online to order more honey."

Ryan followed her and leaned his hip against the edge of the kitchen island. "This is sounding a lot like work."

That was good because otherwise she might start to imagine a different sort of evening with Ryan. One that included secrets shared. Hand holding. And hearts falling. "There's still so much to be done before this weekend."

"That can wait." He touched the petal of a gardenia floating in a vase she'd filled with water that morning. "If you don't stop, Elsie, and smell the flowers, you're going to get to New York and fall over from exhaustion."

The thunder rumbled outside. The rain splattered

against the windowpanes. LED candles cast pockets of soft, buttery light into the shadows. It was intimate. Private. New York seemed a world away. But her cowboy was within reach. And when she looked at him, she felt everything. She curled her fingers around the back of a kitchen chair. "That's dramatic."

"That's the truth," he countered. "I look around here and do you know what I see?"

Elsie frowned. "Too many cases of honey with incorrect labels." Too many unpacked moving boxes. Too many fix-it projects to count. A house craving a refresh. A home she always...

"I see you," he said and pointed at the gardenia vase as if to back up his point. "I see you up all night. Unpacking boxes. Putting things away. Restoring this house room by room."

He wasn't wrong. That didn't make what she was doing wrong either. The house was quite large. Elsie feared it was too much for her aunt to keep up on her own the past few years after her Uncle Robert passed. She lifted her chin. "I haven't done that much."

"You've unpacked every single moving box upstairs," he countered. "I know how many there were because I helped Bryce unload his moving truck."

That had been months ago. All the boxes made it feel like Bryce and her nieces were still living in a storage unit. Elsie kept silent. She'd spent two full nights tackling the upstairs and transforming each guest room into an inviting refuge. The kind her brother could fill now with family and friends.

"You gave the girls their own suite and transformed it into a cotton-candy-pink princess wonderland," Ryan continued. "I peeked in when I went to Bryce's room to raid his closet."

"The girls love it," Elsie said, her words defensive. She would gladly trade a week of no sleep to see her nieces that excited again. "Their rooms turned out well, I think."

"Their suite is better than anything in the movies," he said.

She smiled. "That's a nice thing to say."

"It's not a compliment." Disapproval worked across his face. "You need to slow down. It's okay to take a break."

"I can't." Resolve was clear in each syllable. "I'm not in town for much longer. I want the girls to feel comfortable here. To feel settled. To feel like this is their…"

"Home," he said simply.

Don't. Don't do that. Don't act as if you get me. Then she'd like him even more. Still her words flowed out, as if she wanted him to understand her. "I want them to love this place as much as I did growing up."

The grand house had been her secret retreat. Every room a new place to explore. An adventure. Full of light. Rich scents. Textures. An escape where she wasn't an inconvenience. Or in the way. Where she was always wanted. "If you would have asked me to show you happiness back then, I would've pointed at this house. I want Autumn and Gemma to have that same feeling."

"And if I asked you to show me happiness now, where would you point?" he asked.

At you. Elsie touched the front of her throat. "I came here to help my family. That's what I'm going to do. You can do that with me or not."

"Fair enough." He straightened away from the counter. "Anything else?"

I'm going to leave. Knowing her family was good. Knowing it was the right decision. Because her own happiness had to be in the city. Waiting for her. New York was proof she was finally living her life. On her own terms. Stepping out of her comfort zone. That was everything to be happy about, wasn't it?

She released the chair and walked into the pantry. "I have a box of unopened vanilla wafers I'm willing to share if you help me peel off labels."

"Those are my favorite."

"I know." *I know a lot about you. But not enough. Could you tell me more? Anything. Something to take with me. Like a souvenir.* Something she could hold on to during the deepest part of the night when she wasn't always so happy. She shook the cookie box lightly. "How about one cookie for every five labels removed?" Or even better. A cookie for a truth.

He ran his fingers through his beard. One corner of his mouth lifted. "This sounds a little bit like bribery."

"Is it working?" She grinned at him.

"I'll help you, Elsie Marie. No cookies necessary." He walked slowly toward her. "I'll help you because I want to. And do you know why that is?"

Elsie's pulse picked up. She managed the smallest shake of her head.

"Because I like seeing you happy." He stopped just out of her reach. An intensity she hadn't seen before swirled in his hazel gaze. "You never asked me what I think of when I think about happiness, Elsie Marie. Do you want to know?"

Awareness spiked. Elsie's mouth dropped open slightly. Words failed her.

"You." His half grin pressed into his cheek. "When I think of happiness, I think of you."

With that he plucked the cookie box from her weak grip and walked out of the kitchen, whistling.

Elsie grabbed the wine bottle they'd opened earlier and rushed after him into the family room. He was already sitting on the couch. The wafer box open and a case of honey on the coffee table, waiting for labels to be removed. She set the wine on the side table and sat beside him. "You can't say things like that."

"Why not?" He popped a cookie into his mouth. "It's the truth."

Elsie reached for the wine bottle, pulled out the

cork and splashed wine into her glass. "You can't say it because I don't make you happy."

He ate another cookie and took a honey jar from the box. "That's not the point. I don't need you to make me happy."

Whatever this is, Elsie, it's not enough. We don't make each other happy. And I want to be happy. You should want that too. Elsie rubbed her forehead.

"It's not so very complicated." Ryan refilled his wine glass then went to work on the honey label. "When I think of you, I feel happy. Just like when you think of this house, you feel happy. It's simple."

He made it sound simple. But nothing was that cut-and-dried in a relationship. Her first marriage proved that. Elsie reached into the box and took out a cookie. "My ex-husband told me I wasn't enough for him anymore."

Ryan paused and lowered his wine glass. His expression and words suddenly grim. "He told you that?"

She appreciated his anger on her behalf. She bit into her cookie as if the sweetness would mellow her words. Then she picked up a honey jar. "He told me that he wanted more from life than what we had." *This can't be all there is. We settled. Now we're stuck, Elsie, and sinking.*

"What did you have?" He lifted the edge of another label.

"Our careers." She took another jar from the box, ripped the label off and reached for another.

"Work goals like promotions. Partnership for him. We were both career oriented. Motivated and financially responsible. We aligned that way." At least on paper they'd been compatible. A logical fit. Destined to last for the long haul unlike her parents.

"Sounds like it was all work and no play." He crinkled the incorrect label into a ball and tossed it on the floor with the growing pile.

Or rather it'd been all work, no spark. But her parents had sparked brighter than fireworks on July Fourth and look where that had gotten them. The label came off like a Band-Aid being removed. She started on another. "We had plans for fun eventually."

"When you reached your goals," he said.

"Yeah, then we were supposed to be alright." And they'd have that spark. Feel that magic. Remember why they'd even said "I do" in the first place. The label tore in two, leaving half stuck to the glass. "Finally, we would've made each other happy."

Because wasn't that what love promised? A lifetime of happiness. Yet when it was all stripped away, her ex-husband hadn't been wrong. Neither of them had been happy. Not for a while. So, Elsie would find it on her own.

She rubbed her thumb over the glass, removing the last of the label. "That obviously didn't happen."

"Where is your ex-husband now?" He paused for a cookie break.

"He remarried. They're expecting their first child next month." Her ex-husband hadn't taken long to find the life he wanted. She didn't resent him. Rather, she envied him. One more label gone. "I'm glad he found what he was looking for."

Ryan reached over. His hand settled on her leg. When her gaze met his, he said, "You deserve that too."

The warmth from his touch curved through her. Encouraged more than a flicker of awareness. *I like you.* There was that spark. *Will you warn me before you break my heart, please? That's only fair, isn't it?* Elsie swallowed, willed her pulse to slow and backpedaled into that friend zone. "What I deserve is more vanilla wafers. Hand the box over." She swept her arm toward the pile of discarded labels. "I've done twice as many jars as you."

"I didn't know it was a competition." Amusement flickered across his face. He picked up the cookie box and held it just out of her reach. "What are the terms exactly?"

She snatched it and said, "Most labels removed in an hour, which happens to be bedtime around here. Loser comes back and makes breakfast for everyone tomorrow morning."

"I already promised the girls waffles." He held out his hand for a cookie.

Elsie pressed a wafer into his palm. "When did you do that?"

"When we were building the princess fort and

they told me I needed to sleep over in case you got scared during the storm tonight." He tossed the cookie in his mouth and grinned.

Elsie touched her cheek. Glad the dim lighting hid her blush.

"They even told me what room I need to sleep in," he continued. His words casual. "The one right across the hall from yours is apparently the closest to you. I won't have to run far to reach you."

The idea of having him close appealed a little too much. "That's good to know." She cradled the cookie box and considered him. "When you get scared tonight, I'll know where to find you."

"Or, we could leave our doors open and just talk across the hall." He lifted his wine glass and took a sip. "Save ourselves all that unnecessary running around."

She laughed. "Or we could just work through the night." *Sit right here. Together. Like this.*

He shook his head. "We've got one more hour of work. Because the royalty in this house needs their rest. Consider it like a royal decree."

"We should get to it." Elsie sat up and straightened. "What about those terms?"

"Let's make it more interesting," he mused. "Seeing as how you are making me work after normal business hours."

"There's no normal business hours on a farm," she chided then waved at him. "Fine. Let's hear it."

"If I win, I want a day." He watched her over the

rim of the wine glass. "If I win, you spend an entire day with me. From sunrise to sunset. No work. All play."

All day with her cowboy. That spark flared. Unstoppable. Unbidden. Not so very unwelcome. She worked the catch out of her words. "Fine, but if I win you take me horseback riding."

His eyes widened. He considered her for a beat then said, "Deal. Start the timer."

Elsie opened the timer on her cell phone, set it for an hour then glanced at him. "Go."

The only sound for the next sixty minutes was the ripping of stickers off glass. Over and over. One jar after another. They were both efficient, fast and focused. Finally, the timer chimed on Elsie's phone, and she called a stop. Stiff from leaning over the coffee table, Elsie stood and stretched her arms over her head, then looked at the discarded piles of labels that appeared equal. "I'll count those to see who won."

"I'll check on the girls." Ryan leaned down in front of the blanket door of the princess fort. His voice dipped into a regal and extremely formal tone. "Cowboy Prince would like to request an audience with Princess Gem and Princess Autumn."

Muffled giggles drifted from the fort. Then Autumn announced, her words equally stiff and starched, "Cowboy Prince, you may enter now."

Elsie chuckled and marveled again at how comfortable Ryan was with the girls. Her cowboy would be a great father one day. She flopped onto the couch, picked up a pile of crumbled labels and told herself it was just a passing observation. The kind one friend makes about another. Nothing that toppled her over those friendship borders, of course. The labels clung to her fingers. Sticky and unavoidable like her growing feelings for her cowboy.

"Can we play a game, Cowboy Prince? Please." Gemma's blond head peered out of the opening. "Autumn finished all her homework and now our movie is over too."

"Unfortunately, your aunt has overruled me and declared it a school night." Disappointment spread through Ryan's words. "That means we don't have time for a board game."

"But we always read before bed," Autumn chimed in. Hope drifted through her plea. "Can you read to us? Please."

"And use all the different voices like you do," Gemma pleaded. "That's the best part."

There were a lot of parts to her cowboy she was discovering. Hard to declare the best. Elsie tugged off those labels. But her feelings, well, those still stuck.

Ryan glanced over his shoulder. "That okay with you, Elsie?"

No, she wasn't okay. But she would sort that all out in the morning. For now, she had the night to keep her secrets and she had her cowboy. She stood up and smiled. "Only if I get to join you guys too."

The girls cheered.

"Make room," Ryan said. He lifted Gemma, making her squeal with laughter and plopped her down on one of the blankets. Then he scooted carefully inside the fort. Too tall to sit without toppling the fabric ceiling, he stretched out on his back and propped several pillows behind his head.

Elsie squeezed in, surprised the interior was bigger than it appeared. She laid on her side and curled herself around Gemma. Autumn handed a book to Ryan then adjusted herself until her head rested on his shoulder. Ryan read the first line, his deep voice filling the cozy space, blocking out the thunder rolling on outside and captivating his audience.

Elsie fell into the story. And fell a little bit more for her cowboy.

Then promised herself, tomorrow when the sun rose, she would heed those caution signs. Tomorrow in the morning light, when her head was clear, her heart would see it too. That falling for her cowboy was a bad idea.

But for tonight. For right now, she let herself be enchanted.

CHAPTER SIXTEEN

IT WASN'T AN alarm that woke Elsie the following morning. Or even her cowboy with a soft hello and an even softer good-morning kiss. Not that Elsie expected that. Wished perhaps.

No, it was her phone vibrating in her sweatshirt pocket that jarred her awake. She slipped her phone out and blinked at the screen. *Mom.*

She crawled out of the princess tent where she'd spent the night nestled between her nieces under several thick blankets. Her nieces only rolled over into the space she'd left and kept on snoozing. Ryan wasn't on the couch where she'd last seen his silhouette stretched out when she'd woken in the middle of the night. She sighed. Finding her cowboy had to wait.

And those wishes in her heart, well, those had also disappeared. The sun shone through the windows, brightening the room. The view was clear now. Her eyes were open, and her heart was closed. Lifting her phone to her ear, Elsie greeted her mom and frowned at the clock on the mantel. She'd overslept.

Rushing upstairs to change, Elsie listened to her mom detail their trek through the Egyptian pyramids. And noted the door to the guest bedroom across from her room was closed. Cowboy located. When she came out of her bedroom, her phone tucked in her legging pocket, the door across the hall was open yet the room was empty. Elsie dashed downstairs, heard dishes clanking in the kitchen. But had no time to investigate. She woke her nieces and hustled the slow-to-rouse pair back upstairs for showers.

Autumn was dressed for school and downstairs without delay. Gemma requested French braids to match her new friend Madeline. And that required Elsie to watch a how-to video for a quick refresher. When they finally made it downstairs, their plates with waffles and fresh strawberry slices waited on the island. The syrup was still warm. The girls' lunches were packed. And her cowboy was nowhere in sight.

There was little time for disappointment. Teeth needed to be brushed. Backpacks loaded and seat belts buckled. Then it was straight to the elementary school with minutes to spare before the late bell rang. A pit stop at the gas station for diesel to fill the generator and Elsie headed back. In the driveway, she disconnected her phone call with Bryce and spotted Smarty Marty already perched on the top of her moving van like a sentry. Then

Ryan rounded the path near the greenhouses and her smile stretched wide.

Her cowboy was still there. Back in his jeans, boots and cowboy hat. Wearing another one of her brother's pullover shirts. The fit snug across his broad shoulders. And all Elsie wanted was to wrap herself back in his embrace. Confirm her theory that the deep forest green color of the shirt complemented his hazel eyes. Not exactly the appropriate greeting for a simple friend.

A flash of caramel behind her cowboy caught her attention. Elsie chuckled. Butter-Belle trailed him like a loyal pet. She couldn't fault the goat. Spending more time with her cowboy was becoming more and more appealing.

Elsie grabbed the baggie of grapes Gemma had left in the cup holder, opened her car door and forced herself to slow down. Lean back into that friend zone where hearts were safe.

"Good news. You're off the hook." Elsie opened the back gate on the Jeep. She grinned at Ryan. "You can go back to being a silent partner." And she could go back to being resistant to her cowboy. Uninterested. And unaffected.

He lifted the portable gas container out. "Is that so?"

"Bryce just called." Elsie shut the gate, offered a grape to Butter-Belle and congratulated herself for not reaching for her cowboy. Nothing to it. "Bryce is being discharged today. The girls and I are going to pick him up when they get out of school. Since Bryce is on limited duty, I figure he can finish removing labels and put on the new ones."

Ryan nodded and walked toward the generators located on the far side of the house. "What about the festival booth?"

"My mom called this morning." When Elsie had still been content to put off facing the day and her misplaced feelings for her cowboy. She touched her sunglasses, fearing she might still be hiding. Yet he was there. And she was delighted. That hardly meant she couldn't stick to the friend zone, right? "They changed their flight out of London. They'll be home tomorrow afternoon. And they couldn't have been more thrilled about the festival."

"Busy morning." He refilled the generator fuel tank.

"Looks like you've been busy too." She gave Butter-Belle more grapes. "Sundancer is already grazing in the pasture. I saw Midnight Rose almost fully out in her paddock. And if I'm not mistaken both the tractor and UTV have been moved."

"I drove out to the bee pasture." Ryan glanced at the sky as if looking for rain. "It'll be a few days before the seeds can be planted. Soil is too wet. Caleb dropped off a load of hay. I used the tractor to load the bales into the stable loft."

"What's left for me to do?" Elsie asked.

"I thought maybe that horseback ride." He

tapped the spout of the gas can and replaced the cap on the generator fuel tank. The brim of his cowboy hat shaded his expression. "You won."

She won. Elsie touched her cheek, stalling her frown. She didn't have time for a no work, all play day with him anyway. No reason to be let down. Besides, her family was coming home. That meant she would be on her way soon enough. Spending an entire day with her cowboy—what would that solve? She pressed her fingers against her chest. "You counted the labels then."

"Woke up early. Couldn't sleep. Call it my version of counting sheep." His words were light and playful. But there was a reserve to his movements as if he wasn't quite certain where they stood.

Or perhaps that was only more wishful thinking. Elsie wanting to believe he might be considering more than a friend situation too.

"What do you say?" he asked. "Ready to ride?"

With him. "Definitely."

Half an hour later, Elsie was in the saddle on Sundancer. Without her cowboy. Not exactly what she'd meant last night when she'd made the wager. Nothing for it now. If she clarified, she risked revealing too much. Right now her feelings for her cowboy were private. Her own. She meant them to stay that way. She adjusted her position and loosened her grip on the reins. "What do you want me to do?"

"Just walk around the pasture." Ryan sat on the

fence that connected Midnight Rose's paddock to the pasture. Butter-Belle grazed near his boots. "I want to watch his gait walking. Just keep it easy for now. Then we'll move to trotting."

Elsie guided Sundancer into a circle. She'd surprised Ryan earlier when she'd mounted Sundancer without assistance. She'd taken riding lessons years ago, then continued to ride for pleasure in college whenever she could get out of the city. Later, work and marriage had taken her away from the saddle completely. Now she was counting on muscle memory to keep herself properly seated to impress her cowboy.

Four turns later, Ryan nodded as if satisfied with Sundancer's gait. Elsie passed by Ryan and whispered, "Midnight Rose is coming."

Ryan never moved. Kept his focus on Sundancer. The pleasure was there in his words. "Her curiosity is overwhelming her nerves. Don't pay attention to her."

Ryan's current position on the fence was no accident. He had an unobstructed view to the pasture. And Midnight Rose had a full view of him. He was observing Sundancer as much as he was waiting out the mare.

Elsie praised Sundancer softly and expanded to circle more of the pasture. Dozens of turns later, Ryan finally okayed the gelding to trot. Sundancer transitioned easily, seeming more than ready. More than eager. Ryan finally smiled. "It's good to see he's back to himself."

What about you, cowboy? Elsie pulled back her words and slowed Sundancer.

Midnight Rose had finally joined Ryan. He held his lower body completely still. No doubt to keep from startlingly the mare. The only constant was his continuous words of affection and praise for the horse.

Elsie held her breath. Mesmerized by the pair. By his extreme patience. By how he gave the mare his undivided attention. As if he had all the time in the world to sit there. With her. Until she was comfortable. Until she trusted him.

Carefully, he raised one arm. The movement slow. Quiet. For one gentle stroke along her sleek neck. He rewarded her with a carrot. More praise. Time stilled or perhaps it was that Elsie could've sat there and watched the pair all day. There was something extraordinary—and touching—in the simplicity of a horse and a cowboy. Healing each other.

The mare nuzzled his shoulder. And Ryan beamed as if he'd just won the greatest prize. He offered the mare an apple. "Sorry, Midnight Rose, I'm out of treats. You'll have to settle for grass like Butter-Belle."

The mare snorted and shook her beautiful mane. Her thick tail twitched higher. Ryan chuckled. "You're definitely a beauty. And I'm going to be spoiling you something bad, I can already see it."

And Elsie could already see the bond forming between the pair. She nudged Sundancer closer to the fence. "You're really good with horses."

"I like the connection." Ryan watched Midnight Rose extend her head over the fence to graze near Butter-Belle. He grinned. "Don't get me wrong. The thrill of riding a bucking bronc for eight seconds is quite addicting. But this connection, it's special."

"And it's lasting." Like the connection she was beginning to feel with her cowboy.

"Exactly." Ryan braced his hands on the fence and studied her. "There's no pretense. They give so much more than they ever take. If you take care of your horse, they will take care of you."

Could I trust you to take care of my heart? I could take care of yours. Elsie urged Sundancer into a trot around the pasture as if that would prod her thoughts back into line.

When she passed closer to him again, he said, "You ride well." He paused then added, amusement and a touch of impatience in his words, "Let me guess, Josh taught you to ride, didn't he?"

She caught her laughter, but couldn't stop her smile. "Why would you think that?"

"Well, Carter taught you to drive, and Caleb taught you to dance." His words sounded surly. "You learned something from all my brothers.

So, it makes sense. Josh is a well-known horse trainer."

"But your brother wasn't a trainer back then." She chuckled then added, "Josh gave me tips, but I took lessons." She slowed Sundancer to a walk in front of him. Then as they moved away, she glanced over her shoulder and called out, "I wanted to impress a cowboy I liked."

Then she urged Sundancer out of talking range for another loop around the pasture. On her return, she checked her grin. Now her cowboy definitely looked surly too.

At her approach, he straightened slowly on the fence. "And was your cowboy impressed?"

Elsie shrugged. Passed him. Then circled Sundancer back around and met Ryan's gaze. She said, "He never asked me to ride that summer. I never got to show him. Then I left for college."

Something shifted over his face. Her breath caught. He eased off the fence. His boots landed softly in the grassy pasture. Her heart thumped in her chest.

He watched her. She watched him. Neither moved. Both waited.

Her pulse raced. Her stomach wobbled.

They'd been circling around this moment for a while. She should've held on to her secrets. She wasn't a risk-taker. Not with her heart. But here. With him. She wanted...

Wanted to know if she could be enough for this

cowboy. Even if only for one moment. This one. Because they only had this one.

Finally, he stepped forward. Slow. Easy. As if giving her the opportunity to back out. Elsie exhaled, slow and deep. It was only one small risk. A test of that spark she felt. Surely that wasn't too much. Nothing she couldn't come back from, right?

He was beside her. His focus on her completely. Fully. He said, "I think that's enough for Sundancer today."

But they were far from finished. Her words were breathless. "I can get down myself."

"I'd rather help you." He reached up. His hands settled around her waist.

His touch gentle. Steady. But the choice was hers. Lean in. Lean away. One risk. Her pulse pounded. Her hands fell to his shoulders. One minute she was seated on Sundancer. The next, his arms wound around her waist. He held her closer than the evening before. Impossible. Perfect.

His thumb brushed across her cheek. "Who was the cowboy?"

"You already know." Elsie curved her arms up around his neck. Curled her fingers in his hair touching his collar. Curiosity appeased. Her heart raced faster. Surely, he could feel it too.

He drew her tighter against him. "Why didn't you say anything?"

No backing out. She was where she wanted to

be. She whispered, "You never looked my way that last summer."

"But I always saw you." His palms cupped her cheeks. The heat in his gaze skimming over her face was better than a caress. His voice was rough. "Same as I'm seeing you now."

"It was for the best." She searched his gaze.

"Says who?" he asked.

She no longer knew what was best. Knew only she was lost to him. In him. She trailed her fingers over his bearded cheek. "I want to kiss you, but we both know it's a bad idea."

He leaned into her touch. "Does it make it worse to know I want to kiss you too? More than anything I've ever wanted."

Her heart tumbled. She wasn't falling alone. But who would catch them after? "Somehow it makes it better."

"Are you going to kiss me then?" he asked, his words hesitant. Tentative as if he feared her reply.

"I shouldn't." But she wanted to. Despite all the reasons not to. "What about you?"

"I should let you go." He tipped his head toward the gate. "Walk on out of this pasture. And keep on walking."

She stayed anchored in his embrace. "Why don't you?"

"Gran Claire always told me that I never did what I should." That half grin returned. The one she found so appealing. The one she thought of as hers. For her. He added, "Seems I haven't gotten over that flaw quite yet."

"We should both move away." Her words were too breathless to carry any force. Any conviction.

Still, he nodded. His fingers flexed around her back as if he was preparing to let go. He cleared his throat. "Say when."

"On three."

"One." He leaned toward her.

"Two." She met him halfway.

And their lips connected. That spark flamed. And caught. Surrounding them both. He wasn't reluctant. She was far from shy. It was remarkable. Thoroughly perfect. And over entirely too soon.

The kiss slowed. Still her heart beat too fast. Her knees wanted to buckle. Her mind was scattered.

Yet, she wanted another kiss. Just one more.

Elsie opened her eyes. Their gazes collided. Held.

And they both said, "Three."

CHAPTER SEVENTEEN

EVEN THE DEVIL was laughing now. When would Ryan ever learn to walk away?

Ryan released Elsie. Before he kissed her again. Before he got swept up in her completely.

Once was…not ever going to be enough.

Now he knew that with the same certainty that he knew being thrown from a twelve-hundred-pound bucking bronc was going to sting. But a fall from a bronc he would recover from. Something told him there might be no getting over Elsie. If he let himself fall.

He looked at her. Her cheeks flushed. Her silver eyes wide. Her lips parted. Part flustered. Part mystified. As if she was as unbalanced by that kiss as he was. She was adorable and captivating. And everything he could want. If only.

He rubbed the back of his neck, searched for words. How was he supposed to make this right? When everything he wanted to say was wrong.

I don't regret that.

I can't apologize.

Can I kiss you again?

But he had to say something. Anything. He started, "Elsie…"

She bit into her bottom lip and shook her head. Her gaze imploring. "Don't. We can't." Pause. "We knew." Another pause. "We shouldn't."

Ryan closed his mouth. He wanted to pull her back into his arms. Convince her they should. But she was right. He couldn't. She was leaving soon. And his heart had never been up for grabs. Never been on the line. And one world-tilting kiss wouldn't change that. "What now?"

Before she could answer, his phone chimed. The sound crackled between them like a divide.

"You should answer that," she said.

"It can wait." He kept his focus fixed on her.

"At least see who it is," she urged. "It could be someone important."

You're important too. To me. More words that would only make a complicated situation even more so. *You're important, but I can't give you what you deserve.* He sighed and took his phone out of his back pocket. He frowned at the screen. Talk about impeccable timing.

"Who is it?" Elsie prodded.

"My mom," he replied.

"You have to answer her," she said, her voice insistent. "It's your mom."

"It's complicated between us," he admitted. Seemed he had a talent for finding complicated relationships.

"Ryan," she said, resolve in her words. "Answer it."

He pressed the accept button on the screen. Maybe—just maybe—when he finished this conversation, he would have the right words for Elsie. The video call opened, and Ryan greeted his mother. He turned, adjusting the angle of the phone until the sun wasn't blocking his mother's face on the phone screen.

"Fletcher has been texting you all morning, Ryan." His mother skipped over any pleasantries and got straight to the point, as was her style. She continued, "He has a new list of places he wants to show you."

Ryan squeezed his forehead with his other hand.

Unfazed, his mother asked, "Are you free in the next hour?"

He lifted his gaze over the phone and caught sight of Elsie's moving truck in the distance. Well, it looked like he was free for the rest of his life. He said, "Sure. I can meet him."

"Alone?" his mother said, displeasure in her expression.

He wasn't entirely sure he wanted to be alone. But Elsie was moving to New York for the life she wanted. Besides, what did Ryan even know about sticking around? He'd only ever stuck to one thing—the rodeo. Once he was back on the circuit, he'd be on the move again too. Just the way he always preferred it. "I'll be fine."

His mother frowned. "Surely there's someone who can go with you, for both our sakes."

For both their sakes, Ryan hoped this house-hunting endeavor ceased soon. He already had one woman turning his world upside down. At least Elsie had warned him from the start that she was leaving. It wasn't a goodbye he wanted to face. Still, he didn't need his mom coming in only to back out of his life all over again as well.

"Ryan." His mother's sharp voice pulled his attention to her. "Who is that behind you?"

Ryan shifted, realized Elsie and Sundancer were standing in range of the camera lens. "That's Elsie Parks. She is Marlena Doyle's niece. They are our neighbors."

His mother leaned closer to the camera. "And she's a friend of yours?"

Of sorts. The lines were certainly blurred now. He scratched his cheek. "I'm helping her at the farm. Her brother had an accident last week."

"How serious?" The physician Lilian Sloan stepped forward. "Is he okay? Recovering at home?"

"He fell through the greenhouse roof. His ankle suffered the most damage, but Grant already did surgery," Ryan explained. "He's being discharged this afternoon."

At Grant's name, pride washed over his mother's face. "Well, it's fortunate Grant is there. Her brother will no doubt be walking again soon, thanks to your brother." She paused and seemed to check her appearance in the camera then said, "Introduce us, please."

"Mother," Ryan started.

"Ryan," she interrupted then continued patiently, "It may come as a surprise to learn that people do like me. That I have more to offer than a medical prognosis."

He wondered what his mom's prognosis would be for his heart. Lost cause, most likely. He didn't need a medical degree for that. He said, "Hold on." Then lowered the phone and twisted around. "Elsie. She wants to meet you."

Elsie moved beside him. He whispered an apology and then completed the introductions.

To his surprise, his mother was correct. Elsie seemed to like Lilian Sloan almost immediately. At least their conversation flowed easily, as if they understood each other. Within minutes, Elsie had his phone in her grasp and full control of the conversation.

It was both bewildering and fascinating. Ryan had Sundancer's saddle and gear removed before the conversation between the women had even wound down. It was several more minutes before Elsie disconnected. She joined him, reached over to rub Sundancer and grinned. "Your mom is going to help me locate an apartment in New York. Can you believe that?"

There was so much he didn't want to believe. Like Elsie really was leaving. He lifted the saddle and started for the gate. "My mother has lived in New York for decades and she's well-connected. You couldn't ask for a better resource than her."

Unless of course you wanted to stay here. Then I could show you... Ryan ground his teeth together. There was nothing more to show Elsie. Except that he was as temporary in town as her. His boots sank in the dirt as if testing the ground for roots. But he was too restless. Too much of a cowboy rambler seeking his next adrenaline-fueled ride. And more likely to trip over those roots than plant them. He lengthened his strides, heading for the stable.

Elsie kept pace beside him. "So, in exchange for her help in New York, I'm going to join you for those house showings today."

"You definitely don't have to do that," Ryan managed, even though relief loosened his shoulders.

"It's already decided." Elsie opened the door to the stable for him. "You're stuck with me for a while longer today."

Would you mind being stuck with me for something like, say, forever? He frowned and ducked into the tack room. He was seriously in bad. But not too deep he couldn't still get out intact.

He just had to set things straight between them. Ensure they were both on the same page as it were. How hard could that be?

As IT HAPPENED, one simple conversation was proving very hard to have. And not through any fault of his own, actually. It was simply a matter of bad timing and no privacy.

Ryan had left Elsie after his mother's video chat to shower and change. Fletcher had picked Ryan up. And Elsie had agreed to meet them in her own car, as she'd planned to collect the girls and head to the hospital for Bryce's discharge afterward. That meant between Fletcher's escort and the multiple video calls to his mother, Ryan had no alone time with Elsie.

Then he'd returned home only to find his entire family preparing to descend on the Doyle farm that evening. Tess thoughtfully prepared dinner for the group to bring over before she and Carter headed to Belleridge to purchase more supplies for the babies' room. His grandfather and uncle made their special dessert. And Grant claimed he wanted to check on his recently discharged patient. Then Caleb decided he was perfectly content eating a meal he didn't have to prepare himself. Worse, his grandfather pressed the butterscotch and rum bread pudding dish in Ryan's hands, ushering him back to his truck before Ryan could come up with an excuse not to attend dinner at the Doyle farm.

Now he was standing on the front porch of Elsie's house with his family, holding a glass casserole dish and realizing that conversation with Elsie was going to have to wait a while longer. He only hoped he could keep his attraction to Elsie in check a few more hours. If his family caught on, there would be nothing but more problems.

Maggie jumped out of her truck and joined them on the porch as Elsie opened the front door.

Maggie's irritation was obvious and directed solely at Ryan. She frowned and said, "Ryan, we were supposed to practice this afternoon."

One more thing he hadn't dealt with yet. The tinfoil crinkled underneath his tense grip.

Elsie stepped in and eased the dish from Ryan's grasp. "Sorry, that was my fault. I promised Lilian when Ryan and I spoke to her that we'd see as many houses as we could today." Then she added, "I also told Lilian's real estate agent, Fletcher, that we had time to look at a few more houses before I checked with Ryan to make sure that was okay with his schedule."

Maggie appeared mollified.

As for Ryan, he appreciated the save. But he couldn't keep hiding. Especially not behind Elsie. Not only was she not going to be there. It just wasn't right. At least he'd had one small victory that afternoon. A short ride on Mischief, his mustang. It was a step.

"Wait." Grant moved beside Ryan and slung his arm over Ryan's shoulders. "Elsie talked to our mother. With you. Today."

Ryan nodded.

"We had a very nice conversation in fact," Elsie stated. "Lilian was very appreciative of our assistance. We even found several places both Ryan and Lilian agreed on."

"Elsie, you're a miracle worker." Grant squeezed Ryan's shoulders then followed Elsie into the house.

Caleb laughed and joined the pair. "I seriously think this might be the first time Ryan has ever agreed with our mother on anything."

Ryan held back, let his grandfather and uncle inside before him and put more distance between him and Elsie. How was it possible she looked even prettier that evening? In another flowy sort of sundress. With her long hair twisted into a casual bun, showcasing her mesmerizing silver-gray eyes. He wanted to pull her into his arms and get lost in her all over again. He feared it was going to be a long night.

Unfortunately, his sister-in-law lingered too. Maggie eyed him and toyed with her wedding ring on her finger. "Rumor has it you didn't come home last night."

Ryan tipped his head back and stared at the white shiplap ceiling over his head. "It's not a rumor, Mags. You and everyone in the family know I was here with Elsie and the girls last night."

"Of course, we know where you *were*." Maggie chuckled. "But I want to know where you *are*."

He dropped his chin and eyed her. "I'm standing right here."

"Don't do that. We've been friends for far too long." She punched his shoulder lightly. "You know exactly what I'm asking."

He also knew he had no good answer. Certainly not one he believed Maggie would buy. They had been friends too long. Traveled too long on the rodeo road together and shared more than one secret with each other over the years. But Maggie was head-over-boots in love with his brother and Grant with her. Couples like that tended to color every situation with love-tinted markers, wanting everyone to have what they shared.

Yet love couldn't be what was between Elsie and him. Because Ryan had only ever committed to things where his success was guaranteed. If he believed, worked hard enough and trusted in himself, that is. But he never trusted love. Not enough to believe in it for himself.

He gripped Maggie's shoulders, turned her around and gently nudged her inside. Then he followed her. "I'm right where I was the last time we discussed this, Mags. Firmly in the friend zone."

That was where he belonged. And if he dwelled on the incredible kiss he'd shared with Elsie that morning for the rest of his days, well, that was his business.

Maggie opened her mouth.

Ryan shook his head. "Let it go, Mags." He certainly was. "Trust me, it's better this way."

And if his heart disagreed, well, that was of no consequence. He couldn't remember the last time he'd ever truly paid his heart any mind anyway.

CHAPTER EIGHTEEN

ELSIE WAS RUNNING out of patience. Not that she wasn't grateful for the delicious meal the Sloan family brought over so she didn't have to cook that evening. Leaving her free to see to her brother's comfort on his first night home from the hospital. Really, she appreciated every one of the Sloans.

However, what she didn't appreciate was not having one moment—not even a minute—alone with her cowboy. There were things that needed to be said. Things she needed to tell him.

That was why she was stalling in the kitchen, trying to catch Ryan's attention through the wide window that looked out over the porch.

Her brother had decided he wanted to eat outside. They'd set him up on one of the cushioned chairs with his ankle propped at the appropriate height on pillows stacked on an end table. Then they'd adjusted the large outdoor table near enough for him to reach his plate. Dinner had been lively and entertaining and animated. Despite Elsie and Ryan being seated at opposite ends of the table. Again.

"Dessert is served." Sam walked into the kitchen and interrupted Elsie's third slow pass in front of the wide window.

Startled, she spun around and took in the two older cowboys.

Sam's grin stretched into his white beard as if he knew exactly what she was up to. Then he motioned toward the island. "We just came to pick up our bowls and make sure you were joining us too, Elsie."

"We'll help you clean up those dinner dishes before we leave," Roy promised. He scooped a large dollop of whipped cream over a piece of butterscotch bread pudding and handed the bowl to Elsie.

"And we just wanted to thank you while we have you to ourselves for a moment." Sam plunked more whipped cream on his dessert.

"I should be the one thanking you for this meal." And so much more. Elsie passed out spoons.

"Ryan told us it was you who convinced him to prep our dandelion field," Sam admitted. "We sure do appreciate you."

"And the dandelion seed you found us too." Roy took a bite of his bread pudding and grinned around the mouthful. "We'll be planting that soon enough. And just waiting on those dandelions to bloom."

Elsie pictured the wide field of yellow blossoms. Now the pair would have something to remember her by. She knew she wouldn't be forgetting the two cowboys anytime soon. "Well, don't forget to save me some wine from your first batch."

"You can count on that." Sam held his arm out to escort her back to the porch. "We will have a bottle for you ready and waiting for when you come on back home to us."

Back home. The words swirled around Elsie, yet she was afraid to let them settle fully.

Roy held open the door. "And we will share a few glasses together."

"I can't wait," Elsie said and meant it. She was already looking forward to coming back and hadn't even left yet. She slid into her chair and told herself not to make anything of it. Her brother and nieces lived there now. Of course, she would want to return.

"Auntie, where is Marty going to sleep when you leave?" Autumn asked from the other end of the table where she slipped Butter-Belle a grape and gave the goat a quick pat. "Marty sure likes your moving truck a bunch."

The other conversations around the table quieted at Autumn's question. Elsie's spoon stilled in the butter rum sauce pooled around her bowl of butterscotch bread pudding. The sweetness was suddenly too heavy in her mouth. Too cloying in her throat. She reached for her water glass and searched for a conversation detour.

"Maybe you could leave that truck and get a different one," Gemma offered. She plucked a cherry from the top of her ice cream sundae with her fingers. "Then Marty can still sleep on it, and he won't be sad."

"I'm afraid that truck has to come with me," Elsie said gently. Then took another sip of water. Already foreseeing the conversation slipping where she hadn't wanted it to go. Not yet. Not before she talked to her cowboy alone. "It has all my stuff in it."

"You could keep your stuff here." Gemma watched her from her seat beside her sister. Hope lifted her words an octave. "Then you could stay too."

Elsie set her spoon down and kept her gaze on her nieces. "I've got a job and people waiting for me in the city."

Autumn rubbed her nose and frowned. "But we'll be waiting for you here."

"So, you have to come right back," Gemma declared then nodded as if it was all settled.

But nothing was settled. Elsie chanced a glance at Ryan. He sat across from the girls and next to Elsie's brother. He leaned back in his chair as if he'd extended his long legs out under the table. His posture was casual. His fingers tapped a silent beat on the armrest. He never looked her way.

"How about we let Aunt Elsie get to New York and get settled," Bryce suggested then brushed his fingers lightly across Gemma's nose. "Then we can talk about when she can come back to see us."

Gemma wrinkled her nose.

Autumn straightened in her chair and grinned, the way she did when she solved a hard math problem. "How about we go with Auntie when she leaves Monday?"

There it was. That bit she'd wanted to tell Ryan. Before anyone else. She slanted her gaze toward him. He'd gone still. Even his fingers stopped tapping. *Look at me. Please.*

Bryce smoothed his hand over his mouth then smiled at his daughters. His words sympathetic. His expression affectionate. "I'm afraid Monday is a school day."

"And we can't miss school." Gemma jammed her spoon into her ice cream sundae, looking defeated.

Elsie felt a bit defeated herself. "You can come visit me," she suggested. Ryan's gaze collided with hers across the table. *You could too, cowboy.* To what end? Another goodbye. Best to leave whatever it was between them right here in town. She smiled at her nieces. "I would really like to show you the city."

Autumn perked up. "Can we, Dad?"

"Yes, we will certainly plan a trip to visit your aunt this summer," Bryce assured his daughters.

The girls returned to their ice cream bowls with more enthusiasm than before.

"You're leaving Monday." Maggie sat on the porch swing with Grant. Her husband dipped his spoon into Maggie's bowl. Maggie handed Grant her dessert to finish and frowned at Elsie. "That's so soon, Elsie. I was hoping we'd have more time to spend together."

Elsie nodded then explained, "I got a call late this afternoon from my new boss. The Heartscape Foundation lost its venue unexpectedly and my hotel agreed to host their gala. It's in less than three weeks with a guest count of over five hundred. They need my help now." Elsie paused and added, "I already have several video conferences scheduled for tomorrow and Friday."

"Elsie is calm under pressure." Bryce grinned at her. "She's exactly who they need. She'll make the gala a big success."

Elsie appreciated her brother's support.

"Then it's good timing with your aunt and mom returning from their travels tomorrow," Sam mused.

Yet it felt mostly like really bad timing. Still, it was one kiss that Ryan and she had shared. Not a promise exchanged. Not the start of something. They'd both known that. Accepted it. Elsie pushed her bread pudding bowl away and forced herself to smile. "I'm looking forward to hearing about their trip."

"We need to sit down and discuss your budget, Els." Bryce stacked the girls' empty sundae bowls into his bowl. "I've worked out several scenarios to help with your apartment search."

Yet Elsie hadn't worked out one scenario where it worked between her and her cowboy. Elsie collected Sam's and Roy's empty bowls. Caleb gathered the other dessert bowls like a trained waiter and headed toward the sliding glass door. Elsie added, "No business talk tonight, Bryce. You just got home."

"I must say it's good to be out of that hospital bed and outdoors again. Breathing fresh air." Bryce stretched his arms over his head then pressed his palm against his stomach. "But I think I ate enough for the next week."

Murmurs of agreement rolled across the table.

Caleb returned and swiped a hand over his mouth. "Elsie, if you're not going to take advantage of your brother's skills with numbers and finances, can I?"

Elsie laughed and waved toward her brother. "He's all yours."

"How about we play some cards while we chat?" Bryce ran his hand through his hair. "I seem to recall I need to win back the money from the last time we played."

"Deal me in." Caleb rubbed his hands together. "I don't want your wallet to be too heavy. It might slow down your recovery."

Bryce laughed. "Not a chance."

"Count us in too." Maggie stood then grabbed Grant's hand. "We really like beating you guys."

"Don't be counting those winnings before

you've collected 'em," Sam said then he pointed to his place mat. "Deal Roy and me in too, Bryce. We've bested all you more than once."

"Tonight won't be much different." Roy chuckled.

"Elsie," Sam said. "You in?"

Elsie looked at Ryan.

Just then Autumn skirted around the table and took hold of Ryan's hand. "Cowboy Prince, can you take us to say good-night to Midnight Rose and Sundancer?"

"We gotta give 'em good-night wishes," Gemma added. "So they have sweet dreams."

"I would love to do that." Fondness softened across Ryan's face. He stood, kept his hand in Autumn's and took hold of Gemma's. Then the trio stepped off the porch and walked away. Butter-Belle trailing after them.

And something twisted in Elsie's chest. Nothing that hurt her. Nothing she couldn't handle. She rolled her lips together then offered the table a small smile. "Just give me a minute." *To work that catch out of my chest.* She added, "I'll go inside and find those playing cards."

Elsie returned and handed the deck of cards to Caleb. She glanced at her empty chair and admitted she was too restless to sit. Too out of sorts to pay attention. Checking to see if her guests needed anything else, she offered an excuse that she wanted to check on Ryan and the girls then retreated before anyone stopped her.

She took her time walking to the stables. Wandered by the greenhouses. Checked on the seedlings. Peeked into the goat pen. Noted Smarty Marty was still out carousing somewhere on the property. The stable door swung open. She heard the girls' giggles before she saw her nieces. They rushed toward her for quick hugs, then decided to go on a hunt for Smarty Marty. Each one certain they knew where Marty was.

And like that, Elsie had what she wanted. Her cowboy alone. All she had to do was open the stable door. Step inside. Yet she hesitated. *Come on, Elsie. City girls are stronger than this.* Elsie pushed her shoulders back and walked into the stable.

The interior was dim. The sun minutes away from setting completely. She made her way toward Sundancer's stall. Ryan's quiet murmurs drew her to Midnight Rose's stall instead. She stopped and held her breath. Not wanting to interrupt the pair.

Midnight Rose's dark head was bent, resting against Ryan's shoulder. His hands rubbed her elegant neck. And Elsie captured the image in her mind. She knew when she thought of the pair, this was the moment she would always remember.

Seconds passed. Minutes. It seemed the bond between cowboy and horse only strengthened. Right before her eyes.

Midnight Rose's ear twitched. The horse's head

lifted. Ryan twisted and looked right at Elsie. Caught, Elsie stilled and offered him a small smile. "Sorry. I was checking on the girls."

Ryan nodded then gave the Arabian one more rub and more whispered words. Then he walked to the stall door.

Elsie watched him. "What did you tell her?"

The corner of his mouth twitched. His expression secretive. His gaze unreadable. "I told her that she's going to be okay."

The same words Elsie had given him last night.

He stepped out and slid the stall door closed. "I also told her I'm going to be okay too."

"You sound like you believe that?" Elsie strolled beside him toward the main door.

"I rode today. Bareback." He held the door open for her. "Just for pleasure. Nothing formal. Nothing fast."

But he'd gotten back on a horse. Elsie liked to think she had some small part in that. That maybe she left some small lasting impression on her cowboy. She smiled. "This is good news."

"I found myself inspired recently." He seemed amused. His shoulders relaxed. His words rolled out easily. "It felt right. Better than that actually. I can't remember the last time I rode for fun. For the pure joy of riding."

He was finding his way back to where he belonged. She could see the joy in his gaze and the relief in his expression. He even stood a little straighter as if he'd found that footing he'd been missing. He'd be practicing soon enough. She'd bet on it. After that, back to the circuit full-time. "I'm really glad for you, Ryan."

"Thanks." He sobered, tucked his hands into the back pockets of his jeans and moved toward the house. "So, Monday is the day then."

His steps were slow. The pace unrushed. Easy for her to keep up. "I wanted to tell you earlier. Several times."

He nodded then said, "It sounds like you're needed. They'll be lucky to have you on their team."

Enough. Enough with the polite. Enough with the courteous. Elsie turned, stepped right in front of him. Stopped him completely. Her words dropped like a challenge. "I'm not sorry we kissed this morning."

"Is that so?" He crossed his arms over his chest and rubbed his cheek.

She notched her chin higher. Like a dare. "Yes."

"That's good to know." He stepped around her and continued on toward the house.

Elsie jumped and grabbed his arm, turning him back to face her. "That's all you have to say?" That can't be all. One kiss. Nothing more. *You're leaving, Els. Of course, there isn't more. Get it together.*

"Elsie Marie." His sigh was wrapped around her name like a ribbon. His gaze trailed over her face. One corner of his mouth finally lifted but barely enough to dent his cheek. "Elsie Marie, I'm not sorry for any time I've gotten to spend with you. And I'm especially not sorry about our kiss."

Her breath escaped. The breath she hadn't realized she'd been holding. Behind her, she heard voices and laughter on the back porch. Still, she searched his gaze. For what, she wasn't certain. His words should be more than enough. Yet a tremor passed through her smile. "Then we are okay?"

"Yeah." He eased around her again. "We're okay."

CHAPTER NINETEEN

ELSIE TOLD HERSELF she was still okay four days later. Despite not a single run-in with her cowboy. Or even a fly-by sighting of the man. Even though he'd been around the farm. That she knew thanks to her family's reports.

Aunt Marlena had a lovely visit with him in the stables the morning after her return from overseas. Bryce talked hive management with him just yesterday. Gemma and Autumn fed the goats lettuce with him before school both days. And even Elsie's mom ran into him on her morning nature walk. *Two days in a row.*

Her cowboy had certainly been around. He just hadn't been around Elsie. At least not close enough for her to test out exactly how okay she was.

I'm fine. She was fine. Nothing wrong with reminding herself that a couple dozen times a day.

Besides, she'd been busy herself. Mostly on video conference calls with her new team at the ritzy hotel. Organizing the last-minute charity gala for the Heartscape Foundation and getting familiar with the other upcoming events already on the schedule. The workload would be far from light. But she was ready for the challenge. Welcomed it like always because she was fine. *I'm fine.*

Good, really. It was better not to see Ryan again anyway. This way she would leave with bruises on her heart, not broken pieces. And some day in the future, when she thought of him, she'd even feel happy. That was enough.

Elsie straightened the postcards then the bottles of honey on the display she'd created that morning when she'd set up the Sweet House of Bees booth at It's Blooming Spring. That had been hours ago. Lunch had passed and dinner was approaching and still, she manned the booth.

Her mother and aunt had floated in and out with Autumn and Gemma throughout the day. But they'd left to bring the worn-out girls home for the night. Noticing her mom and aunt both looked equally weary, Elsie had told them to stay home too. Promised them that she was perfectly fine closing up the booth herself. As it was, the crowd was thinning as the first of several live bands scheduled to play that night had taken the stage.

Elsie greeted a cheerful couple and handed the wife a honey sample. Then she spotted a familiar foursome approaching the booth and her smile widened. She waved to the Baker sisters and the older cowboy duo accompanying them.

Sam Sloan worked his way into the booth and

gave her a hearty hug. Then he leaned away, his hands still resting on her shoulders. His gaze twinkling, he asked, "You know what day it is, Elsie?"

"Saturday," Elsie said. The others piled into the booth and surrounded Sam.

"Do you know what Saturdays are good for?" Gayle asked. The lively retiree had traded her usual denim-colored overalls for a pair of poppy-red ones. Underneath she wore a cream-colored shirt with flowers embroidered down both sleeves. Her eyebrows spiked higher, revealing her matching pink-red eyeshadow.

Elsie shook her head.

"Dates." Breezy smoothed her fingers through her short hair as if fixing herself for said dates. Then she leaned forward, set her hand on the side of her mouth and whispered loudly, "And we have it on good authority that you and Ryan already have a Saturday date night scheduled."

"Well, that was just…" A silly thing with her nieces. Ryan hadn't been serious. Elsie touched her ponytail then the back of her neck. Then finally tucked her hands into the pockets of the yellow apron Aunt Marlena had made with the words: *It's a bee thing.* "Who told you about that?"

"The most reliable sources in the Doyle household," Roy chimed in then fluffed his salt-and-pepper curls. "It was Gemma and Autumn, of course. When we shared cotton candy and funnel cakes with them at lunch today."

"My nieces are wonderful, but I'm not sure they're the most reliable of sources." Elsie winced. Although they'd been correct. Tonight was Ryan's and her supposed date night.

"Don't worry about not being dressed in your fancy date clothes," Breezy assured her and linked her arm around Elsie's. "The best dates are the ones that are spur-of-the moment. Everyone acts more like themselves. More natural and genuine instead of stuffy and reserved."

"Isn't that the truth." Gayle nodded and grinned as if remembering her own spontaneous date nights.

Not that anyone would ever consider the Baker sisters standoffish or unfriendly. They were more dynamic and persuasive. And for two petite older women, decidedly determined. Like right now. Breezy guided Elsie out of the booth with a single-minded precision. That didn't break until Elsie found herself standing right in Ryan's path.

He was there. Her cowboy. She was fine. Better than that. She couldn't stop looking at him. Clean jeans. Polished boots. Pressed button-down sky blue Paisley-print shirt. Cowboy hat. *Where have you been? I missed you.* Elsie swallowed, her throat suddenly dry. *But I'm fine.*

"Well, it seems to me that your date has arrived, Elsie." Delight circled around Breezy's bright announcement before she released the bow holding Elsie's apron around her neck.

"What about the booth?" *What about my heart? The one I wasn't going to break.* Elsie caught the apron, but Breezy snatched it out of her grip.

"We've got it covered," Sam called out and appeared at Elsie's other side. "We're going to take turns manning the booth for the evening."

"That way we can sneak over and dance a quick-step or two," Breezy confided and patted Elsie's arm. "Then we'll come back and let the others have a turn on the dance floor too."

"But you two take all the turns around the dance floor that you like." Gayle spread her arms and completed an intricate series of dance steps weaving between Ryan and Elsie. Then the spry retiree grinned wide at Elsie. "I've found the dance floor is one of the best places to get swept off your feet."

But Elsie didn't want to be swept off her feet. She wanted her feet on the ground. Firmly. And solidly. She watched Ryan. Surely, he wasn't interested in a date. With her. Where could that lead?

"A commitment is a commitment," Sam said with pride and determination. "You gave your word to take Elsie on a Saturday night date, Ryan. Gran Claire would be sorely disappointed if you broke your word. Same as I will be."

Ryan held out his hand toward Elsie, his smile compassionate. "I really don't think they're going to let this alone."

Elsie dropped her hand in his. And, too late, discovered her error. Their hands fit. In just that right way. No readjusting. No awkward finger maneuvering. Just a simple slide and joining as if their fingers were always meant to link. Just that way. The way she'd always been searching for. *Let go.*

Ryan's grip tightened as if he felt it too. And Elsie allowed him to lead her away. Her hand in his. As if she never meant to let go.

"Are you hungry?" he asked, breaking the silence between them. "We can eat. Or dance if you want."

"Dance," she said. Then there would be no words. Nothing revealed she might later regret. Nothing said she would want to take back.

He nodded and guided her out onto the dance floor. The music was upbeat. The steps quick. He danced as well as his brother Caleb. Partnered her like no one ever had. And Elsie escaped into the moment. Twirling. Laughing. Matching him step for step. Beat for beat.

Then the music slowed.

He didn't release her. Simply brought her into his embrace and said, "Elsie."

"Let's not." She reached up, touched his cheek. "Can we just dance?" *Can you hold me? Just for now. Then I can pretend you'll be holding on to me forever.*

He pulled her in closer. Close enough she tucked her cheek against his chest. Close enough she felt the beat of his heart. And pretended her own wasn't breaking.

Pretended she really was fine after all.

CHAPTER TWENTY

TAILLIGHTS. THAT WAS the last Ryan thought he'd see of Elsie.

They had danced until the last set the evening before. Then they'd closed up the festival booth together with his uncle and grandfather. Afterward, he'd walked Elsie to her car. Then he'd waited in the parking lot, watching her taillights disappear down the road. The last he'd heard from her had been a text, letting him know she'd arrived home safely. His reply: a thumbs-up emoji.

And that was where it was supposed to end with Elsie Marie Parks. A thumbs-up emoji. Proof they were okay. Just like he'd told her they were the other night at the stables.

They'd both known there couldn't ever be more between them. One kiss. One moment. One goodbye. And they were both okay.

Or so he'd assumed.

Never would he have imagined that his girl from the city would be the one to get him back in the saddle and riding no-holds-barred into the night.

But he was in the Sloan stables at that very moment, saddling his mustang, Mischief. Trying not to panic. Trying not to worry. Trying not to let his fear override every bit of common sense. *I'm okay. She's okay. They're okay. Repeat.*

"We're going to find them." That from his younger brother. Caleb worked quickly and efficiently to saddle Whiskey Moon in the neighboring stall.

Ryan forced himself to slow down. No sense rushing only to find himself sliding out of the saddle later when he galloped across Sloan land. And he would be galloping. And not slowing until he found Elsie and her nieces.

Less than fifteen minutes ago, Bryce had called Ryan. Worry and desperation thick in his voice. Elsie had taken the girls out on one last UTV ride around the property after dinner, but the trio hadn't returned. It was now more than an hour past sunset. More than four hours since they'd left the house. And the night was settling in faster and deeper.

Carter and Grandpa Sam had already jumped into a UTV and left. Grant and Maggie were en route from their house to the Doyle property. While Uncle Roy stayed behind with a concerned and very pregnant Tess. Ryan and Caleb had determined they could cover more ground on horseback.

There had been nothing to consider. Nothing

to hesitate about. Ryan had to get to Elsie. Had to know she was safe. Unharmed. He had to hold her. Check her over for himself. And that meant getting in the saddle and riding harder than he ever had before.

Ryan led Mischief out of the stable, mounted and curved his fingers around the reins. Steady. Focus. *Please be okay.*

He reined in his worry. His fear for her and the girls. It was time to ride. Just ride.

With that, Ryan urged Mischief into a run with the barest pressure of his knees and settled into the saddle. Rode with one purpose: Elsie. Caleb rode beside him, his palomino quarter horse keeping pace. At the property line dividing Sloan and Doyle land, the brothers slowed, nodded to each other and rode in separate directions as they'd agreed on earlier. With the plan to send up a flare when one of them located Elsie and the girls.

And the search began.

WHAT HAD SHE been thinking? That she'd driven a tractor. Plowed a field. And that suddenly qualified her for UTV exploration on open land she wasn't the least bit familiar with? *You're a fool, Elsie.* And a lost one at that. Not exactly the memory she'd wanted to leave her nieces with. *Hey, it's Auntie Elsie. The one who got you lost in the woods that night with no supplies. That was fun, right?*

Elsie grimaced and dug through the toolbox

in the bed of the stalled UTV. Roy Sloan hadn't been wrong at the mud pit last week. The toolbox was woefully understocked. She dropped into the driver's seat and looked at her nieces. "Well, we've got a flashlight and a tire jack."

Autumn propped her feet on the front passenger seat and wrapped her arms around her raised knees. "But we don't have a flat tire."

Good thing that. There wasn't a spare tire anywhere. She passed the flashlight to Gemma in the back seat and said, "You're in charge of our light, Gemma." And hoped being in control would keep her niece's fear from getting the best of her.

Gemma straightened and her shoulders went back. Her face relaxed as her distress receded. Relief eased through Elsie.

"Auntie," Autumn said, her voice low as if she didn't want to disturb the night. "How lost are we?"

"Not so lost they won't find us." Elsie stretched as much optimism through her words as she could muster. But the truth was she couldn't exactly tell how lost they were.

They'd been headed to the waterwheel barn. But a wrong turn put them on the opposite side of the stream. After the mud pit fiasco, Elsie was leery about driving into the water to cross it. So, they had searched for a bridge. Never found one and instead ended up losing sight of the stream when the woods swallowed them. Then the UTV died. Just stopped running. No warning. No heads-up.

Her phone battery had less than ten percent left and worse, no signal. Now Elsie wasn't sure what to do next. Or which way was home. *Can't read your way out of this one, Els.*

"But Dad can't find us." Gemma leaned between the two front seats. "Dad can't walk or ride a horse."

"And Grandma's eyes are bad in the dark. That's what she always tells us," Autumn added then flung her arm out. "And Aunt Marlena's arches hurt from walking all over Egypt and back."

Panic washed out any lightness Elsie might've found in Autumn's pitiful declarations. Worse, Autumn wasn't wrong. It wasn't the strongest of search teams for certain. Still Elsie held out hope. It was all she had. Her nieces were too precious. "They'll get help."

"Cowboy Prince," Gemma declared and lifted the flashlight like a baton. "He'll come get us. Right, Auntie?"

If ever she needed her cowboy, it was now.

"What if he doesn't see us?" Autumn hunkered down in her seat. "It's getting awful dark out here."

I see you. I've always seen you, Elsie. That's what Ryan had claimed. Well, Elsie was starting to see now too. Even more clearly. That she didn't belong here. How many people did she have to put in danger to realize that? First Sam and Roy at the mud pit. Now her nieces. If she'd had any doubts—any second thoughts—about leaving last night, those were gone now.

After all, she hadn't required one cowboy rescue in all her years living in the city. Out here in the country, she couldn't claim the same. She reached over and took Autumn's hand in hers. "We are going to be fine."

"Because we are together." Gemma hopped out of the UTV and squeezed into the seat with her older sister. "Dad always tells us that we're stronger together."

Yet Elsie wasn't feeling quite so strong right now. She was worried she was something she'd never wanted to be—an inconvenience. Because of her, people were most likely out in the woods when they should be at home, safe with their families. One more reason she was better off alone. Even if she'd forgotten that this past week.

"I hope Cowboy Prince hurries." Autumn hugged Gemma. "We didn't get to tell Sundancer and Midnight Rose good-night. I hope they are okay."

Okay. That was how Elsie had ended the previous night with her cowboy. Ryan had hugged her outside her car last evening. Then he'd framed her face in his hands. His touch impossibly gentle. Impossibly tender. While she'd held on to him, finding it almost impossible to let go.

When their gazes had connected, he had said simply, "Okay."

And Elsie had swallowed everything she didn't want to say, like *Goodbye.* Everything she couldn't say, like *Come with me*. She'd nodded and managed a heartfelt "Okay" in return.

Then she'd climbed into her car, driven away and refused to look back. With her heart bruised, not in pieces. Small victory there.

Now she needed Ryan again. Elsie pressed her palm against that ache in her chest and concentrated on her nieces. "You know what? I think we should sing."

"We don't have any music." Autumn frowned.

"That's okay." Elsie tapped a beat on her leg. "I'm thinking if someone can't see us, then they might hear us." And if they were all belting out the words to their favorite songs, there would be no space for the worry.

"Cowboy Prince has good ears," Gemma confessed. "He heard me sneaking my broccoli to Butter-Belle at dinner one time."

There were a lot of things her cowboy hadn't heard from Elsie. But what good would sharing her feelings do if she wasn't sticking around? Or worse, what if she walked away from her career, left her life behind and instead bet it all on love? What happened when he realized she wasn't the life he wanted? When he gave up her love and her. After she'd lost her whole heart to him. Who would she be then?

Thanks, but no thanks. Not a risk she could take. That was a heartbreak she just might not get over. Besides, she hardly had a track record for success when it came to love. No, she was better off betting it all on her career and life in New York, not on love and her cowboy.

"Still, we should sing super loud," Autumn decided. "Just in case Cowboy Prince is far away."

How far away would be far enough for the pain in her chest to dull? Elsie looked at her nieces. "What song do we all know?"

"'Happy birthday,'" Gemma shouted.

"Good one." Elsie launched them into the birthday song. Followed by "The ABC Song," half a dozen nursery rhymes.

Until Autumn found her inspiration. "Christmas songs. We all know those."

"Those are my favorite." Gemma swayed in the passenger seat with her sister.

And they were off. Decking the halls. Rockin' round the Christmas tree. And dashing through the snow.

Elsie lifted her voice above her worry. And hoped for one last cowboy rescue.

CHAPTER TWENTY-ONE

ALMOST AN HOUR into the search, Elsie and the girls still hadn't been located.

The wheelhouse had turned up empty. Not even a sign they'd been there. Ryan had been convinced that was where Elsie would've gone.

He slowed Mischief. Searched the night sky for the green laser rescue flares that his family carried. Nothing. He checked his cell phone. No signal. He angled his flashlight toward the ground. Scanning for tracks—for anything really.

That was when he heard it. The first chorus of "Jingle Bells." He knew those off-key voices. Relief flooded him. He might have dropped to his knees if he wasn't seated atop Mischief. As it was, he dropped forward and hugged the reliable, loyal mustang. Then he stilled and listened. Got his bearings and followed the direction of the carolers. It was the sweetest off pitch rendition he'd ever heard.

When he was close enough to see the parked UTV and the shadowy figures huddled inside, he joined in with the carolers. Dismounted, continued his approach and his harmonizing.

It only took the first line of the chorus. Four words. Then silence from the UTV. Then a mad scramble. A shout for Cowboy Prince. Pounding footsteps. Two small figures careening into him. And he held his ground, waiting for the third.

Elsie never hesitated. Stepped straight into his arms. Buried her face against his chest then shuddered. Full body and powerful. So much so he tremored in turn. Then he pulled the trio even closer. Tethered them all together within his embrace. Grounded himself.

They're okay. They're okay. They're okay.

It was several minutes and several deep breaths all around before anyone spoke. Then they surrounded him in a half circle and talked all at once. As if getting the story out faster got rid of all their pent-up fear.

A drive. Sunset. Wrong turn. Another wrong turn. The stream. Too deep. No gas. Stalled. Lost. No signal. Flashlight. Tire thing. Together. Strong. And singing. Finally, Gemma cheered and exclaimed, "Then you found us, Cowboy Prince!"

Ryan decided to leave the retelling at that for now. He'd get the details filled in later. "And I'm glad I found you. How about we tell the others?"

"Others?" Elsie asked, worry skimmed across her pale face.

"Everyone is looking for you," he replied. "You have a lot of people who care about you guys."

"I caused a lot of trouble for everyone." Elsie

rubbed her forehead. She looked weary and miserable.

And much too far away. Before Ryan could pull Elsie back into his arms and reassure her, Autumn captured his hand and tugged.

Distress filling her face, Autumn said, "The phone doesn't work out here, Cowboy Prince."

"We don't need a phone. I have something better." Ryan lifted Autumn into his arms and squeezed her gently. "Want to see?" At her nod, Ryan walked over to Mischief and opened the saddlebag. He took out two handheld laser flares and gave one to Autumn. "We're going to shine these green beams into the sky. And then they will use the light to locate us. Watch."

Gemma and Autumn both finally grinned, equally fascinated by the green laser beams extending toward the stars. Ryan positioned the flares on the UTV and patiently answered their questions about how the lasers worked. Then he gathered the trio back into the UTV. Gemma ran first to sit with him. Autumn sat with Elsie in the passenger seat. And Ryan skimmed his gaze over each one. Told himself again that they were all okay. It was all he needed. It was enough. For now.

"What should we do while we wait?" He flipped on the UTV headlights. One more signal for his family.

Gemma pointed at the sky. "We can wish on falling stars."

"We have to watch the stars, Gem." Autumn yawned loudly. "We can't look away or we might miss it."

"I'm watching." Gemma yawned too then burrowed into Ryan, flattening his shirt until it was comfortable under her cheek. Settled against him, she mused, "Auntie, you should watch for a shooting star too. Then you can wish to stay with us forever."

Elsie looked at Ryan. Her eyes shimmered from the tears pooled there. But her will was strong enough not to allow the escape of a single one.

And just then Ryan was certain Elsie would not be making that wish. Not tonight. Still, he reached over and linked his fingers with Elsie's. As if all he had to do was hold on tight enough.

Elsie didn't pull away. She kept her hand in his and buried her head in Autumn's hair.

Her skin was cold inside his. Her grip steady, if not distant. And Ryan knew. Knew to his already chilled core. This goodbye was going to hurt. He ached already.

His family arrived before a shooting star was spotted. Before wishes could be made. That was fitting. Ryan's heart wanted one wish. His head recognized the folly. Good thing, he'd never been a fool for love.

He loaded a sleepy Gemma, then an exhausted Autumn into the back of his family's UTV. Then covered the pair with the blankets Tess had tossed in back at their house. Carter and Sam left with the girls, eager to get them to their anxious dad. Meanwhile, Caleb refilled the gas tank on the stalled UTV and checked it over.

Minutes later, Caleb dropped the empty gas can into the UTV bed. His gaze passed from Ryan to Elsie and back, then he said, "The UTV is good to go. Started right up. I can take Mischief with me, and you can drive Elsie back to her place."

Elsie turned toward Ryan. Her gaze unreadable and her expression reserved. "Ryan, could we..."

No. Don't ask me. Please. He held his breath. Held her gaze. Willed her not to ask. Anything but that.

"Could we ride Mischief?" Her words were faint, but all too clear in the crisp evening air. "Could we take that ride together? I'm not ready..."

Her words fell away. He wasn't ready. Not to hold her in his arms one last time. Not to say goodbye again. He was already sinking. Already knew where this was leading. It was there in everything she wasn't saying. Ryan glanced at his brother, seeking a save.

But Caleb shook his head slightly then eased back and offered, "We can get the UTV tomorrow. No one is going to bother it out here tonight."

Tears pooled in her eyes again. Her whisper was as fragile as she looked. "Then we can ride together."

Together. All he wanted. All he couldn't have.

Ryan squeezed his eyes closed briefly, then nodded. "Caleb, you take the lead."

His brother looked all too relieved. Caleb was in his saddle and walking toward the trail before Ryan guided Elsie onto Mischief. Ryan swung up behind Elsie. Wound his arms around her, took the reins and urged Mischief forward.

"Thanks for coming for us." Elsie's soft words broke the silence.

I will always come for you whenever you need me. "I'm glad everyone is..." *Okay.* He lost his voice. Cleared his throat then managed, "I'm just glad everyone is safe."

"And you're back in the saddle." She shifted and glanced over her shoulder at him. Concern was there in her face and words. "How does it feel?"

But he didn't want her to worry about him. He wanted her to... He pressed mute on that thought and gathered her closer. Then he whispered in her ear, "It feels like home." *You feel like home.*

She kept her head pressed against his. Her words were just above a murmur. "Then perhaps I wasn't too much of an inconvenience after all."

"You were never that." *Not to me.*

She settled back against him as if she no longer wanted to resist. He did the only thing he could. Tucked her fully against his chest. Held her as close as he could. And wondered how exactly he was supposed to let her go.

This was why he always left his emotions alone.

This was everything he hadn't ever wanted to feel. He willed his heart to remain detached. Put his feelings on lockdown. Then maybe the fallout wouldn't be more than he could handle. Then perhaps he would be okay.

TOO SOON, the lights at her family's house flickered through the trees. Too soon, they'd walked the horses into the driveway. Too soon, Caleb dismounted, led the horses away and left Elsie alone with Ryan on the front porch.

And it was too late. Too late for Elsie to ask Ryan to keep on riding. To nowhere. To anywhere. *Just take me with you.*

Elsie lingered under the dim porch light in front of the double doors.

Ryan held back near the top stair. His fingers curved around the handrail as if he needed an anchor. "What time are you leaving tomorrow?"

"Before sunrise." She cleared her throat. Twisted her hands together in front of her, keeping herself from reaching for him and anchoring them together. "I'm hoping to make it to St. Louis. I made a hotel reservation for the night there."

"Sounds like you have it all planned out then." He stepped down to the next stair, farther away from her.

Elsie clenched her hands tighter. Looked away. They'd both known she was leaving. They'd both known this was all they'd have. But her heart hadn't listened. Now she hurt. And she had only herself to blame. "You know I can't stay."

He stilled. His fingers tightened on the rail. Then he countered, "Can't or won't?"

"Both," she said and leaned into the facts. The logic that would smother the splintering of her heart. "I don't fit in here any more than you fit in the city."

"You don't know that." He lifted his gaze toward the sky as if searching for a star to wish on. Perhaps to wish that things were different between them.

But they were beyond wishes. Beyond whispers inside hearts. *Stick to the facts. Now isn't the time to follow your heart.* She watched him. "If I asked you to leave all this behind, I'd be asking you to leave a part of yourself behind too. I won't—I can't—do that."

A muscle tensed along his jawline. His lips pressed together. He offered no argument. No denial. He knew the same truths.

Time for more. Time to face what they had known along. She lifted her chin, ignored that ache in her chest, like the first crack in her heart. "And I don't belong here." *Even if in your arms everything felt right. As if for the first time, I found where I belonged.*

"Are you making that determination because of tonight?" He paused and studied her. "Even experienced trail guides get lost. It happens. It's not a good reason to leave."

But you haven't given me a reason to stay. "I should've known to check the gas tank. To pack better supplies. I should've been more prepared. I know better." *I knew better than to fall for you. But I fell anyway.*

"You will be next time," he offered.

There would be no next time. It was time to walk away. When all she was leaving behind was a piece of her heart. A sliver. Surely, she wouldn't miss that. Surely, she would recover. "I'm better in the city. It's where I belong. Same as you belong on the circuit."

"Seems like you have it all figured out for the both of us." He remained still. Contained. Out of her reach.

Where she wanted him. Why was she hurting so much? She pressed her palm against her chest. "How many cowboy rescues do you have to make before you admit I'm right?"

"That's just an excuse." He shook his head and wiped the back of his hand over his mouth. But his frown remained. "You're just scared to stay here and take a real risk."

He meant her heart. He wanted her to risk it all. For him. But she wasn't falling alone. He would have to risk it all too. *Give me your heart, cowboy.* She charged, "What about you, cowboy? You're scared too."

He brushed his fingers over his bottom lip. "Is that so?"

"Yeah." She never backed down. Hearts were on the line. Hers. His. She said, "You're scared to commit to something outside the arena."

His gaze widened and flared.

Her words had hit their mark. Little satisfaction there. No victory.

"What do you want, Elsie? Do you want me to ask you to stay?" He moved back up the stairs toward her. "Fine. Elsie, stay here. Stay. Don't go to New York. Is that what you want me to tell you?"

No. Don't do it. Don't open your heart, Els. Turn around. Walk away. But she was already charging down that path, following her heart. At warp speed. "I want you to tell me that you love me."

"Love you." He scrubbed his palms over his face. Then settled his gaze on her. Steady. Direct. Unflinching. "I've always loved you, Elsie Marie."

No. Not like this. His words challenged. His confession was filled with impatience. More like a warning than an ardent declaration.

If he loved her then she would be soaring through the sky. Touching the stars. Never wanting to come down. Not falling. Not tumbling without a net, without someone to catch her. Completely alone.

No, this couldn't be love. It was heartfelt. But in all the worst possible ways. It hurt too much. She hurt too much.

"I love you, Elsie, but I can't ask you to stay." His words were resigned and composed. Same as he was. "Because this place isn't what you want. It's never been what you wanted."

That ache expanded inside her. Her throat tightened.

He gave her no reprieve. "All I've ever wanted for you, Elsie, is to be happy." He retreated. Back down the stairs. Away from her. "So, go, Elsie. Head to that big city and be happy. Not for anyone but yourself."

"Don't do that." *Don't shut me out. Ask me to love you. Let me love you.* She swept that scratch from her words. "What about you?"

"Don't worry about me." A ghost of a smile filtered across his face. There and gone. "I've got my horses and rodeo. What more could a cowboy like me need?"

Love. My love. She crossed her arms over her chest and refused to sway. Then she searched his face for more than indifference. A dent in his composure. Saw something there in his narrowed gaze. A faint flicker that gave him away. "It's not love that scares you, is it?"

"I already told you how I feel about you." He met her stare. Again, so steady. So very stoic.

But his words were cavalier. Almost careless. And so not freeing. For either of them. They felt more like a trap. Like a weight on her chest. He loved her, but who cared? He looked far from moved by his declaration. Far from love struck. Far from enchanted. He loved her but it wasn't enough. Not for her. And her own heart broke a little bit more.

"You love me." She shrugged. Three easy words. Simple to toss out there. Like flower seeds in a field. "But you're scared to commit to something outside the arena." *Or someone.* And what was his love if she didn't have her cowboy too? Same as that flower seed without water. Nothing special.

"I've got a career I'm dedicated to." He swiped his hat off, tapped it against his leg. "Obligations. People counting on me. Same as you."

"You're allowed to be happy outside of the arena too. That doesn't make you any less of a cowboy," she said. "You can be more than a bronc rider. It's not all or nothing."

"You're happy outside the city too," he countered.

But for how long? She wasn't happy now. Far from it. "But this was always temporary."

"It doesn't have to be." His cowboy hat rested against his leg. His words as always were earnest and for a moment he wasn't quite so withdrawn. "You could choose to stay."

"What if I stayed? Gave up everything." *For you. Would you give me everything in return?* She wanted his love and more. She wanted him to stand by her. Never give her up. No matter what. And she wanted to love him the same. *All or nothing, cowboy.* She continued, "And when you decide I'm not the life you want? What will I have then?"

"I can't promise, but I can…" he started.

"You're right. You can't promise." She stopped him and shook her head. She couldn't take the risk. No matter how much her heart begged her to. No matter how much she ached now. "And I don't trust love. I won't. Not enough for both of us."

"Then we know where we stand." He smashed his cowboy hat on his head.

Apart. Alone. Like they both preferred. Like they both wanted. She ached all over. The pain pressed on her. Love wanted to lay her low. But still she fought it. She swallowed her tears and held herself together. "City streets never were good for horses or cowboys."

His eyebrows flexed. Up. Down. He nodded slowly as if absorbing her words. Then he was back to impassive. Back to contained. Unreachable. "Then I guess there really isn't anything left to say, is there?"

"Only goodbye, cowboy." She barely kept herself from choking on her words.

He stiffened and considered her. She met his stare. Clamped her jaw together to stop the tremor. Still the quiver in her chin. He had her heart. He would not get her tears too.

Finally, he touched the brim of his hat and said, "Goodbye, Elsie."

Then he turned and left. Simple as that. As if

there was nothing to it. And nothing more he cared to say. Simple as that, he let her go.

Yet Elsie stood there. On that porch. Under that dim light.

Watched her cowboy walk away. And held her chin high.

Watched her cowboy mount his horse. And kept herself standing tall.

Watched her cowboy ride away and never look back.

Not her cowboy. Not anymore. Just a cowboy.

And still she stood there. Waited for the last piece of her heart to fall. Right there on that front porch. Where she intended to leave it. No good could come from dragging it with her.

She'd known better than to follow her heart. Known better than to believe in love.

Finally, she went inside. Climbed up the stairs and collapsed face-first on her bed. And cried. Long and hard and from the deepest parts of her.

She cried for the scare she'd caused her nieces that night. For the family she was leaving in the morning. For the friends she would miss. For the goats she'd come to adore. And the horses too.

Her tears kept falling. And she kept finding reasons for each one. Because girls from the city knew better than to cry over cowboys. Especially cowboys who loved with limits.

CHAPTER TWENTY-TWO

EIGHTY-FOUR. RYAN NEEDED to score eighty-four to win the saddle bronc event at Rodeo Rides for A Cause.

It was time to do just that. Win.

Ryan exhaled. Beneath his legs, Midnight Star Catcher shifted. The black-and-white paint was more than anxious to leave the chute. More than eager to make Ryan work for every single one of those points. More than willing to buck Ryan right out of the standings.

Ryan relaxed in the saddle. Let everything around him fall away. The sold-out crowd in the Belleridge arena. The noise. His own thoughts.

He had eight seconds. Just him and a horse. No more time to think. Only react. One jump. Then the next. Eight seconds to forget. To ride in the moment. Adrenaline sparked along his nerves. Welcome and addicting. It was all he ever wanted to feel.

Ryan adjusted his grip around the thick braided rein. Lifted his head. Gave the okay.

The gate opened.

Midnight Star Catcher launched out of the chute.

Jumped high. Kicked fast. Bucked harder. His cowboy hat hit the dirt. Another midair kick. Ryan held on. Found his center. Found his rhythm. Kept his seat. One powerful horse. One determined cowboy. A clash of wills that somehow synchronized. Against all odds.

Eight seconds. And it was finished.

Ryan accepted an assist from his brother Caleb. One of two pickup riders in the arena. His boots landed in the dirt. And his score flashed on the screen. Eighty-five.

Cheers erupted around the arena. A win for the hometown cowboy. He caught his breath. Felt that adrenaline recede. Struggled to hold on to it. Just a few more seconds. It'd been a reprieve. But it was over. Ryan swiped his cowboy hat from the ground, waved to the excited crowd and headed out of the competition area.

His family surrounded him. Laughter. More cheers. Congratulations. Ryan soaked in every word. Clung to each heartfelt job well done. Yet a part of him felt eerily hollow inside. More hugs. More embraces. A kiss on the cheek from Breezy. Then Gayle Baker. But the void remained. Firm handshakes. Squeezes on the shoulder. Nothing filled him completely.

But he had won. Doing what he loved. What he'd always loved. For the people he loved. The horses he loved. That was supposed to be enough. More than enough.

Ryan smiled wider. Accepted more congratulations. Convinced himself it was just the aftereffects of an adrenaline rush. That he would get to his true happy soon enough. Surely after the team roping event.

An hour later, Ryan checked the saddle on Tango one last time and mounted the muscular horse. The gelding belonged to Maggie's older sister and former team roping partner and had helped the sisters become a top women's roping team. Now Ryan was counting on the talented quarter horse to help him win again.

"It's you and me, cowboy." Maggie mounted Lady Dasher and eyed Ryan. Her smile bright. "Don't forget what I taught you this past week. I won't be satisfied with second. We're here to win."

"Got it." Ryan guided the horse into the header roping box. Exhaled. Steadied himself in the saddle.

Maggie moved into the second box on the other side of the chute holding the steer.

One more ride. One more chance to win. Only this time with Maggie—his family and his friend. What could be better?

Less than ten seconds later, Ryan and Maggie clocked the fastest time. Ryan had another first-place finish. Another win. But that happy place seemed even further out of reach. Good thing Ryan was a master at masking his true feelings. Same as he had for the past week.

Once again, he smiled through the cheers from the crowd. The congratulations from friends and peers. The hugs and pats on the back from his family.

He was back. At the top of his riding game again. That was something to celebrate. He supposed he had Elsie to thank for that. It seemed a broken heart saved his career.

Ever since he'd walked away from Elsie that night, he had doubled down on just about everything else in his life. From practicing for the rodeo to repairing the old wheelhouse barn to working with the horses at the sanctuary. Even clearing land for the new stable barn and seeding the dandelion pasture. He'd stayed later. Pushed harder. Right into exhaustion. Whatever it took to numb the pain of losing Elsie.

And he'd discovered two important things:

Physical pain had nothing on heartache.

And Elsie was wrong. It was all or nothing.

He had to give his all to keep from feeling like he had nothing without Elsie.

But she was back in the city where she wanted to be. He would soon be back on the road to the next rodeo. Everything was as it should be. As it'd always been. Soon enough his heart would fall back in line too. All he had to do was wait it out. Good thing he was a patient man.

"We missed you in the hospitality tent tonight." Maggie leaned against the stall door in the stables at the Belleridge arena. "It was quite the celebration in there."

"I was getting Tango and Lady Dasher ready for their victory ride home." Ryan ran his hand over Tango's sleek neck and avoided looking at Maggie. The problem with having a best friend turned sister-in-law was that she saw too much and wasn't afraid to call him on it. But he wasn't ready to talk. Same as he hadn't been ready all week. And might not ever be.

"Grant is pulling the truck and trailer around now," Maggie offered.

Ryan nodded then kept his words light and up-beat, and the conversation away from himself. "I'm thinking I should take up roping too, Mags. We could tear it up on the circuit together."

"I might take you up on that." Maggie slid the stall door open for him. "But for now, I'm afraid I need to give you a nine-month rain check on your offer."

Nine months. Ryan paused and glanced at his sister-in-law. Her eyes sparkled. Her smile was looking hard to contain. Ryan said, "Mags, are you pregnant?"

"Yes." Maggie tossed herself into his arms. Her joy overflowed into her words and her expression. "I'm pregnant. Grant and I are having a baby. A baby," she marveled, then pressed her palms against her mouth and caught her squeal inside her hands. She rushed on, "But you can't tell anyone, Ryan."

"Wait." Ryan's own grin spread wide. Watching Maggie, he was starting to feel a sense of that happiness himself. He decided to hold on to it a bit longer. He said, "I'm the first one to know?"

Maggie nodded and bit her bottom lip. But her bright smile couldn't be contained. A pregnant Maggie took happiness to a whole other level. "Grant and I are going to tell everyone tomorrow night at the house party to celebrate the rodeo."

"But I know first," Ryan clarified. "Before my entire family."

Maggie's eyebrows pulled together. She pushed on his shoulder playfully. "Don't make me regret telling you."

Too late for that. Ryan waggled his eyebrows at her. "You know what this means, right, Mags?"

Maggie set her hands on her hips and eyed him.

"It means I'm the favorite uncle of course." Ryan spread his arms wide then patted his palm against his chest.

"The baby isn't even here." Maggie shook her head. But there was amusement in her words. "You can't claim favorite uncle status yet."

"I just did." Ryan stepped beside Maggie and dropped his arm around her shoulders. "It's fate, Mags. If favorite uncle was meant to be Caleb or Carter or Josh, you would've told them first."

Maggie jabbed her elbow into his ribs. "I'm beginning to wonder why I told you."

He squeezed her tighter. "Because I'm your favorite too."

"What about Grant?" she countered. "My husband."

"Well, besides Grant," Ryan qualified. Then he gave her a quick side hug and said, "Seriously, Mags, I'm thrilled for you and my brother."

"I'm kind of thrilled myself." She lifted her hands and pressed her fingers against her cheeks. "And, I admit, I'm a little bit terrified too. I'm going to be a mom, Ryan."

"One of the best ones out there," he said, believing it and wanting to assure her of it too. "And you'll have lots of help from us."

"Speaking of letting family help," Maggie started then glanced up at him. There was concern in her gaze, understanding in her words. "We're here for you too. I'm here for you, Ryan."

"I know." Ryan dropped his arm and stuffed his hands into his back pockets. "I'm good though, Mags."

"You're not, despite how many times you say it." She stopped and faced him. "We can all see it. You're in pain, Ryan. You can't keep pushing yourself like this. This pace you've set. It's not sustainable."

But it had to be. All he had to do was outlast his heartbreak. He rubbed his chest then grinned at Maggie. "Look at you, Mags. You're already acting like a mom. I knew you were going to be good at it."

Maggie frowned at him. "I'm serious, Ryan."

So was he. Being a cowboy on the rodeo was all he knew. Now all he had. He had to make it count. Had to make walking away from the best person in his life count. "I just won twice this weekend. First place, Mags. That means something must be working right."

"But you're not happy," Maggie stressed.

"Of course, I am," he declared, perhaps with a little too much intensity if Maggie's raised eyebrows were any indication. Still, he kept on rolling with it and added, "The sanctuary is getting that new stable. Fully funded. Five more retired rodeo horses will have their forever home. That's fulfilling. That's everything to me."

"But that's not everything, Ryan." She stepped closer to him and set her palm over his heart. "You're not happy in here. That matters."

But Elsie and Ryan had gotten exactly what they wanted. That was something to be happy about, even if his heart hurt a little. But it was nothing he couldn't manage. On his own, like he always had. "I'm alright, Mags."

Maggie studied him then shook her head. "I hope my child isn't as stubborn as you Sloans."

"Good luck with that." Ryan laughed. "Grant's middle name should've been stubborn."

Maggie chuckled.

"Speaking of names, you do know Ryan works for both a boy and girl name, don't you?" Ryan started walking again. "It also makes for a strong middle name. Like for instance Samuel Ryan Sloan or James Ryan Sloan. Or Olivia Ryan Sloan or even Elizabeth Ryan Sloan."

"Those actually aren't bad suggestions." Maggie walked beside him.

"I know, right?" Ryan grinned at her some more. "Leave it to Uncle Ryan. I've got a barrel full of suggestions."

"Why do you have all these name ideas?" Maggie slanted her gaze toward him and frowned. "You already pitched these names to Tess and Carter for their twins."

"Can you blame me? They are good solid names," he countered. "I need to hedge my bets. Have a namesake niece or nephew. Now I've got three chances to get my name in the conversation."

"Or you could keep these names and use them for your own kids," she suggested quietly.

Ryan barely had time to dodge that hit. It struck right inside his chest where his heart used to be and knocked him slightly off-balance. He managed, "I'm proud to be a favorite uncle, Mags. That's enough for me." He spotted Grant climbing out of their truck with the horse trailer attached. Saved. And just in time. He jogged over to greet his brother and said, "Well, if it isn't the dad-to-be."

Grant hugged Ryan then wrapped an arm around Maggie and tucked her in close. Grant said, "You told him."

"Of course, Maggie told me," Ryan said. "And now I know I really am your favorite brother."

Grant frowned at Maggie. "He's not going to let this go."

"And to think I know a full twenty-four hours before the rest of the family." Ryan wedged himself between the pair and linked their arms with his. "Come on, you two parents-to-be. We can discuss baby names while we load up the horses."

And Ryan could keep pretending he really was alright.

ONE WEEK AFTER she left Three Springs, Elsie spent her Sunday night ironing. For the second night in a row. Last night, she'd spent her Saturday evening with takeout from the nearby Thai restaurant and a stack of work blouses. Tonight, it was takeout from the local deli and a stack of work pants. Her entire business wardrobe would soon be pressed and wrinkle-free and ready to wear. She would be all set for the many weeks ahead.

She hung a pair of navy suit pants in the closet and stubbed her toe on her farm boots. The ones she hadn't put on in over a week. There'd been no reason. The same ones she meant to pack away but hadn't yet.

Rubbing her toe, she considered the boots. When she'd been in Three Springs, she hadn't picked up an iron once. She'd cooked every meal. And loved every minute of it. Of course, she had. It was only temporary. Like a vacation. A reprieve from her normal, everyday routine. Sure, there had been stress, but it was nothing she had to take on fully. She'd only been a stand-in for the short term. What wasn't there to like about that?

Sure, life in Three Springs seemed enticing. More than a little appealing. Even now. She supposed it always would until she had to live it full-time. Then there would be stresses and burdens she couldn't begin to imagine. And that life would be less than charming.

But in Three Springs, she wouldn't be alone. Like she was now.

Elsie sighed and glanced around the clean but sparsely furnished studio apartment. The short-term rental was her temporary living quarters until she found a place she could afford. Boxes were stacked to the ceiling, filling the already cramped space. She made a mental note to follow up with the real estate agent Lilian Sloan had recommended. She needed to pick up her house hunt. Surely once she was settled into her own place, unpacked, and put her own spin on the decorating, then it would be better. Then she would start feeling like she was home.

The tape on one of Autumn's pictures Elsie had hung around the apartment came loose. The drawing of Sundancer and Midnight Rose drifted to the floor behind the couch. Elsie set her iron on standby on the ironing board and went in search of the picture. It wasn't like she didn't have others. The girls' drawings filled the walls and even stuck to the outsides of her moving boxes. Elsie picked a different drawing to stare at each night and fall asleep too. Wishing for those fun dreams Gemma claimed she'd find. And hoping she'd wake up in the morning happy.

Unfortunately, her nights were restless. She was awake more than she dreamed. And the morning sunlight only seemed to highlight her discontent. Still, she was undaunted. Her heartache might have followed her to New York. She accepted that. But surely, she didn't have to hurt all day and all night. Not because of a cowboy.

She located the picture and stuck it to the lampshade. Within sight of her pillow. Telling herself tonight she would find that good night's sleep. That cowboy would become a memory. Not someone she couldn't get over. Not someone she didn't want to get over.

The video app on her tablet lit up the screen. Elsie grinned. Just the distraction she needed. She grabbed a blanket, propped the tablet on a pillow on her lap and accepted the video chat. Her nieces' adorable faces filled the screen. Their bubbly greetings filled her heart.

Quick enough, they launched into a detailed retelling of the past two days since their last video chat on Friday evening, when the girls and Bryce had called to tell her that they'd found Smarty

Marty in her bedroom, bleating so loud he'd woken everyone up. Gemma was convinced the goat was looking for Elsie. And all Elsie wondered was if a certain cowboy was looking for her. The same way she'd been searching for him on the city streets.

The girls quickly shifted the conversation from their Midnight Rose and Sundancer update to their weekend. Elsie steeled herself and anchored her smile in place. She knew what was coming.

"We got to sit in the front row at the rodeo, Auntie," Autumn said cheerfully. "'Cause Ms. Maggie got us special seats. 'Cause she runs the rodeo. Did you know that?"

Elsie smiled and nodded. She'd been texting with Maggie and Tess on the daily since her arrival in New York. And if she was honest, she felt even closer to the two women now. She'd also been talking more with her brother. Sending him articles on beekeeping and best honey producing practices from her research in the evenings. Even more they'd been sharing with each other, getting to know each other better and Elsie liked to think becoming friends too.

"The rodeo was so fun," Gemma added, stretching out every word into multiple syllables. "Did you see Cowboy Prince win?"

Only several dozen times. Her brother had opened a video chat during the different rodeo events. Elsie had watched live for Vivian's barrel race, Ryan's saddle bronc ride and finally Maggie and Ryan's team roping. Then Bryce had emailed the video of Ryan competing to Elsie. And she couldn't stop watching him. She'd been terrified, anxious, excited and in awe. Then incredibly relieved when Ryan had gotten off the magnificent black-and-white paint without getting thrown or injured.

She'd wanted to be there. Wanted to check Ryan over herself. As it was, she'd made Maggie and Bryce and Sam assure her Ryan was in fact fine. Then she'd asked them all not to say anything to Ryan. She was just a friend concerned about another friend after all. Still, she wasn't entirely sure who she was trying to convince—them or herself. And feared that she hadn't fooled anyone, including herself.

"Guess what, Auntie? Ms. Maggie says I can rope like her one day." Gemma wiggled her way farther onto the video screen. "And I can race barrels like Ms. Vivian too. They're going to teach me how to ride fast like them. They told Dad I'm not too young to learn."

Elsie concentrated on her nieces. "I think you will be very good at whatever you decide to do, Gemma. And Ms. Maggie and Ms. Vivian will be excellent teachers." Elsie watched Autumn chewing on her bottom lip. "What about you, Autumn? Did you pick your rodeo event too?"

"Cowboy Prince took me riding with him on

Mischief last week," Autumn said and nibbled on her bottom lip a bit more. "Cowboy Prince told me that I don't have to compete in the rodeo if I don't want to. I can love horses all the same and ride them whenever I want."

A sigh swirled through Elsie at Ryan's kindness and awareness. He understood Autumn's reserve and her nature then offered her something of her own. Elsie smiled. "Cowboy Prince is right, Autumn. Horses need your love and attention and care. They'll be better for it."

Autumn smiled wide then peered into the camera lens. Her face filling the screen. "Auntie, are you sick?"

"No, I'm fine," she said. Or she would be. In time. With a decent night's sleep. One she intended to get that very evening.

Autumn scratched her nose and leaned away again. "But you're all wrapped up in that blanket."

"It's just a little chilly in my apartment," she hedged.

"That's the blanket Cowboy Prince got you," Autumn announced. Her eyes widened and her smile grew. "I remember 'cause I found the bag by the door that night after dinner. The night you and Caleb danced. Remember? That was so fun."

Elsie nodded and curled her fingers around the blanket. She remembered more than she wanted to. Remembered too much. Like dancing with Ryan. Laughing with Ryan. Kissing Ryan.

"And then we used that blanket in our princess fort when Cowboy Prince stayed over," Gemma added, seeming as thrilled to see the blanket as her sister. "It's so soft and warm and cuddly."

It was all that. And if it still smelled faintly of Cowboy Prince, well, that was for Elsie to know.

"Cowboy Prince is back from the stables." Autumn lifted her face out of the camera view. Then she leaned back in, "Gotta go, Auntie. Cowboy Prince is showing us how to make proper s'mores now."

Good-nights and air kisses exchanged. The video call disconnected. And silence filled the studio apartment in the high-rise building once more.

Elsie buried herself in the plush blanket, drawing it up around her face. Told herself she never really liked s'mores anyway. She always burned the marshmallow to something past blackened. The melted chocolate made her fingers too sticky and she ultimately had more of a mess than a delicious dessert.

No, she never much liked s'mores. But unfortunately, she still liked her cowboy. More than she should.

CHAPTER TWENTY-THREE

IT WAS MIDWEEK and Ryan hadn't slowed for the past ten days. Not since he'd accepted his belt buckle at Rodeo Rides for A Cause. He'd spent last week working at the wheelhouse barn and the sanctuary. With his demo of an old storage barn on-site and land prep done, the new stable barn build was ahead of schedule. Then he'd collected one more belt buckle that past weekend in Tulsa, Oklahoma and took second place in Dodge City, Kansas one day later.

And no matter how many miles he traveled or how well he competed or how hard he worked, that heartache stuck to him like a persistent shadow. So, he did what any sensible cowboy could. He kept moving. Kept forging ahead. Certain the pain would call it quits soon. It had to, right?

Now he was back home, touring more properties for his mother. And sticking to his Keep Busy motto. He walked through the single-story house and panned his video camera on his phone around the family room. "Just to recap. The cottage sits on just under four acres. The barn is small, but relatively new. It could house three horses and maybe a pony. No more." He turned in a slow circle. "The kitchen could hold our entire family if the weather was in our favor and the back porch could be used too for additional seating."

"Ryan." His mother's voice was crisp yet thoughtful on the speaker. "Is this house for you or me?"

Ryan stilled then flipped the phone toward himself, putting him in the camera view and allowing himself to see his mother.

"This property sounds more suited to your needs," his mother said, touched the pearl earring she always wore and tilted her head. "Are you asking my opinion?"

"Maybe," he hedged and dropped onto a stool at the island. The property was staged for a sale. There he propped the phone up against a cookbook holder. "I don't know."

"But you're looking for your own place," his mother pressed.

"I can't live with Tess and Carter forever." He linked his fingers together on the cool countertop. "They will need the bedrooms if they have more kids."

"That may be so, but let's look at this particular home you're in right now a bit closer." She lifted her fingers and tapped against them in a precise count. "First. You've already outgrown the stables there and you've yet to move in. What with Mischief, Sundancer and Midnight Rose needing stalls. I doubt you'll be able to turn down another mare or gelding in need in the future."

Ryan worked to keep his mouth closed and not gape wide-open. Still, surprise shifted through him and was hard to contain. His mother knew his horse's names. Knew also his affinity for rescuing the animals.

"Second. That house, while quaint, is just that… Quaint," his mother continued. "There's no office. Where will you go to discuss contracts with your sponsors and deal with the business of bronc riding? And what about your workout equipment? I suppose you could put it in the garage, but that's hardly ideal."

Now his mouth did drop open. Just a parting of his lips.

"Lastly there's the location." His mother shook her head slightly. Her precision-cut hair swayed across her jawline. "It's on the other side of Belleridge. Not exactly close to your brothers or grandfather."

Ryan lifted his arm and rubbed the back of his neck. It was rare he'd found himself dumbfounded. But he was. Right then. Right there. On a video chat with his mother of all people.

His mother's eyebrow twitched. One side of her mouth ticked up. "I seem to have surprised you."

"Caught me off guard," he admitted.

"Well, I like to think I know some useful things about my own sons," she added then motioned to the screen. "Now, tell me. What is it about this particular place that appeals to you?"

He wasn't exactly certain. He just knew he needed to find a place of his own. Ryan scratched his cheek. "It is priced well. Affordable."

"If it's money that is the issue—" she started.

"It's not the money," he interrupted. Not exactly.

He'd invested a portion of his rodeo earnings from his first cash payout years ago. At Bryce's direction. As he'd won more, he'd invested more, always with Bryce's wise and watchful guidance. His investments performed well—again, thanks to Bryce—and he'd had the funds to invest in Carter's distillery, then recently in Josh's equestrian rehabilitation center and Bryce's Sweet House of Bees. He'd been thrilled to help his family and friends. Yet never gave much thought to how he would fund his own future. Until now.

He ran his hands over his jeans and looked at his mother. "It's about proving I can commit to something outside the arena."

"Then you should commit to Elsie," his mother said, direct and on point as was her style. "Don't buy a house that isn't suitable just to prove a point."

Commit to Elsie. Ryan stretched his legs out. His boot tapped on the tile floor. "This isn't about Elsie."

"Isn't it?" his mother asked. "I've spent a good deal of time with Elsie the past few weeks. She's as miserable as you are."

"I'm not miserable," he argued. He just wasn't

happy. At all. Not like he'd been with Elsie. "This was supposed to be about a house."

"Things are never what they seem." His mother chuckled then considered him, her voice pensive. "You and I are not so very different."

They were also nothing alike. Ryan braced his elbows on the countertop and stared into the screen. "How is that exactly?"

"We're both considering a complete change of lifestyle," she explained then leaned toward the camera as if imparting a sage secret. "We're both terrified of what that means. And even more terrified we'll get it wrong and fail. We're comfortable doing the things we know we're good at."

He wanted to deny her claims. Tell her that she was entirely wrong. Completely mistaken. That she did not in fact know him at all. Instead, he tugged at the hair covering his cheek. Even hidden behind a thick beard, his mother saw him. Understood him. It was nothing he would have ever foreseen. "I don't intend to leave the circuit."

"But you intend to live outside of it too," she countered. "Just as I intend to live outside the operating room."

Ryan swiped his hat off and dropped it on the countertop. Nothing seemed to be fitting right. Or sounding right. He eyed his mother. "You're seriously leaving New York and your practice?"

"I believe the term is retiring," she said. A faint smile creased her lips and disappeared. "I'm still getting used to the word myself. I won't be practicing. I will be guest lecturing at the college, speaking on panels and consulting with peers when asked. But I will be retired."

"It's all you've ever done," he said. All she'd ever known. *How* she was known. Dr. Lilian Sloan, renowned heart surgeon. Same as him. He was a cowboy. Only ever known as a bronc rider.

"I've come to realize my medical career isn't my entire identity," she said. Her face softened. "I'd like to believe there is more to me than a medical degree. And it's time I find out what that is."

It's not all or nothing, Ryan. He reached for his hat, pressed it on his head. At his core he was a cowboy, but was there more to him? Elsie seemed to believe so, but did he? Suddenly restless, Ryan stood and said, "Okay, Mother, I think we should find you a home, so you at least have a place to start your new journey."

"What about you?" she asked.

"You're right," he said and reached for his phone on the countertop. "This place won't suit either of us."

"Then let's continue our search, shall we?" His mother smiled. "And, Ryan, thank you for being part of my journey. I hope I can return the favor one day."

SEVERAL HOURS LATER, Ryan added more two-by-fours to his growing stack inside the wheelhouse barn. He'd already repaired two of the walls and practically rebuilt the entire workbench. The safety violations were dwindling with every repair. With luck and a bit more renovation, the barn would be safe for his grandfather and uncle to produce their dandelion wine in the summer.

The door creaked open, and his grandfather stood in the doorway. "Thought I might find you here."

"How'd you know where I was?" Ryan brushed his hands on his jeans. He hadn't told anyone what he was doing. He'd wanted to surprise his grandfather and uncle.

"You can sneak around behind your brothers' backs." Grandpa Sam smiled and stepped inside. "But your grandmother taught me how to pay attention to you boys years ago. I've not forgotten, even if I get around a bit slower these days."

"Gran Claire was certainly watchful." Ryan checked to make sure the floor was clear where his grandfather was stepping then added, "She never did miss much."

"But I think she fretted over you the most." Sam stopped beside the workbench and ran his hand over the newly sanded top.

"Me?" Ryan said.

"You were always comforting your younger brothers." Sam leaned against the workbench and considered Ryan. "But you never let your gran fuss over you. She always worried about that. She worried you weren't getting enough of her care and attention."

"I never felt like that." Not once. He always welcomed Gran Claire's embraces. Always felt stronger after one of her warm hugs. Reassured and loved too. He'd felt something similar recently with someone else. *Elsie*. Ryan adjusted several two-by-fours, rebalanced the stack and his thoughts. "If anything, I felt like I got more hugs from Gran Claire than anyone else."

"That's because you stopped her fussing at hugs." Grandpa Sam chuckled. "No matter what it was, your gran would give you a hug then you'd proclaim you were fine. Even when you were sick. Broke your arm. Fell off a horse too many times to count. You had a one hug limit, then you always told her not to worry about you."

"You both had five young boys to look after," Ryan said. "You already had too much to worry about."

"But that was for us to decide where we wanted to put our worries." Grandpa Sam watched him. A knowing gleam in his gaze. "When you love someone the way your gran loved you, the worrying and the fussing are all part of the package."

Ryan knew something about that kind of worry. He'd worried about Elsie. And wanted to fuss over her. Take care of her, not because she couldn't take care of herself. But because he...

"You're fussing and worrying about this old barn because you love your uncle and me," Grandpa Sam continued as if he already knew what Ryan was fighting. "Same as we love you."

"I just want it to be safe." Ryan paced around the barn, picked up an old nail and tossed it into the debris pile in the corner. "I want to make sure you're okay."

"We appreciate that." Grandpa Sam braced his arms on the workbench as if more than content to watch Ryan pace circles around the barn all day. He added, "But I'm here to make sure my grandson is okay."

"I'm fine." Ryan completed another circle. Picked up another nail.

Grandpa Sam held his silence but kept his vigil.

"Or, I will be." Ryan stopped and faced his grandfather then qualified, "I want to be. I'm trying to be."

"What's the problem?" Grandpa Sam asked.

"I wished to be a real cowboy all those years ago," Ryan blurted. As if somehow in this barn, with his grandpa, the past still mattered. Maybe it was talk of his Gran Claire. Maybe it was needing someone else to understand. Maybe he needed to understand. Whatever it was, Ryan spilled those secrets he'd kept locked away. "After you taught me to ride that summer and I fell in love with the rodeo. Then the next summer, Mom left us here and never came back. And my wildest wish came true."

"And you thought the bad stuff was your fault." Grandpa Sam smoothed his fingers through his white beard. Wisdom and compassion in his gaze. "The divorce. Your mom leaving you and your brothers. You blamed yourself because you wanted the rodeo, horses, being here so badly."

Ryan nodded. "Ever since, I wanted to prove it wasn't the wrong wish. That I truly belonged here." Ryan speared his arms to the side. "I had to be fine for my brothers. For you and Gran. I had to look after you all and I couldn't do that if I wasn't fine. And to be that I had to be the best cowboy I knew how."

"Now you are the best bronc rider and an even better brother and grandson." Grandpa Sam waited a beat and said quietly, "Isn't it about time you let yourself off the hook?"

Ryan lowered his arms. "I don't know how."

"I imagine if your Gran Claire was here now, she'd tell you it's simple." A small smile curved across his grandpa's face.

Ryan waited.

"Your gran would tell you that you can start by letting someone look after you," Grandpa Sam said, his eyebrows lifted toward his head as if he wanted to make sure Ryan was paying attention. "And then your gran would tell you to let someone love you."

Love him. That meant letting someone in. Completely. Fully. Trusting his heart to another. It meant more than words. It meant showing up. Proving it. "And if I'm going to let someone love me, it's only fair to love them fully in return." No half measures. *All or nothing.*

"Now you're catching on." Grandpa Sam grinned then pointed out the window. "Those dandelions out there will start to sprout soon. They'll go from seed to seedling to a plant to a flower. And eventually they'll become wine. We're on a similar path of growth that includes our successes and our failures. It's what your uncle and I like to call the journey of a life well spent. Falling in love is a blip, but staying in love, well, that's the reward of a life well spent. A journey worth taking."

But was he ready for that journey? Ryan stepped next to his grandfather and stared out the window at the dandelion field.

"You've always been in for only eight seconds," Grandpa Sam mused beside him. "Maybe it's time to try something that'll last a bit longer. Like a lifetime perhaps."

That meant committing to Elsie. Ryan's words sounded wry. "That seems to be the theme today. Mom told me something similar this morning."

"Then what's the problem?" Grandpa Sam asked.

Ryan channeled his mother and kept it right to the point. "I seem to have a bit of a commitment problem when it comes to things outside the arena."

"I don't believe that's true." His grandpa shifted to face him. "You've never wavered on your commitment to this family."

"That's family, Grandpa. There's nothing to waver about," he said. "I was talking about my track record with relationships. I'm not known for sticking around long."

"That's not a problem. It just means you weren't willing to commit to the wrong person." His grandpa set his hand on Ryan's shoulder and drew

Ryan's attention to him. "But when your heart knows, Ryan, there's nothing to fear. And that's when you'll want to stick."

Ryan flattened his palms on the workbench top. "How do I know Elsie is the right one?"

"Listen to your heart." Grandpa Sam squeezed his shoulder. "It didn't steer you wrong before. It won't now either."

What was in his heart? Ryan stilled, quieted his mind inside the old barn with his grandfather beside him. And beyond the pain and hurt he discovered love. A whole bunch of love for one woman. Elsie. So much love he hurt from not knowing what to do with it.

He was in love with Elsie.

He drew a deep breath, feeling freer than he had in weeks. Lighter, yet stronger. He knew what he wanted. He wanted to take that journey. He wanted to prove he could love Elsie for a lifetime. And that would be a life well spent.

"I know what I need to do," Ryan said then pulled out his phone.

His grandpa grinned wide. "And your family is here for you. Whatever you need."

Ryan tapped a name on his contact list, set the phone to his ear. His mother answered on the second ring. He offered a quick greeting then got right to the heart of things. "Mom, it turns out I could use that favor after all."

CHAPTER TWENTY-FOUR

IT WAS FRIDAY and Elsie had officially completed her first full week on-site at her new job. With the drive from Texas to New York last week, she'd hoped her early days in her office would be a quiet chance to get settled. But it had been one meeting after another. Coordinating with her staff and cross-checking last-minute details for the weekend's events at the hotel, including a high-profile gala.

Elsie picked up the embossed invitation for the Heartscape Foundation's Annual Charity Gala. The one her boss had delivered not ten minutes earlier at the request of Dr. Lilian Sloan. Elsie was expected to attend as the personal guest of Lilian's. Turned out Dr. Sloan sat on the Heartscape Foundation's board and was partially responsible for the foundation reaching out to Elsie's hotel when the nonprofit lost their original venue.

Elsie's boss was more than grateful for the event and the exposure for the hotel. Elsie was to attend the ball and not worry about staffing. Her boss assured her all would be covered for the evening. All Elsie needed to do was enjoy herself.

Looked like Elsie would be going to a gala tomorrow night. If only she was feeling more excited. She appreciated the invitation. Yet feared seeing Lilian again would only make her think of Lilian's son even more. And Elsie wasn't sure she could think of Ryan much more than she already did. And here she was supposed to be moving on.

Her cell phone vibrated on her desk. Elsie glanced at the screen, saw her brother's contact picture and quickly answered. Setting the call on speaker, she said, "Bryce. You're calling early. Is everything okay? Are the girls okay?"

"Everyone is fine. We're all really good. My ankle is getting stronger every day according to my physical therapist," Bryce assured her then added, "I wanted to talk to you before I picked up the girls from school. If you haven't noticed I can hardly get a word in when they're on the phone with you."

Elsie chuckled and relaxed into her office chair. "Yes, they have a lot to fill me in on. And I must admit I don't mind."

"They miss you," Bryce said. "I do too."

"Thanks. I feel the same." Elsie stared out her second-floor office window at the busy street below. "I've already been looking at my calendar to see when I can slip in a weekend trip." *Home*. She left that out. New York was her home now.

"That would be wonderful." Bryce's words came out in an excited, somewhat nervous rush. "If you could perhaps come around the end of May that would be very helpful."

"What's happening at the end of May?" Elsie flipped open her calendar notebook on her desk.

"I'll be moving into my new office in Belleridge the last week of the month," Bryce said. Then he paused but his words tumbled out. "Because of my official open date for Parks Investment Services the first day of June."

Elsie straightened in her chair and stared at her phone. "What? Did you say Parks Investment Services?"

"Yes." There was a scratch across the speaker then her brother's voice strengthened. "It's what I called to talk to you about."

"I'm listening," Elsie said.

"The short version is I'm not a farmer, Elsie," Bryce said, his words matter-of-fact if not slightly sarcastic.

Elsie slapped her hand over her mouth to catch her burst of laughter. She managed a muffled, "Okay," then a more clear, "Go on."

"It's fine if you laugh," Bryce said, not sounding the least bit offended. "I've learned to laugh at myself quite a bit since we moved here. I've also learned to face some hard truths about myself."

"Like the fact that you're not a farmer," Elsie supplied.

"Like the fact that I'm really good at numbers, money and planning for the future," Bryce explained. "But the everyday things trip me up. The marketing, the customer service, the actual selling of the honey. Not to mention the grocery runs, the elementary school homework and the girls needing their dad."

Elsie sobered. With certainty, she said, "You're a really good dad, Bryce. One of the best. Never doubt that."

"I want to be," Bryce said, his words sincere and heartfelt. "I want to be the dad you never had, Els. The one you deserved."

Elsie squeezed her eyes closed. Still, she felt the tears pooling behind her eyelids. "You already are that dad, Bryce."

"Well, I need to go back to what I'm good at, Els, so I can continue to be that dad for my daughters. The farm, the bees, the house. It's all more than I can handle while trying to be present for the girls too. I want to do this right."

"You are," Elsie assured him. "You will."

"Thanks," Bryce said. "Believe it or not, I already have clients lined up from the rodeo and the hospital for my financial planning services."

"I believe it," Elsie said, pleased for her brother. "I'm excited for you, Bryce. But can I ask what will happen to the house?" Their aunt and mom had already booked three more monthlong trips for later in the year. And last she'd spoken to the travel-bug-bitten pair, they were already discussing next year's vacation itinerary as well.

"That's the other thing I wanted to talk to you about," Bryce said. His words picked up speed as if he wanted to get everything out in one breath. "You made this place more of a home than I ever could, Els. You've always loved it. I think you should come back and manage it."

"Me?" Elsie gaped at her phone even though her brother couldn't see her. "Manage a farm? Did you forget that I'm your sister, Bryce? Neither one of us are farm grown."

"It doesn't have to stay a working farm." Bryce's amusement was clear over the speaker. "The house is too large already. You could turn it into a real venue for all sorts of events and still have plenty of private space for yourself. No reason you can't start your own business too."

Her own business. Surely, she couldn't do that, could she? Elsie rubbed her forehead then set her palm flat on the desk as if things were starting to tumble too fast around her.

"Aunt Marlena and I talked about using the greenhouses as a venue for weddings and such," Bryce continued. "Did you see the pictures of the charity gala Aunt Marlena hosted there last Christmas?"

Elsie nodded. Set her other palm on her desk. Told herself to slow down and not to get ahead of herself. This was just an idea being tossed out.

Bantered about. Not a viable, actual solution. Elsie managing Doyle Farm. Full-time. And as a proper business too. The idea was impractical, but very tempting. She said, "Yeah. The greenhouses looked spectacular for that Christmas ball."

"And now with Three Springs hosting more rodeos and events in their local arena, there are more people coming to town and venue space needed," Bryce explained. "And the closest halls and ballrooms are in Belleridge. There isn't anything in Three Springs."

"I didn't know that," Elsie said and told herself to stay objective.

"Look, I've run some numbers," Bryce continued. He slipped into his professional, business tone. "Just preliminaries if you want to see them. The other way I figure it is if Aunt Marlena and me decide to sell the place, we could use the information to entice a potential buyer. Additional income streams are often appealing to certain buyers. This could certainly help with a sale."

Sell the farm. Elsie tensed her fingers on the desk, fought the slow roll of her stomach. That idea did not sit well. Not even a little bit. She said, "Send me what you've put together and I'll review it."

"Really, Els?" Bryce said, hope in his tone.

"I'll look it over, but I'm not saying I'll do it," Elsie countered.

"But you'll think about it," Bryce said. "At the very least consider it."

"That I will agree to." She was already thinking about it. Already turning it over in her mind. And it wasn't objections she was coming up with.

"While you are considering things, can we please talk about you considering how you might work things out with Ryan?" her brother asked.

Elsie stilled. "What do you mean?"

"Come on, Els," Bryce said. His words were not impassive. And far from indifferent. "You're my sister. Ryan is one of my best friends. It's obvious there's something between you two."

"There was something." Elsie rubbed her chest then added, "That's past tense in case our phone connection was bad."

"Are you sure about that?" Bryce challenged.

"I'm sure we don't have a future," Elsie said.

"But how do you feel about Ryan?" Bryce asked, seeming intent to keep pressing her. "Do you still love him?"

Elsie closed her eyes, but her words still slipped out before she could catch them. "Yeah, I do."

"Then it's not so past tense," Bryce argued.

"But Bryce, I've got one failed marriage," Elsie argued right back. "Where I got love entirely wrong. Then there's Mom and Dad. And what about you? We aren't exactly lucky in love in our family."

"Luck has nothing to do with it, Els," Bryce

countered. "Love. Marriage. It takes two to make it work. And two people can't put their careers before their marriage and expect it to last."

That was what Elsie and her first husband had done. Careers first until they were ready to focus on the marriage portion. But they'd waited too long and there wasn't much left to work on. "But what about that spark Mom always talks about?" Like the one she felt with Ryan. "The one Mom claimed burned out too fast."

"I suspect it's not about the strength of the spark, Els," her brother said, his words pensive. "But instead, it's about actively choosing to keep that spark lit. Choosing love first. Always."

Choosing love. Always. Elsie closed her mouth and rolled her lips together.

"And if one person doesn't want to put love first, how can it work?" There was a pause then her brother continued, "Sometimes love is about letting go. When, sadly, you know your love won't ever be what the other person truly needs."

Her brother was talking about his ex-wife. The one he'd loved and let go for her happiness. Elsie was hesitant. "Bryce, how do you know when to let go?"

"When you both stop wanting to fight for love and your partnership," he said quietly.

Elsie squeezed her eyes closed.

"But, Elsie." Her brother's voice was strong

across the speaker. He added, "You have to fight for love first."

She'd fought. Hadn't she? *No.* Not exactly. She had walked away from Ryan. Driven away. Fled to New York. She hadn't wanted to take a risk on love. Hadn't wanted to stay and fight for what Ryan and she might be. She'd been out before she'd ever been in. But she loved Ryan.

I love him. But she hadn't given love or him a chance. She hadn't given them a chance. *I love him.*

Everything inside her suddenly settled as if falling into place. She loved Ryan. She wasn't tumbling. Or hurting. Or running. She was ready. To love.

Elsie snapped her eyes open and picked up her phone. "Bryce."

"I'm still here," her brother said.

"Send me those numbers for the farm today," she said, an urgency to her words.

"Does this mean…" her brother started.

"It means I've made my choice, Bryce," she said, her smile drifting into her words.

She was going all in on love. It was time to win her cowboy and his heart.

CHAPTER TWENTY-FIVE

A PILE OF dresses lay on Elsie's bed. Several more were draped over the back of the love seat couch. A longer black satin gown hung on the open bathroom door. Panic about what to wear to the charity gala that evening had driven Elsie out of bed too early for a Saturday morning. Within minutes of waking, she had most of her closet strewn across her bed. And not long after that, she had more than one open moving box as she'd attempted to locate the coordinating heels for her formal outfits.

For the past hour, she'd been trying on and discarding one gown after another. Finally, she'd given up, propped her tablet on the short kitchen counter and dialed for help, Now Tess and Maggie were on video chat, considering and eliminating one dress after another.

Elsie twirled in front of the camera then stopped and set her hands on her hips. "What about this one?"

"That dress is nice." Tess sipped a cup of tea.

Beside her, Maggie frowned and shrugged. "But

that's all it is. Nice. There's no flash or sparkle or anything memorable about it."

"But it's formal," Elsie argued and trailed her fingers over the nondescript deep navy sheath gown that lacked a bold plunging neckline. Or a daring open back. Or even a shimmery sheen. She added, "In my defense, I'm usually working at these events too. So, my outfits need to do double duty. It's not easy to clear buffets or help my people in a princess ball gown."

"That's it, Elsie." Maggie lifted her hands, pointed at the screen and smiled wide. "You should wear a princess ball gown tonight."

Elsie scanned her dresses. "I definitely don't own one of those."

"Time to go shopping." Tess smoothed her hands over her very pregnant stomach and sighed. "I wish I was there. I love a good shopping day. I want one after these babies arrive. Ladies, promise me."

Maggie and Elsie both laughed. Elsie walked closer to the camera, leaned in then said, "Tess, we promise to take you on a full day of pampering and shopping after the babies are born."

"Wonderful." Tess picked up her cup and fiddled with the tea bag. "Now back to you, Elsie. I'm afraid you need a new gown for tonight."

Elsie's shoulders drooped. Her frown followed. "I was worried you were going to say that."

"It's fine." Maggie waved her phone at the screen. "I've already been looking up dress stores near you ever since you put on that not quite salmon, but not really orange dress earlier."

Tess laughed. "Definitely don't wear that one, Els."

"I already explained that. The dress was part of my putting-color-back-into-my-wardrobe phase," Elsie said, but she couldn't quite stop her own laughter from spilling free. She reached out and touched the not quite silky, not quite satiny fabric and shook her head. "Although I'm not sure why I chose to start that color change with this dress."

"Well, there's nothing wrong with classic, bold colors," Tess said and grinned. "Besides, Elsie, it's you that brings the color to everything, not the gown."

"That's a very kind thing to say," Elsie said.

"It happens to be true." Tess toasted her with her teacup. "And remember, if you can't name the color immediately, maybe it's not the dress for you."

"Good advice." Elsie dropped an oversize sweatshirt over her head and let her dull strapless gown slide to the floor in a puddle. Much like her enthusiasm. But her mind wasn't on shopping and ball gowns and galas. It was on winning back her cowboy.

"We can't be there, but we can guide you." Maggie paused then grinned a satisfied grin. "There. I just sent you the addresses to three highly rated boutiques close to you."

"Call us when you've narrowed down your options," Tess ordered. "We will be here on standby and can help you decide."

Elsie pulled the black sheath gown with cap sleeves off the bathroom door and held it up in front of herself for one last shot. She asked, "Are you certain this won't work?"

"No." Maggie shook her head. "Sorry, Els. It looks like a bridesmaid gown."

Because it was. She'd worn the dress years ago for a former college roommate's wedding. Elsie shoved it back into her closet.

"You're going to a black-tie event as a personal guest of Dr. Lilian Sloan, Elsie," Tess said, her expression thoughtful, her words firm. "You've got to level up, Els."

"What if I made up an excuse," Elsie offered. She hadn't told her two friends about her plans yet. She was still working out the details with her brother. And she could use the evening to finish finalizing her strategy before she presented it to them for their input. She already knew winning back Ryan was going to be a team effort.

Alarm filled both women's faces.

"You have to go, Els." Maggie shook her head. "You can't bow out on Lilian."

"Right, she's your mother-in-law." Elsie nodded. "And Lilian has been really kind to me since I arrived." She reached for her purse. "Looks like I'm going shopping."

Maggie and Tess cheered, wished her luck then

ordered her to text as soon as she had options for them to consider. With that, Elsie tied her running shoes, checked her phone for the first boutique's address and headed out.

Two hours and a dozen dress samples later, Elsie twirled around in an elegant sequined royal blue gown. The hemline swept just so across the floor. Her tablet was propped on the dressing room chair.

"Do you feel like a princess?" Maggie asked. "You certainly look like one from our view."

"Yeah, I kind of do," Elsie admitted and propped her hands lightly in the pockets on the skirt. She couldn't quite believe she'd found a dress in her size that fit so perfectly. As if it was meant for her. She said, "That sounds silly, doesn't it?"

"No. It's perfect," Tess gushed. "And everyone deserves to feel like a princess, Elsie, especially you."

"Well, your compliments make me feel like royalty," Elsie said then smiled into the camera. "I think this is the one."

"Now, find yourself a pair of fancy slippers and head to the ball," Maggie said. Enthusiasm stretched across her face. "Who knows? You might even meet your prince tonight."

Her prince. He was back in Texas. Elsie held on to her smile and said, "I'll stick to feeling like a princess tonight and attending that gala."

"Whatever you wish." Maggie waved her hand

as if she held a magic wand. "It's your night. Just have fun."

"Don't forget to send lots of pictures," Tess ordered. "So I can feel like I'm at that ball with you."

Elsie thanked her friends and disconnected. She'd head to the ball and, like a fairy-tale princess, skip out early. After all, she still had a cowboy, not a prince, to win.

RYAN SLIPPED HIS arms into a black tuxedo jacket and walked over to the full-length mirror in the guest bedroom at his mother's penthouse flat in New York City. He stared at his feet. Dress shoes were polished and gleaming. The tuxedo pants pressed perfectly. The waistcoat vest buttoned. The silver cuff links his grandfather had surprised him with were in place and secure. He adjusted the silk lapels of the formal jacket. Then finally looked at his face.

Gone was the thick beard. Gone was the shaggy hair that had touched his collar. The wavy strands were cut and styled, not smashed and flattened on his head from his cowboy hat. Gone was the cowboy.

Ryan inhaled. Exhaled. Considered the tuxedo again. Not bad, he decided. And if it helped him convince Elsie to let him love her forever, well, he might consider wearing it all the time.

He turned around, felt the stiff insole of the dress shoes cut into his foot. Then amended that thought about all the time. He'd wear the fancy tuxedo but with cowboy boots. After all, he could be polished up, but he'd always be a cowboy.

He picked up a black slender necktie from the bed and left the bedroom. He stopped in the doorway and took in his mother standing at the floor-to-ceiling corner windows across the flat. She wore a floor-length black gown with brilliant white lace and sequin embroidery on the top that extended down her arms. She looked elegant, attractive, and yet there was a shadow of loneliness wrapped around her. Nothing obvious, but perhaps he saw it because he'd felt the same too without Elsie.

He looked at his mom and decided then he'd do whatever it took to find her a home near Three Springs. Perhaps then she too might find a way out of that shadow of loneliness. He walked farther into the room and cleared his throat.

His mother spun around from the windows and gasped softly.

Ryan held up the ends of his slim black silk tie. "I need some help with this and then I think I'm ready."

His mother smiled affectionately and walked over. Her movements graceful and effortless even in her formal attire. She said, "I'm surprised your grandfather or grandmother didn't teach you how to properly tie a tie."

"They tried." Ryan touched his cheek. Surprised when he felt skin and not his beard. That would take getting used to. He added, "But I never paid much attention. Never thought I'd have to put one on."

"You wore a tie for Maggie and Grant's wedding." His mother eyed him.

"Only for the ceremony and photographs. And Grant tied it for me." Ryan grinned. His family always stepped in to help him, but they weren't there now with him in New York. It was surreal that his mother was. And she never once hesitated to assist him. She'd jumped right in and offered a few tips of her own. He cleared his throat again. "Thanks."

"I'm not an expert like your brother and grandfather, but it'll do." She adjusted the knot then smoothed her palm over the tie. Her gaze was tender, her words warm. "I wouldn't have believed it was possible for you to be any more handsome than you already were."

Ryan took her hand and squeezed her fingers. "When I said thanks, I meant for all this. For everything you're doing for me."

"Thank me after you win back Elsie." His mother tipped her chin and regarded him. "Otherwise, I won't feel quite so good, and you might not feel quite so grateful."

Ryan didn't release her hand. Instead, he tucked her arm around his and said, "Whatever happens tonight, I appreciate this and you, Mother."

"That's quite lovely to hear." She reached up and touched the corner of her eye. "I'm delighted you asked me. Now, shall we get to that gala?"

"I can't think of any place I'd rather be," he said, certainty in his words.

Wherever Elsie was, he wanted to be.

CHAPTER TWENTY-SIX

ELSIE SMOOTHED HER hands over the sparkling skirts of her gown and took in the crowded ballroom. One circuit. That was her plan. She'd complete one full circuit of the ballroom. Greet guests, check on her staff then make a quick exit. She needed every minute for her win-back-her-cowboy strategy. Hearts were at stake. And she wanted it to be foolproof. That wouldn't happen at a gala.

Even if she did feel slightly like a princess. And the chandeliers sparkling over the dance floor made her want to indulge in a waltz. With a prince. That she still needed to win back first.

Elsie navigated to the far end of the ballroom away from the dance floor. There the buffet tables were arranged and the food presented exactly to her specifications. She was more than pleased with how the event turned out, especially given the tight timeline. She greeted one of the catering staff then moved in to shift empty appetizer dishes around.

"I was told you would have enough staff here tonight," a familiar voice said behind Elsie. The woman added, a hint of amusement in her words, "I was also assured that you wouldn't need to work."

Elsie brushed her hands together and turned around to greet Lilian Sloan. "I was just checking with my staff quickly."

"You were working, dear." Lilian chuckled and waved her hand lightly in the air. "I won't tell anyone, but tonight can't be all work and no play. There's little joy in that."

But if she was working then she wasn't dwelling on a certain cowboy. Her host's son, in fact. Wondering where he was. What he was doing. Was he thinking about her too? She had already spent the car ride over trying to decide which rodeo he was competing in that weekend. She'd narrowed it down to possibly Santa Fe, New Mexico or Colorado Springs perhaps.

"Come with me, dear." Lilian wrapped her arm gently around Elsie's and guided her effortlessly back into the crowd. "There are some people I'd like you to meet."

Lilian stayed by Elsie's side the entire time and completed one introduction after another. Each one thoughtful and insightful about the guests. The chair of the foundation's board was an accomplished CEO, but an even more talented violinist. The director of the cardiac unit at the local hospital was a forerunner on cardiac advancement, but also a trivia expert. And on the intro-

CARI LYNN WEBB

321

ductions went. Soon Elsie had a champagne glass pressed into her hand and she was looking forward to meeting the next person to discover their unexpected talent. There didn't seem to be a person Lilian Sloan wasn't acquainted with. It was impressive, even more so was her poise and elegance.

Elsie sipped her champagne and enjoyed a lively debate about the latest superhero movie from several of Lilian's colleagues.

"Oh, if it isn't Elsie *please-dance-with-me* Marie Parks," a male voice drawled behind her.

Elsie lowered her champagne flute without taking a sip. Her heart suddenly raced. Her palms suddenly felt damp. She very carefully, very delicately turned around on her brand-new three-inch strappy heels.

Let it be him. Please.

Her gaze collided first with a tuxedoed chest. Her breath caught.

Please. Let it be him.

She lifted her chin. And gaped. Mouth wideopen. Eyes even wider.

Her cowboy was there. He was there.

Only her cowboy looked like he had stepped out of the pages of a men's fashion magazine. Pictureperfect. Impeccable. Handsome. Her gaze traveled all over him, yet she couldn't seem to stop staring. Finally, she swallowed and found her voice. "Ryan." She blinked at him, barely held back from reaching up and touching his smooth cheek. "You look more like a prince than a cowboy."

"That was the plan." One corner of his mouth hitched up into his cheek, revealing a dimple. "I wanted to show you I can fit into your world, if there's room."

Room. Elsie wasn't certain there was enough room to breathe. Her cowboy was there. Within reach. And how had she forgotten he had dimples? *Dimples.* Once again, she found herself speechless.

"Elsie Marie, may I have this dance?" he asked, clearly not struggling for words. "In truth, I want your first dance. Your last dance. And every single one in between, but we have time for all that." He held out his arm, opened his hand. Then he leaned closer. "By the way, you look absolutely stunning. I would've gotten to you sooner, but I had to catch my breath first."

That's what she needed to do. Catch her breath. Everything seemed to be happening so fast. She eyed her champagne flute, wondering what to do with it.

Lilian eased the crystal glass from Elsie's grip and smiled warmly at her. "It's time to find the joy portion of your evening, my dear."

With that, Elsie set her hand in Ryan's. And finally found her anchor. Found her center. She linked her fingers with his. Found her reason.

He led her to the dance floor, turned to face her and drew her into his arms.

"Ryan. What are you doing here?" She braced her hands on his shoulders and held herself back to look into his eyes. "Not that I'm not thrilled." And stunned. Delighted. And nervous. Anxious. All those feelings Ryan stirred inside her came rushing back through her.

"I promise to explain." He curved his arms around her waist. His touch gentle, yet secure. "But can I please have this dance? I missed you, Elsie."

His confession softened her. The affection in his gaze melted through her.

Elsie moved fully into his embrace. Close enough to feel his heartbeat under her cheek. At the end of the song, Elsie held on to him and said, "Now it's my turn. Dance with me, cowboy, and let me hold on to you."

"Whatever you want." He tucked her even closer into his embrace then added, "This is your night."

It was a dream come true. But too soon the song drew to a close. And Elsie knew dreams ended and dreamers woke, even princesses. She walked with him off the dance floor toward the wall of windows where the music and crowd were muted. Where it seemed like it was only her and only him. Elsie eyed him. "Ryan, what rodeo is here this weekend? I didn't see one even close to here."

"I was supposed to ride in Santa Fe this week-end." He rubbed his cheek then pulled his hand away as if surprised at the lack of a beard. "But I pulled out."

"Why?" Her gaze drifted over him. "Are you injured? I saw you ride last weekend. It was clean. You weren't thrown on either day."

"You watched me?" He grinned at her and leaned closer. "Elsie Marie, are you following me?"

"I've been following Maggie and Vivian on the circuit," she said. And checking up on him every chance she got. In truth, she'd seen every single one of his rides more than once. There was something fascinating about watching her cowboy compete. The strength. The determination. The dedication. It was all a part of him.

"To be fair, it seems I'm following you now." He tucked his hands behind his back and watched her.

She did the same. Clutched her hands behind her back. But she really wanted to reach for him. Pull him back to her. But he was holding himself away. "What do you mean?" she asked.

"I'm here for you, Elsie Marie." He motioned toward the crowded ballroom. "I'm here to prove I can fit into your world."

Elsie's throat tightened. Was he giving everything up for her? "But what about the rodeo?"

"You're more important to me." He stepped closer to her and held her gaze if not her hand. "What we have is more important to me. I don't want to lose you, Elsie. I want to be wherever you are, whether it's New York or the North Pole."

Elsie searched his gaze and saw only sincerity on his face. Heard only honesty in his words. "What are you saying?"

"What I should've told you the night before you left." He wound one arm around her waist. His hand connected with hers and linked. "I love you, Elsie Marie Parks. I want to share a life with you. Put down roots. Have a family. I want all of it with you."

"Ryan," she said. "Are you sure?"

"That I want a life outside the arena with you." He pressed their joined hands on his chest. "With all my heart."

Tears swelled in Elsie's eyes. For this man who'd given her his heart. For the love she had for him. For the gift he was. "I love you, Ryan Sloan."

He pressed his forehead against hers. His eyes closed briefly then he focused again on her. There was a sheen in his gaze. "I won't ever get tired of hearing those words."

"I love you," she said again. Felt him sigh. Felt his heartbeat steady and strong under their joined hands. She straightened and curved her other arm up around his neck. "Will you be happy here?"

"I'll be happy with you," he said, confidence in his words and resolve in his expression. "And if that's here then I'll make it work. I want to make us work, Elsie."

So did she. Very much. She chose them. She

chose love. She asked, "What if I told you there's this other place I'm considering?"

"Yes," he said, without hesitation. Without pausing.

She laughed and squeezed him tight. "You haven't heard anything about it yet."

"Will you be there?" he asked.

She nodded.

He pulled her into his embrace. Lifted one shoulder and said, "Then that's all that matters."

Oh, how she loved her cowboy. She brushed her fingers against the back of his neck and considered him. "Let me tell you about it anyway."

He pressed his lips against hers. Gentle. Tender. Perfectly. Then he grinned and said, "Sorry, I'm listening. I've just been wanting to do that since I saw you."

She framed his face in her hands and leaned in for a longer kiss. One filled with love. One that promised lifetimes. That joined two hearts. Slowly she pulled back and smiled at him. "I've been wanting to do that since I saw you."

His quiet laughter shook his shoulders. "I love you, Elsie Marie Parks."

She pressed her hand on his chest, held him in place. "I can't think when you kiss me. And I want to tell you about this place."

He shifted, pressed a kiss to her cheek. "Absolutely."

She took a deep breath and dived in. "There's

land. Quite a bit. That we'd need to tend together. Are you okay with that?"

He nodded.

"And a stable that needs updating if we decide on more horses," she continued and held his gaze. "Hives that need looking after."

He shifted slightly. Suddenly alert. His focus fixed on her.

Oh, she had his full attention now. She added, "And there's a rather large house. It needs work too. And it has rooms that need to be filled."

"Filled," he said, his voice low.

"With family and friends." She lifted one shoulder, tried to sound indifferent, but failed. "Kids, one day. It's a house that wants to be a home. That's when it's happiest."

His gaze lit. His slow drawl stretched out. "Is that so?"

"Yeah," she said. "So, what do you say, cowboy? Do you want to build a home with me there?"

"Every day," he promised and held her impossibly close. "Every day I choose you, Elsie Marie."

She smiled at him. Felt love swell inside her. Finally knew where her happy was. It wasn't a place. It was what she shared with him. It was the life they would build together. She kissed him and said, "And I choose you, my cowboy prince."

Today. Tomorrow. Always.

EPILOGUE

One Month Later

"Do you have the ring?" Caleb turned from the window in the wheelhouse barn where he was keeping watch for Elsie and her nieces.

Ryan patted the front pocket in his jeans. "It's in my pocket."

"Well, pull it out," Caleb ordered and closed the distance between them. He motioned to Ryan. "We have to see it. You have to know you have it."

Ryan glanced around the barn, filled with his family and Elsie's. Everyone looked at him expectantly. Several even nodded as if to encourage him to display the ring. He obliged, slipped the ring box carefully from his pocket and opened it.

"Put it away," Caleb said, looking suddenly worried. "You don't want to drop it."

"And whatever you do, do *not* drop it in the stream either." That from Grant.

"I won't drop it," Ryan said then tucked the box back into his pocket.

"Do you know what you're going to say?" Maggie stood in the shelter of Grant's arms and smiled at him.

"I imagine I'll say…" Ryan started.

"Don't." Caleb cut him off then added, "Don't tell us. Save it for Elsie."

Ryan eyed his younger brother. Watched Caleb pace around the barn, weaving in and around the others. He looked restless and nervous. But that should be Ryan. He was the one proposing. He set his hands on his hips and stepped in front of his younger brother's path. "Caleb. What is wrong with you?"

"This is about Elsie." Caleb tugged at his wavy hair. "Elsie is like my little sister, Ryan. I taught her to dance. This has to be perfect."

No pressure there. Ryan eyed his sibling.

"I taught her to drive," Carter offered from his post near the ladder to the loft. "It does need to be perfect."

Not his big brother too.

"I shared my books with her." Grant grinned. "And it really needs to be perfect."

Of course, Grant would join in. If only his other brother Josh was there, he could add to it. Ryan took it all in stride. His brothers would watch over Elsie like their own sister. That was more than enough. Once again, he was grateful for his family.

"And she really is my baby sister." Bryce turned around from the window and eyed Ryan. "So, they're right. It has to be perfect. It's one of those important life moments she'll remember and talk about."

He would too. And if it wasn't perfect, they'd talk about that as well. Hopefully laugh about it and keep as one of many memories they'd gather in their life together.

"Don't be nervous, big brother." Caleb dropped his hand on Ryan's shoulder. "Then you will drop the ring in the water."

Ryan seemed to be the calmest one in the barn. He had Elsie's heart. And Elsie had his. There was nothing to be nervous about. Nothing to second-guess. Nothing to question. He knew what he wanted. Who he wanted. For the first time, he knew the future he wanted. He said, "I'm not going to mess this up. I promise. Elsie is my everything."

"Don't tell us." Caleb squeezed Ryan's shoulder. "Save it for Elsie."

Ryan saw his mom press a tissue to her eyes then hand another tissue to Elsie's mom and one to Marlena. Grandpa Sam and Uncle Roy joined the three women.

"I had a great plan to tell Elsie, but you all wanted in." Ryan eyed his brother.

"We had to make sure it was perfect for Elsie." Caleb shrugged and walked back to the window to stand beside Bryce.

Ryan had talked to Bryce, Elsie's mom and her aunt about his intentions and asked their permission to marry Elsie. He would swear he hadn't made it to his truck when they'd called his family and told them. He'd arrived home to find his family waiting for him with ideas and suggestions for his proposal.

Fortunately, Ryan already had a plan, and the two families were more than willing to help him with the proposal. Of course, that hadn't stopped any one of them from offering advice and tweaks to make it better. More special. Perfect, as it were.

"Okay, it's time. Elsie and the girls are in the dandelion field." Bryce motioned to the door. "Get to the bridge, Ryan. And don't drop the ring."

Finally. Ryan eased out of the barn. He heard Autumn, Gemma and Elsie laughing and talking in the dandelion field next to the barn. He snuck around the corner of the barn and headed for the new bridge spanning the stream. Quickly and quietly.

Although he would've liked to shout his love for Elsie to the fields. He didn't care how it looked. He wanted the world to know he loved one woman. Cherished one woman. He'd tell everyone and anyone who wanted to know. But first, he wanted to tell Elsie. Because when he cut through all the noise only one person mattered. *Elsie.*

Ryan waited in the center of the new bridge and rested his arms on the railing. The wheel spun slowly behind him. The water splashed and trickled over the rocks and along the stream bed. The sun was out. The sky that perfect blue. And the winds were more breezy for once. Finally, he watched Elsie round the corner. Gemma and Autumn waved to him before slipping inside the barn together.

And Ryan's day was suddenly perfect.

Elsie slowed and paused. She shielded her eyes from the sun. Then her grin spread wide. Her excitement filled the warm air. And she ran. Straight to him. Right into his arms.

"Where did this bridge come from?" she asked and caught her breath. "It's like artwork."

"I built it," Ryan said. "With a lot of help from our families. It joins our families' lands together."

"That's lovely." She ran her hand over the smooth railing. "I'm going to want to spend a lot of time out here with you."

"I'm counting on it," he said.

"Wait. What are you doing here? I got so distracted by this bridge." She framed his face, checked him over as if worried something was wrong. "You're supposed to be in Arizona competing."

"It's next weekend," he said.

"No." She shook her head. "I have it in my calendar for this weekend."

He captured her hands in his before she could pull out her phone and check. "You had it in your calendar for this weekend because that's what I told you."

Her eyebrows pulled together. "Why would

you…" Her voice dropped away when he dropped to one knee. "Ryan."

"It's not easy to surprise you," he said. "You know all our calendars better than we do."

"That's so I can look after everyone better," she said.

"And we all appreciate it," he said and squeezed her hands. "Now I want to look after you and your heart, Elsie Marie."

She bit into her bottom lip. Her chin quivered. Tears filled her eyes. Her words sounded water soaked. "You already do."

"But I want it all, Elsie." He held her gaze. "The kids. The family. The roots."

Those tears spilled free.

"And that all starts with you becoming my wife." He reached into his pocket and pulled out the ring box. Opening it, he said, "Elsie Marie, will you marry me?"

Her reply was part laugh, part sob. She was in his arms before he could slide the ring on her finger. He dropped back onto the bridge and cradled her on his lap. Then poured all the love in his heart into their kiss.

The kiss slowed, but their love only strengthened. Right there on that bridge that connected two families. Joined two hearts.

"I think I was supposed to wait for you to put the ring on my finger." Elsie twisted in his lap and held out her hand. "I'm ready now."

Ryan slid the diamond ring onto her finger and heard her small gasp. Then she whispered, "It looks like something for a princess."

He lifted her hand, pressed a kiss to her fingers and smiled. "A city princess for a cowboy prince. Sounds perfect to me."

* * * * *

For more great romances in
Cari Lynn Webb's latest miniseries,
visit www.Harlequin.com today!